SO-SHIN
(素心)

It is cool ——— Empathy

Soshin Consulting, inc
Toshihiko Kobayashi
Japanese / English

JMP Japan Medical Planning

素心とは

　素心とは、中国は唐代の書家、顔真卿(ガンシンケイ／709〜785)が初めて使った言葉で"平常心でものの本質を見極める心"という。要するに、"事にあたって動じない心"ということである。

What is; So-shin

　So-shin (素心) is a phrase which is said to have been created by a chirographer, Gan - Shin - Kei (顔真卿／709-785) in Tang Dynasty, who wrote "With a Calm State of Mind, Posses the Ability to Identify the True Nature of Any Given Things"

●著者略歴

小林 利彦
(再生医療・文筆家)

現在、東京大学校友会顧問・東京大学薬友会会長、アサシス社―専任上級戦略アドバイザー（クリーブランド、オハイオ州、米国）。米国アップジョン社（副社長）／アップジョン ファルマスーティカルズ（社長、日本、1986〜1994）及び米国E リリー社（副社長）／日本E リリー社（副社長・R&D本部長、1995〜2001）を経て、米国研究製薬工業協会対日技術委員代表（2001〜2010）。東京大学卒（1961）（薬学士）、オーストラリア国立大学医学大学院（博士-医化学、1970）。著書に『国際人になるためのInsight Track』がある。

拙書『素心』は、(株)日本医療企画林諄社長の好意により、『国際人になるためのInsight Track』に続き、私の体験を出版することになった次第であります。

Writer: Dr. Toshi-Hiko (Toshi) Kobayashi
Regenerative medicine and columnist

He is now Advisor for Alumni Associations of The University of Tokyo, and Chairman of Pharmaceutical Alumni Association, The University of Tokyo. And Exclusive Senior Strategic Advisor for Athersys Inc in Cleveland, Ohio, USA. After the career of Vice President (Division) of Upjohn Company, Kalamazoo, Michigan and of Eli Lilly in Indianapolis, Indiana, moved to RhRMA in W.D.C as Technical Representative for de-regulations of Japan, living in Japan. Graduated (B.Sc) from The University of Tokyo and The Australian National University ,John Curtin School of Medical Research (Ph.D. in medical chemistry). He wrote a book : Insight Track for Internationally.

発刊に寄せて

米国アサシス社、CEO・会長

ギル・ヴァン・ボッケレン　Ph.D.

　ここ数十年来、世界は未曾有のスピードで移り変わっています。過去50年は、情報・コンピュータ技術や国際通信の隆盛、医薬・保健分野の驚くべき進歩、その他想像できるすべての分野にわたって画期的なテクノロジーの進歩が見られました。今日の世界では、ほんの二、三十年前に地球上に存在したすべての通信・計算能力より多くの能力を、人々はそのポケットに入れて持ち歩くことができるのです。また、以前には思いもよらなかった医療の前進が、今では普通に行われる当たり前の技術であると考えられています。しかし、多くの人が「これからもっとすごい事が起きる」と考えているのです。

　私は情報通信技術、金融、バイオテクノロジー、製造、材料科学、その他の重点領域において、こうした進歩の多くを可能にした、いくつかの集約的傾向が存在すると考えます。しかし、「各傾向の中心にあるのは何といっても国際協力の基本原則である」というのが私の思いです。これは、国際貿易や誠実な協力活動を基礎として培われてきたものであり、現在こうした取り組みの必要性はかつてなかったほどに高まっていると考えます。

　近年、私は良き友人である小林利彦博士(Toshi、アサシス社—専任上級戦略アドバイザー)と共に事業に取り組み、Toshiから様々なことを学ぶ機会を得ました。Toshiは私が知る日本人の誰からも深く尊敬されていますが、それは、彼が非常に誠実で高潔な人物であることを皆が知っているからに他ならないと思います。彼は無私であり、思いやり深く、謙虚で、探求心の強い人物です。彼はどんな話題でも臆することなく問

Recommendation

Gil Van Bokkelen Ph.D.
CEO • *Chairman, Athersys Inc.(USA)*

The world has evolved at unprecedented pace in recent decades. In the past fifty years we have witnessed the rise of information and computational technology, global communications, amazing advances in medicine and healthcare, and other innovative technologies across almost every area imaginable. In today's world, people are able to carry in their pocket more communications and computing power than even existed on the entire planet only a few decades ago, and advances in medical treatment that once seemed unthinkable are now commonplace and taken for granted. But many of us believe the best is yet to come.

I believe there are several major convergent trends that have made many of these advances possible, in information and communications technology, finance, biotechnology, manufacturing and materials sciences and several other important areas. However, at the heart of each of these trends, in my view, is the core principle of international collaboration, which has been built on a foundation of international trade and genuine collaboration – something that I believe the world needs even more of than ever before.

Over the past few years I have had the great honor of working alongside and learning from my good friend Dr. Toshi Kobayashi(Exclusive Senior Strategic Adviser, Athersys Inc). Toshi is deeply respected by almost everyone I know in Japan, and I believe this is because all who know him understand that he is a man of tremendous integrity and principle. He is selfless, caring, humble and inquisitive – utterly unafraid to ask questions about almost any topic. He displays the relentless curiosity of a true scientist, which is appropriate given his background and training. Since his ear-

小宮山宏三菱総研理事長・元東大総長と共に
Dr. H. Komiyama, A former President of the University of Tokyo

いかけをします。Toshiは真の科学者としてのひたむきな好奇心を示しますが、それも彼のバックグラウンドや受けてきた教育を思うと頷けます。彼は若い頃より、自立した思想家となること、イノベーションを推進し、国際的な科学・学術協力を強化することに尽力していました。

　Toshiは誇り高い日本人ですが、多くの意味で彼こそ真の世界市民であると言えます。彼は世界各国の事情に通じており、世界の様々な地域を旅しています。また、世界のほぼ全域に友人や研究仲間の国際的なネットワークを築き上げています。これは彼がこれまで辿ってきた科学的・専門的道筋を反映したものでもあります。Toshiは名門東京大学を卒業し、その後、名高いオーストラリア国立大学で大学院生として過ごしました。同大学のJohn Curtin医学研究所のAdrian Albert教授のもとで博士号を取得しました。その後数年間にわたりToshiは創薬化学の分野でのキャリアを積み、新技術や新薬の開発に従事しました。その中には今日もなお臨床の場で使用され、患者さんの助けとなっているものがあります。Toshiは幾つもの大手製薬会社で着実に実績を積み、三菱油化薬品在籍時代から、米国アップジョン社副社長兼アップジョン ファルマスーティカル（日本）社長を経て、米国E リリー社の副社長兼E リリージャパンのR＆D担当本部長を務めるに至りました。彼はまた米国研究製薬工業協会（PhRMA、W-DC）の在日技術代表を務めた経験もあり、アジア医薬化学連合（AFMC）の創設メンバーでもあります。また、長期にわたり東京大学の薬友会の会長も務めています。日本の大手製薬会社の重要な役員の中で、彼と共に研究を行った人、また、彼から指導を受けた人は数多く、私は彼らから直接、小林氏（Toshi）の指導や物の

ly days he has been committed to the concept of being an independent thinker, of promoting innovation, and of promoting international scientific collaboration.

While Toshi is a proud citizen of Japan, in many respects he is a true citizen of the world. He follows global affairs closely, has travelled the world extensively, and has established an international network of friends and colleagues that touch almost every corner of the globe. In some ways, this is a reflection of the academic and professional path he took. Toshi completed his early academic training at the prestigious University of Tokyo, and subsequently completed his postgraduate work at the renowned Australian National University, where he earned his Ph.D. at The John Curtin School of Medical Research, training under Professor Adrian Albert. Over the ensuing years, Toshi had an accomplished career in the field of medicinal chemistry, working to develop new techniques and medicines, some of which are still in clinical use today, helping patients. Toshi rose steadily at his time in multiple leading pharmaceutical companies, from his time at Mitsubishi Yuka Pharma, to his role as Vice President of Upjohn Research Laboratories, Upjohn and Company and President of Upjohn Pharmaceuticals in Japan, and his tenure as Vice President of Eli Lilly Laboratories, Eli Lilly Company in USA, and Executive Vice President at Eli Lilly-Japan. He also served as Technical Representative in Japan for the Pharmaceutical Research and Manufacturers Association (PhRMA, W-DC), was a founding member of the Asian Federation for Medicinal Chemistry, and has been the longstanding Chair of the Alumni Association for the Pharmaceutical Sciences at the University of Tokyo. He has worked with and trained many leading executives at major pharmaceutical companies in Japan, and I have seen firsthand how they value his input and perspective.

Dr. T. Kondo PMDA Chief Executive
近藤達也独立行政法人医薬品医療機器総合機構（PMDA）理事長

Toshi's extensive experiences and accomplishments reflect his genuine and heartfelt commitment to work with others in the collaborative pursuit of making the world a better place, both through technological advancement, and simply by being a good person. He is an optimist, and also a realist – someone that understands that while we will always have challenges, each challenge represents an opportunity, and if we work together, we can effectively address them, and make the world a little better

見方がどれほど価値のあるものかを伺っています。

　Toshiの幅広い経験と業績は、「テクノロジーの進歩と人間の善性」という2つの側面を通じて世界をより良い場所にするため、人々と共に取り組んでいきたいと願う同氏の心からの想いを反映したものと言えます。彼は楽天家（オプテミスト）であり、かつ、リアリストです。「困難は常に存在するだろうが、その一つひとつは前進へのチャンスでもある」こと、そして、「私たちが力を合わせるなら、それに効果的に対処し、世の中を少しずつでも改善できる」ことを理解しています。

　私は、畏友であり信頼できる助言者でもあるToshiと共に務めを果たす機会が得られたことを非常に光栄に思います。日米の協力体制の強化や、継続的改善という原則への確固たる取組みについて、私たちは共通のビジョンを持っています。私たちはいつも互いに新しいことを学び合い、その知識を、世界をより良い場所にする機会を捉えては活用しているのです。Toshiこそ、まさにその理念に向かって邁進している人物なのです。この理念は、本書に年代を追って記された様々な所見を通して詳しく説明されています。私はこの推薦文を読者諸氏に捧げることができ、非常に嬉しく思います。Toshiは英知にあふれ、その知識を惜しみなく与える人物です。私自身の経験からも言えるのですが、彼と旅するのは本当に楽しいものです。ぜひ、皆様がこの旅路と彼の慧眼を楽しまれますように。

in the process.

It is my great privilege to have Toshi as my dear friend and trusted advisor, and to have the opportunity to work alongside him. We share a common vision of greater collaboration between the United States and Japan, and a steadfast commitment to the principle of continuous improvement. We can always learn something new from others and apply that knowledge in our pursuit of opportunities to make the world a better place – Toshi is deeply committed to that ideal. Those themes are reiterated throughout the observations chronicled in this book, and it is my honor to provide this recommendation to you, the reader. Toshi has much wisdom and guidance to offer, and I can say from personal experience it is a pleasure to travel with him – so please enjoy the journey, and his observations.

発刊に寄せて
―ちょっとジェラシー―

北海道大学病院長
北海道大学大学院医学研究科・医学部
脳神経外科教授
寶金 清博 M.D., Ph.D.

人生は、たくさんの人々との出会いという「ピース」で構成されるジグゾーパズルである。

そのジグゾーパズルを埋めるピースの数は、人それぞれである。数多くのピースで複雑なパターンを作る人生もあれば、数個のピースで作られる比較的単純な一生もある。どちらが良い、あるいは、幸せな人生かは、もちろん、誰にも分からない。

例えば、僕の叔母などは、ほぼ一生を小さな集落で、おそらく、100名くらいの知り合いとの狭い世界で一生を終えた。しかし、叔母の人生は、とても幸せなものであった。

僕の人生は、おそらく、極めて登場人物の多い人生、つまり、ピースの多いジグゾーパズルだ。子供の頃から、友人が多く、大人にもいろいろ可愛がられた。成人してからは、臨床医として、あるいは、大学人として、そして、留学を経て、世界中に友人や恩師を持つこととなった。世間からははじきだされた「変人」とか、正体不明、やや怪しき人々も僕にとっては大切なピースである。

ただ、僕の年齢になると、もう新たに埋め込むピース、つまり、登場人物はなかなか現れないものである。もちろん、今、病院長などという仕事をしていれば、毎日、毎日、多くの人々との出会いがある。しかし、60年以上生きて来ると、もう類型化がしっかり出来ていて、「Aさんは、

Recommendation
— I'm a bit jealous —

Kiyohiro Houkin M.D., Ph.D.
President of Hokkaido University Hospital

Life is a jigsaw puzzle consisting of many "pieces" in the name of "encounters" with people.

The number of pieces to be put into the jigsaw puzzle varies depending on the person. There is a life that has a complex pattern with numerous pieces and there is another that is relatively simple and made of a few pieces. Of course, nobody knows which is better or which is happier.

One of my aunts, for example, spent almost all her life in a small village, with her small world probably consisting of 100 people or so. Yet, her life was a very happy one.

Mine is probably a life connected by a lot of characters, or a jigsaw puzzle with many pieces. Since I was a child, I have had many friends and been surrounded by adults who treated me kindly in various ways. Once I reached adulthood, as a clinician, as a member of academia, and after studying abroad, I have been blessed with friends and mentors all over the world. Even "eccentrics" who are isolated from society, unidentified figures, and somewhat dubious characters are important "pieces" to me.

At my age, unfortunately, it is no longer easy to find new pieces to put into the jigsaw puzzle, or in other words encounter new characters. Of course, as I work as a hospital president, I meet many people each and every day. However, after being alive for more than 60 years, I have established my own classification system, based on which I unconsciously categorize people as "Mr. A is Type 1" and "Ms. B is Type 2." I was convinced that I would no longer find a new piece that would possibly change my whole pattern of classification.

I apologize for the long foreword.

My presumption was completely shattered by my encounter with Dr. Kobayashi. From the moment I met him, I not only realized that he was my senior in terms of age,

タイプ1」「Bさんは、タイプ2」となってしまう。新たなピースが現れて、全体のパターンを変えてしまうようなことはないと確信していた。

　前置きが、随分、長くなった。

　小林先生との出会いは、こんな僕の思い上がりを粉々にしてしまった。年齢的にも僕の先輩であり、業績の大きさも経験の深さも、僕にとって足元にも及ばないことは、お会いしてすぐに分かった。

　しかし、そういう「大物」には、これまでもたくさん出会ってきた。世界の錚々たる大学の学長、グローバルな製薬会社のCEO、誰もが知っているようなスポーツ選手…などなど。もちろん、上っ面の遭遇ではあるが、類型化の本能が、僕の脳の中で働いて、安易な分類をしてしまう。失礼ながら、「この種類の人には、随分出会った」と思ってしまう。こうして類型化された人々は、僕の人生の新しい種類のピースには決してならない。

　しかし、小林利彦先生は、僕の人生のジグゾーパズルにとって、全く新しい、そして、代え難いピースとなった。小林先生は、数回会っただけで、会った相手を魅了する、暖かい、不思議な引力をお持ちである。深い学識。相手の内面を見抜いてしまうような眼力。何よりも、それが、内側からにじみ出る、引き込むような優しさに基づいていることが格別であった。おそらく、小林先生に出会った人々は、みんな、こうした不思議な引力にやられてしまったに違いない。

　もちろん、神経疾患の細胞療法の治験という、素晴らしい仕事のお話を紹介して戴いたのが、最初のきっかけであった。ビジネスのパートナーとしても、先生は、これ以上はないほど、僕と波長が一致した。かなり勝手気ままを言わせてもらい、あるいは、無理もお願いした。いつも、温かい眼差しで見守ってくれた。

　仕事はまだ、道半ばどころか、悪戦苦闘の状態であるが、先生のアドバイスがあれば、この大きな仕事を成し遂げられそうな希望が湧いてくる。

but also that I was nowhere near him in terms of scale of achievement or wealth of experience.

However, I have met many such "big names" before. There were presidents of eminent universities around the world, CEOs of global pharmaceutical companies, famous athletes, and so on. Of course, many of those were superficial encounters, but my instinct to categorize people is always at work in my brain, making cursory classifications. I can't help but rudely think that "I have met this type of person often enough." People who I classify in this way will never be a new "piece" in my life.

Fluttering young swallow
羽ばたく若きツバメ

Dr. Kobayashi, however, became an entirely new and indispensable piece for the jigsaw puzzle in my life. He has a warm yet curious magnetism that attracts even people who have only met him a few times. He possesses profound knowledge, as well as eyes that see inside the person in front of him. More than anything, he is exceptional in that all these things are based on his kindness, which draws people to him. Perhaps, anyone who has met him has felt the allure of these magical attractions.

My first opportunity to really get to know Dr. Kobayashi was when he invited me to a wonderful project, a clinical trial of cellular therapy for neurologic disorders. As business partners, Dr. Kobayashi and I get along extremely well. Although I stick to my own ways sometimes and I ask nearly the impossible at other times, he always watches over me with kind eyes.

The project is not quite at the halfway point or, more accurately, in a state of struggle, but with advice from Dr. Kobayashi, I feel there is hope that I can accomplish this big project.

Dr. Kobayashi is a feminist. Women who are around or working with me (including my wife!) never fail to become a fan of his even after meeting him just once. His charisma, which attracts not only women but also men, is not something anyone can acquire easily. He always speaks calmly, yet he firmly captures women's feelings and he fascinates them with his sound storytelling. I could never do something like that, and I am a bit jealous of him.

先生は、フェミニストである。僕の周りで仕事をしてくれている女性達（家内も含めてだ！）は、間違いなく、一度会っただけで、先生のファンになってしまう。この男女を問わない魅力は、そうそう得られるものではない。お話はいつも穏やかで、それでいて、女性の気持ちをしっかりと捉える、健康的な語りで、彼女らを魅了する。到底、僕にはない魅力である。ちょっと、嫉妬である。

　小林先生は、また、大変な食通（グルメ）である。帝国ホテルの「天一」も京王プラザホテルの「やまなみ」も先生から教わった。今では、僕の数少ないグルメレパートリーの大切な引き出しである。食後には、必ず、「エスプレッソのダブルと温かいミルク‼」をオーダーする。このこだわりの紳士のマナーを、実は、こっそり、僕も真似てみるが、身に付かない。育ちが違うのである。

　今回、小林先生の魅力が詰まった本が出版された。先生の不思議な魅力の秘密を、この本から、解き明かしたいと願っている。

14 ──── ●発刊に寄せて

Dr. Kobayashi is a food connoisseur, too. He is the person who introduced me to "Ten-ichi" at the Imperial Hotel and "Yamanami" at Keio Plaza. Now, these restaurants are valuable additions to my limited cuisine repertoire. After meals, he always orders a "double espresso with hot milk." Secretly, I try to imitate this gentleman's refined manners, but I have never really been able to. The simple fact is that his upbringing was different from mine.

Now, Dr. Kobayashi has published a book that is filled with his personality and appeal. I am hoping to unravel the secret of his magical charm with this book.

Secretaries ／秘書

発刊に寄せて
小林利彦先生への感謝

独立行政法人医薬品医療機器総合機構(PMDA)理事長
近藤達也　M.D., Ph.D.

　小林利彦先生には、心から感謝を申し上げたいことがあります。2008年4月、PMDAに赴任したとき、つまりはドラッグ・ラグ、デバイス・ラグ、安全対策の不十分さの解決策を探っていた矢先である。米国や欧州の規制当局の優れた機能の実情を理解したいと思っていたとき、米国研究製薬工業協会(PhRMA)の日本における代表のお一人であった小林先生にたまたまご挨拶をいただいた折に、日本はどのような点に努力する必要があるのか、組織の理念作りとは異なり、実際のPMDAの業務における戦略や戦術の課題について伺った。小林先生は、明快に申請前相談事業の充実であるとお話しされ、当時は素人であった私に審査時間における無駄な時の流れの解消のヒントを教えてくださった。既にPMDAは、この相談事業に力を入れ始めた時期でもあり、その業務の遂行を見守ったが、その後、大きなラグの解消に繋がったことは申すまでもない。この申請前相談事業は、日本発の有望なシーズを実用化するためにPMDAの薬事戦略相談の開設を促し、現在は、レギュラトリーサイエンス総合・戦略相談に発展し、今日のイノベーションに関わる大事な事業にもなった。

　その後、PhRMAの米国のトップの方々からも、PMDAの業績に直々にご理解頂くようになり、産学官のスマートな連携の社会的な意義を強

Recommendation
My Gratitude for Dr. Toshihiko Kobayashi

Tatsuya Kondo, M.D., Ph.D.

Chief Executive, Pharmaceuticals and Medical Devices Agency

I would like to take this opportunity to express my deepest gratitude to Dr. Toshihiko Kobayashi. In April 2008, I was appointed as the Chief Executive of the Pharmaceuticals and Medical Devices Agency (PMDA), which coincided with the time Japan just began exploring solutions to drug lag, device lag, and inadequate safety measures. At the time, I was trying to understand the actual circumstances, particularly the excellent functions, of the regulatory authorities in Europe and the US. By chance, I had an opportunity to meet Dr. Kobayashi, who was one of the representatives of the Pharmaceutical Research and Manufacturers of America (PhRMA) in Japan, and ask his insights, such as what Japan should focus its efforts on and the issues concerning strategies and tactics in the actual operation of PMDA that differs from building the philosophies of an organization. Dr. Kobayashi simply and clearly told me that it was to improve pre-application consultations, and gave me, someone who at the time had limited experience in pharmaceutical administration and regulations, a clue to eliminating the wasteful passage of time during the review process. As PMDA had just begun focusing its efforts on consultations, I oversaw the progress with his words in mind. It goes without saying that those efforts eventually contributed to a significant elimination of lag. The pre-application consultations led to the launch of the Pharmaceutical Affairs Consultation on R&D Strategy for the purpose of yielding practical applications of promising "seeds" that originate in Japan. It has now been further developed into the Regulatory Science General Consultation/Regulatory Science Strategy Consultation (R&D) and become an important project involved in today's innovations.

After that, the achievements of PMDA began to gradually be recognized and directly endorsed by the US leadership of PhRMA, which made me strongly aware of the social significance of sophisticated collaboration among the industry, academia,

く感じた次第である。医学会出身である当方にとって、かつては、産学官の連携はタブーであった時代に生き、この業務を引き受けたときに、国民に向かって透明性、公平性、倫理性の確保を常に心に誓い、このタブーの解消に努めてきた。この時の小林先生のスマートな意見は今でも忘れることは出来ない。

　このような産学官の連携というタブーへの挑戦は、小林先生と共感する話であるが、武士の戒めの書として名高い佐賀鍋島藩の『葉隠』への憧れにあるのかと思う。「武士道と云うは死ぬことと見つけたり」。自分の利益の為ではなく公益のために働くという滅私奉公の精神の源である。この気概なくして我々の仕事は達成されるものではなかったであろう。

and government. Although I came from academia and lived in an age where collaboration among the industry, academia, and government used to be considered taboo, since assuming this post I have continuously pledged to ensure transparency, fairness, and ethics for the Japanese people and tried to eliminate this taboo. In this endeavor, I have never forgotten Dr. Kobayashi's concise opinion when we first met.

My fight against this taboo of collaboration among the industry, academia, and government is probably rooted in my adoration of "Hagakure" about the Nabeshima clan in the Saga domain, and a reputed book of samurai's precepts, "Bushido is a way of dying." This refers to the source of the spirit of sacrificing oneself for the good of the nation, which is to work, not for one's own interests, but for the benefit of the public. Dr. Kobayashi has empathy for this spirit and without it our efforts at PMDA would have never come to fruition.

発刊に寄せて

東京大学・北海道大学名誉教授
公益財団法人微生物化学研究会理事長
微生物化学研究所所長
柴﨑 正勝　Ph.D.

　尊敬する大先輩であられる小林利彦博士との出会いは約50年程前に遡る。場所は、明治時代に建てられた東京大学薬学部の研究室であった。私は、これから研究生活を始めようとしていた大学院修士課程の一年生。小林博士は、オーストラリア国立大学医学大学院で博士号を取得され帰国された時。

　オーストラリアの研究室とは比較しようもない程古い実験台に向かい、小林博士が水色のコットンパンツ姿で有機合成の実験をされていた姿が今も鮮明である。その時の最も強烈なインパクトは、小林博士の会話も含めた英語の能力。その能力が前著『国際人になるためのInsight Track』、今回の著書『素心』のベースになっていることは明白である。

　小林博士から"そしん"の言葉を聞いたのは、数年前である。恥ずかしながら"そしん"が素心と書くことも知らなかった。素心コンサルティング代表になられた頃と思う。今回の著書で素心の意味することをやさしく解説されておられる。事に当たって動じない心とのことである。この意味するところは、50年に亘って私が尊敬し続けている小林博士の人間性そのものである。生まれ育った坂東市の家を"素心館"と命名しておられることから、小林博士にとって最も大事な言葉であることは明らかである。何故この言葉が小林博士にとってそれ程の重要性を有しているのか大変興味がある。御両親から生を受けた時より、そのような素晴ら

Recommendation

Masakatsu Shibasaki, Ph.D.

Prof. Emeritus of University of Tokyo and Hokkaido University
Representative Director of Institute of Microbial Chemitry(IMC)

My first encounter with Dr. Toshihiko Kobayashi, who is my senior and whom I respect greatly, dates back roughly 50 years. The place was a laboratory in the Faculty of Pharmaceutical Sciences at the University of Tokyo, which was built in the Meiji Era. At the time, I was in my first year of Graduate School and about to begin my research life. Dr. Kobayashi had just received a doctorate from the Australian National University Medical School and returned to Japan.

I can still remember him vividly – he was in front of an old work table, which was humble at best compared to those he probably used in the laboratory in Australia, wearing light-blue cotton pants, and experimenting with organic synthesis. The strongest impact I felt at that time was his English ability, including his conversation. It is obvious that this ability of his is the foundation of his previous book, "Insight Track - To Become an Internationally - Minded Person" as well as this book, "It is Cool – Empathy" (Japanese title: "Soshin").

It was several years ago when I first heard the Japanese word "Soshin" from Dr. Kobayashi. I am embarrassed to admit that I did not even know how "Soshin" was written in kanji (Chinese characters). I think it was around the time he established Soshin Consulting Ltd.. In this book, he explains what "Shoshin" means in an easy-to-understand manner. It refers to an unwavering mind when doing things and it is exactly the very nature of Dr. Kobayashi, for whom I have had respect for over 50 years.

Judging from the fact that he named his family home in Bando City where he was born and raised "Soshin-Kan," it is obvious that "Soshin" is a very important word for Dr. Kobayashi. I am very interested in why this word has such importance to Dr. Kobayashi. I wonder if he was inherently born with such a wonderful trait or, as he expanded the power of his thinking, he began to see his path in the word "Soshin" and used it as his motto. Probably both. The wonderful relationship of over 50 years that I

しい性格の持ち主であられたのか、それとも思考力がつくにつれ、こうあるべきだとの考えから、素心をモットーとされるようになられたのか、である。おそらく両方であろう。小林博士との50年に亘る素晴らしい関係のベースはこの素心にある。私事になるが、私の弱点は、事にあたって動じてしまう性格にあり、必然的に尊敬する先輩に相談したり、愚痴をこぼすことになる。

　その時の小林博士の返答はまさに素心をベースにしたものであった。2つ程典型的な小林博士のコメントをあげさせて頂くと、1）51％の仲間が支援してくれるのであれば、悩まず柴﨑の考えを実行すべき。2）獲得したいものがあるなら、弱音を吐かず、自分の信念は必ず達成されると思い続けるべき、であろうか。今回の著書『素心』を読ませて頂いて強烈に感じていることは、これほど迄幅広い知識をどのように習得されているのだろうか、です。もちろんその知識にとどまらず、小林博士独自の考えを構築されておられるわけでありますが。

　事に当たって動じない心を考えながら『素心』を読まれることを切に希望致します。

22　———●発刊に寄せて

have been privileged to have with him is rooted in this "Soshin." Though it is a personal matter, a weakness of my personality is that I easily waver when doing things, and it is inevitable that I tend to consult my seniors who I respect or end up complaining.

Dr. Kobayashi's answers at such times are based on exactly what "Soshin" is about. I would like to share two of his typical comments with you: 1) If 51% of your colleagues support you, you should do whatever you think is right without worrying, and 2) If you desire something, do not whine, but believe unwaveringly that if you act on your beliefs, the results will always come to you. After reading "It is Cool – Empathy," what I keenly felt was "How does he acquire such extensive knowledge?" Of course, he is not merely acquiring knowledge, but forming his own unique ideas based upon it.

I sincerely hope that you read "It is Cool – Empathy" while thinking about doing things with an unwavering mind or "Soshin."

発刊に寄せて

東京大学理事・副学長
松木 則夫 Ph.D.

　本のタイトルとサブタイトルが『素心 —ぶれない　やさしい—』ということで、どのような内容か貧弱な想像力では分かりませんでした。宗教を扱った哲学的な本かとも思いましたが、内容はさまざまな課題に対して、小林先生が日頃から考えておられることのエッセンスを綴られた本でした。政治問題、製薬企業など経済界の動向、さらにはiPSやAIなど最近の科学トピックスまでが取り上げられ、実に多様な観点からのオムニバスストーリーとなっています。小林先生の豊富な知識と情報収集力、それらを包括的に判断する慧眼により初めて可能になったことが分かります。

　第1章で取り上げられている「Thanks for Nothing」は英語に造詣の深い小林先生ならではの解説で、この言葉にさまざまな含蓄があることを知りました。また、英語の奥深さ、英語圏の文化や欧米人の気質を知ることができました。「Thanks for Nothing」を何かの機会に気取って使ってみたいと思います。

　政治経済の課題についても表面的な解説ではなく、裏事情も考慮した踏み込んだ解説があるので、どんどん引き込まれていきます。日頃、日本のメディアの情報にしか接していない者にとっては目からウロコの思いです。当時のニュース記事を探し出して読んで比較すれば理解度が深まるでしょう。

On the Occasion of Publication

Dr. Norio Matsuki

Executive Vice President and Board Member
The University of Tokyo

When I first heard the title of the book, "It is Cool – Empathy," I was not able to envision what it is about probably due to my poor imagination. For a moment, I thought it may be a philosophical book dealing with religion, but it is actually a book that reveals the essence of Dr. Kobayashi's daily thoughts on various issues. Covering everything from political issues and trends in business circles including pharmaceutical companies to the latest scientific topics such as iPS and AI, it creates an omnibus from extensively diverse perspectives. Now, I can see that the book could not have been completed without his wealth of knowledge, his ability to compile information, and his keen insights that allow for a comprehensive assessment of that knowledge and information.

In Chapter 1, Dr. Kobayashi touches upon an English phrase, "Thanks for nothing." It is commentary that can only be made by someone like Dr. Kobayashi who is proficient in English. For the first time, I realized such a short phrase could have such various meanings. I also learned the depth of English as a language, the cultures of English-speaking countries, and the temperaments of Westerners. I am secretly hoping to use this "Thanks for nothing" in a cool way when the occasion arises.

Dr. Kobayashi's commentaries on political and economic issues are also by no means superficial, as they take into account the backgrounds and hidden circumstances. I was increasingly drawn into the book as I read it. For someone like me who usually only comes into contact with information as reported by the media in Japan, it was like seeing a light in the dark. My understanding will be deepened further if I find news articles at the time and compare them with his commentaries.

One major feature of this book is that it comes with a parallel translation into English. To be more accurate, I should say that it is not a book with a literal translation

本書の大きな特徴は英語の対訳がついていることです。しかし、単に日本語を英語に逐語訳したというものではなく、日本語と英語の両方で書かれていると言うべきでしょう。直訳ではない「活きた英語」を勉強するための良い教科書・手本となることは、前著の『国際人になるためのInsight Track』で既に実証されています。

　本書は幅広い層の読者から支持されるものと思っております。

of Japanese into English, but a book that is written in both Japanese and English. As proven by his previous book, "Insight Track - To Become an Internationally - Minded Person" it will also be a good textbook or exemplar for those who want to study "living English," not just a literal translation.

I am certain this book will be appreciated by a wide range of readers.

目次

発刊に寄せて：
ギル・ヴァン・ボッケレン／實金 清博／近藤 達也／柴﨑 正勝／松木 則夫 ‥‥‥‥‥ 4

第1章 Thanks for Nothing ‥‥‥‥‥‥‥‥‥‥‥ 33

第1話 Thanks for Nothingとは ‥‥‥‥‥‥‥‥‥‥ 34

第2話 Thanks for NothingとG−Zero ‥‥‥‥‥‥‥‥ 42

第3話 BreakthroughとInnovationは違う ‥‥‥‥‥‥ 46

第4話 黒田日銀総裁と異次元 ‥‥‥‥‥‥‥‥‥‥‥ 50

第5話 人財の引き抜きの表・裏 ‥‥‥‥‥‥‥‥‥‥ 54

第6話 何も無いのが一番 ‥‥‥‥‥‥‥‥‥‥‥‥ 60

第7話 無名の効用 ‥‥‥‥‥‥‥‥‥‥‥‥‥‥‥ 64

第8話 無冠の帝王 ‥‥‥‥‥‥‥‥‥‥‥‥‥‥‥ 68

第9話 小さく考える! ‥‥‥‥‥‥‥‥‥‥‥‥‥‥ 72

第10話 慈善事業の今昔 ‥‥‥‥‥‥‥‥‥‥‥‥‥ 76

第11話 2016年米国大統領選挙の台風の目 ‥‥‥‥‥ 80

第12話 読めなくなった欧米医薬品市場 ‥‥‥‥‥‥ 84

第13話 落としどころが見えた脱ヨーロッパ ‥‥‥‥ 90

第14話 "To think is to Dream：考えるということは、
夢の中に夢を追うことである" ‥‥‥‥‥‥ 96

第15話 "質より量"、それとも"量より質" ‥‥‥‥‥ 100

第16話 Money for Nothing：ユートピアなんてあるの? ‥‥ 104

第17話 トランプ政権下のバイオ医薬産業 ‥‥‥‥‥ 108

第18話 君、ワシントンDCに来ないか! ‥‥‥‥‥‥ 112

第19話 難病と予防 ‥‥‥‥‥‥‥‥‥‥‥‥‥‥‥ 116

第20話 独創か提携か ‥‥‥‥‥‥‥‥‥‥‥‥‥‥ 120

Contents

Recommendation
Gil Van Bokkelen Ph.D ／ Kiyohiro Houkin M.D., Ph.D. ／ Tatsuya Kondo M.D., Ph.D. ／ Masakatsu Shibasaki Ph.D. ／ Norio Matsuki Ph.D. ･････････････････ 5

Chapter I Thanks for Nothing ･･････････････････ 33

First Narrative:What is 'Thanks for Nothing' ･････････････････････ 35

Second Narrative:Thanks for Nothing and G-Zero ････････････････ 43

Third Narrative:Breakthrough is Different from Innovation ･･････････ 47

Fourth Narrative:Bank of Japan's Governor Kuroda and Another Dimension ･･ 51

Fifth Narrative:Executive Pipeline:the Front and Back of Headhunting ･･････ 55

Sixth Narrative:Nothing is the Best ････････････････････････ 61

Seventh Narrative:The Benefits of Obscurity ･･････････････････ 65

Eighth Narrative:A King without a Crown ･･････････････････････ 69

Ninth Narrative:Think Small ! ････････････････････････････ 73

Tenth Narrative:Philanthropy – Past and Present ･･････････････ 77

Eleventh Narrative:2016 U.S. Presidential Election - The Eye of the Storm ････ 81

Twelfth Narrative:The Unreadable European Pharmaceutical Market ･･････････ 85

Thirteenth Narrative:Recognizing the Common Ground of Brexit ･･････････ 91

Fourteenth Narrative:To Think is to Dream: To Think is to Pursue the Dream within the Dreams ･･･････････････････ 97

Fifteenth Narrative: "Quality over Quantity" or it is "Quantity over Quality" ･･････････････････････････････････････ 101

Sixteenth Narrative:Money for Nothing: Why is there a Utopia? ････････ 105

Seventeenth Narrative:The Biopharmaceutical Industry under the Trump Administration ･･･････････････････ 109

Eighteenth Narrative:You, Why Don't You Come to Washington DC ! ･････ 113

Nineteenth Narrative:Incurable Disease and Prevention ･･････････ 117

Twentieth Narrative:Originality or Collaboration ･･････････････ 121

第2章 Changes in the Trend of Globalization······125

第1話　グローバリゼーションの中心になろう·············126

第2話　日本は広いぞ、こちらに来ないか·············130

第3話　日本がトップ！再生医療の科学・技術と規制·············134

第4話　脱EU、英国テリーザ・メイ首相バズーカ発射!·············138

第5話　イノベーションへの道は、険しく一筋ではない·············142

第6話　習政権下の中国バイオ医薬研究開発力を診る·············146

第7話　知的財産権、今昔·············150

第8話　薬価──誰のため·············156

第9話　火中の栗を拾え!·············160

第10話　新英国10ポンド紙幣とJane Austen（逝去200年記念）·············164

第11話　教育の無償化·············168

第12話　AI（人工知能）につき一考·············174

第13話　AI（人工知能）につき一考(その2)·············178

第14話　ダ・ヴィンチ(Da Vinci)とミケランジェロ(Michelangelo)·············182

第15話　弱い人と強い人·············186

第16話　クール・ビズで良いのですか·············190

第17話　習政権の中国は一党支配の立憲共和制である·············194

第18話　ノーベル文学賞に本命 カズオ・イシグロ氏·············200

第19話　後継者は要らない·············204

第20話　新世界に七色の虹を·············208

感謝とあとがき·············212

Chapter II Changes in the Trend of Globalization ·········· 125

First Narrative: Becoming the Center of Globalization ······················· 127

Second Narrative: Japan is Spacious, Why not Come Here ···················· 131

Third Narrative: Japan Leads! Regenerative Medical Science, Technology,
and Regulations ··· 135

Fourth Narrative: Brexit, U.K. Prime Minister Theresa May Fires a Bazooka Shot!
·· 139

Fifth Narrative: The Road to Innovation Is Rough and Nonlinear ············· 143

Sixth Narrative: Examining China's Biopharmaceutical Research and
Development Strength under the Xi Administration ·········· 147

Seventh Narrative: Intellectual Property – Past and Present ··················· 151

Eighth Narrative: Drug Prices – Who are they for? ························· 157

Ninth Narrative: Pick the Chestnut out of the Fire ······················· 161

Tenth Narrative: The New British 10 Pound Note and Jane Austen
(200th Commemoration of Her Death) ··················· 165

Eleventh Narrative: Free Education ································· 169

Twelfth Narrative: Thoughts on AI （Artificial Intelligence） ················ 175

Thirteenth Narrative: Thoughts on AI (Artificial Intelligence),Part 2 ········· 179

Fourteenth Narrative: Da Vinci and Michelangelo ····················· 183

Fifteenth Narrative: Weak People and Strong People ···················· 187

Sixteenth Narrative: Is it okay to go with Cool-Biz? ····················· 191

Seventeenth Narrative: China's Xi Administration is a Constitutional
Republic Ruled by One Party   195

Eighteenth Narrative: Favorite for the Nobel Prize in Literature,
Kazuo Ishiguro ······························· 201

Nineteenth Narrative: There is No Need for a Successor ··················· 205

Twentieth Narrative: The New World, Over a Seven Colors Rainbow ········· 209

A Message of Gratitude and Acknowledgements ····················· 213

表紙・扉／写真:©nobmin55 - Fotolia.com

本書は、国際商業出版株式会社『国際医薬品情報』に2015年1月～2017年1月に連載された「Thanks for Nothing」（全20話）、および2017年2月～2017年12月に連載された「Changes in the Trend of Globalization」（全20話）を初出とし、今回の出版に際して加筆・修正を加えております。

第 1 章

Thanks for Nothing

第1話

Thanks for Nothingとは

"Thanks for Nothing"という言葉は、"哲学的な無から政策的な排他に至る"まで、使い方次第で幅のある言葉である。

一方で生臭くなると、最近起きた(2014年10月29日)欧州最大手製薬会社のCEO追放劇など、追放された方も追放した方も、(きれいサッパリ)Thanks for Nothingに違いない。生き馬の目を抜くビジネスの世界はこんなもので、割り切らなければやっていけない。お互いホッとしているに違いない。

このような表題(Thanks for Nothing)で、現に起きている出来事に見解を述べることで、国際医薬品情報の読者の皆様にお役に立てればと思う次第である。

欧州大手製薬のChairman・会長の立ち位置(positioning)が変わった。会社のオペレーションには関係がないという米国のThanks for Nothing(居ないも同然)とは、欧州大手のChairmanは物言うアクチヴィスト(activist)であると同時に共通点がある(後述)。前述したようにサノフィのCEOであるChris Viebacher／CV氏は、一夜にしてChairman、Serge Weinberg氏に解任された(10月29日)。何故だ？ ドイツ系カナダ人であるCV氏は北米(米国)のなかで育まれてきており、フランス文化とは異質だったかもしれない。CV氏の長年(2008～2014)の偉大な業績にもかかわらず、従来の大手製薬企業からの脱却を目指すSerge Weinberg氏(フランスのエリート官僚出身の投資家)とはソリが合わなかったのかもしれない。フランス政府が株主であるサノフィは、フランス人がCEOであるべきだという。日本の大手企業に招かれた某フランス人も候補者というから、この世界は凄まじい(しかし本人否定)。

Narrative 1

What is 'Thanks for Nothing'?

The phrase 'Thanks for Nothing' can be described as "philosophically nonexistent and thus excluded from policy", and depending upon the situation in which it is used, can be broadly interpreted. However, it is often used in a derogatory sarcastic manner to express displeasure with someone who did not provide what was expected. The situation is sometimes unpleasant, as in the October 29, 2014 ousting of a CEO of a large European pharmaceutical manufacturer. The ousted, as well as the ousters, while making a clean break, were mutually saying 'Thanks for Nothing'. Understanding and accepting that this is part of the highly competitive and brutal business world, it is highly likely that both sides were relieved by the resolution of the situation.

Utilizing the title 'Thanks for Nothing', I will share my observations on several events in the hopes of being of some assistance to the readers or to the followers of developments in the international pharmaceutical industry.

Changes in how companies are run are often evident in the positions taken by the Chairmen of major European pharmaceutical manufacturers. US Chairmen often take a 'hands off' approach toward corporate operations in which 'Thanks for Nothing' is virtually absent. In comparison, European Chairmen, while sharing some similarities with their US counterparts, are vocal activists, as I will explain in the later part of this chapter. As earlier noted, the CEO of Sanofi, Chris Viehbacher, was relieved of his position literally overnight by Chairman Serge Weinberg on October 29, 2014. What happened? Chris Viehbacher is a Canadian of German descent who was raised in North America, which may have alienated him from the French culture. Regardless of Chris's many years(2008~2014) of great achievements, friction appears to have developed with Serge Weinberg, a former elite French bureaucrat and investor who was aiming to have more transparency from Chris. In addition, because the French government is one of the major stock holders of Sanofi, there was a belief in France that a Frenchman should be appointed as CEO. A certain French individual who was employed by a major Japanese corporation was rumored to be a candidate for this now open position, although the individual denied it. These actions reflect the ferocity of this industry. In April 2015, Sanofi appointed Olivier Brandicourt as CEO. Brandi-

Chapter I Thanks for Nothing 35

もちろんそれだけではない。いわゆる"Established Products"（自社特許切れ医薬品）といわれる製品群のビジネス方針も絡んでいる。CV氏は売却の方針であったが、会長のWeinberg氏はそれに反対し、社内にその部門を改めて位置付けた。呼応するかのように、12月はじめに突如、GSKのCEO、Sir Andrew Witty氏が、7月頃から公言していたAuction of Older Drugsの取り消しを表明した。これは、何を意味するのか。話が少しそれるが、日本のアステラス製薬が、後発品を捨て新薬に特化したのを、筆者は高く評価している。Thanks for Nothing of Generic（後発品は要りません）。

　さて、かねてより犬猿の仲といわれたロシュとノバルティスの間に異変が起きている。没交渉だったノバルティス前Chairman、Vasella氏（ロシュ株33％取得）とロシュ前会長、Humer氏がともに退任。ノバルティスには、V氏に追放されたJorg Reinhardt氏が戻り、ロシュには前Lufthanza CEOのChristoph Franz氏が就任した。その両Chairmanの下で有能なノバルティスCEO、Jimenez氏とロシュCEO、Severin Swan氏が経営を担うという構図ができ上がった。両Chairmanは、お互いの利益になるなら、スイス国の発展に貢献できるならという共通点を見出して提携も考えようとしている。合併だってあり得る話である。

　昨年（2014）のM＆Aの話題をさらったファイザーによるアストラゼネカ（AZ社）の買収劇は、いろいろあったが、不成功に終わった。その陰でAZ社CEO Pascal Soriot氏の"耐え忍ぶ"という処方せんを、後方で支えたのはAZ社のChairman、Leif Johansson氏である。J氏は、スウェーデン ビジネス界の大物で、AZ社はスウェーデン国の財産であるという考えである。よろしいですか。フランス国のため、スイス国のため、スウェーデン国のためなのである。単なるわが社のためではありません。ここが共通点である。

　昨年（2014）は、M＆Aに絡む企業納税につき、"inversion"とか"domicile"という言葉がよく使われた。アッヴィによるシャイアーの買収がinversionにより頓挫した。一方、注目されたアラガンの買収が、

court was Chairman and CEO of Germany's Bayer Healthcare AG. I am surprised that Bayer's Marijn Dekkers let him go.

Of course there is more to this matter. It involves the business approach involving products referred to as "Established Products," which are mature off-patent products. Chris's position was to sell off the established product lines, however Chairman Weinberg was against this, and internally re-positioned the division. Almost as a response, in early December, GlaxoSmithKline(GSK) CEO, Sir Andrew Witty, announced the cancellation of plans for the 'Auction of Older Drugs', which had been disclosed around July. What does this mean? It was said that Sir Andrew did not want to give up the steady stream of revenue that these products provided. Although not directly related, I highly praise the decision made by Japan's Astellas Pharma to forego generics and pursue the development of innovative drugs because, while this strategy has higher risk, it also has the potential for higher reward. Thanks for Nothing of Generic.

At about this same time, unusual changes were occurring to the known unfavorable relations of Roche and Novartis. The former Novartis Chairman, Daniel Vasella, and Roche's former Chairman, Franz Humer, both resigned. Jorg Reinhardt, who had been dismissed by Vasella, returned to Novartis as Chairman, and former Lufthansa CEO, Christoph Franz, was appointed as Chairman of Roche. Under these two Chairmen were the capable CEOs responsible for managing the firms: Joe Jimenez at Novartis and Severin Swan at Roche. Both Chairmen saw that a merger might be mutually beneficial. They also understood that their companies had the common factor of contributing to the development of Switzerland, which may have been a key factor leading to discussions about a linkage between the two. In addition, there was talk that a merger was not improbable, given that Novartis owned 33% of Roche shares.

In 2014, Pfizer attempted to acquire AstraZeneca, but after a series of events, ultimately failed to do so. Behind the scenes, AstraZeneca's CEO, Pascal Soriot, was pushing the prescription to "Bite the Bullet" and reject Pfizer's takeover attempt. Backing this stance of endurance was AstraZeneca's Chairman, Leif Johansson. Johansson, a major figure within Swedish business circles, believed that AstraZeneca was the property of Sweden. Is it comprehensible? The common denominator in each of these situations was that management was not merely focused upon ensuring the success of their corporation, but felt a sense of national pride, be it for France, Switzerland, or Sweden.

Terms such as 'inversion' or 'domicile' were frequently used during this time

アクチヴィスト、Ackman氏（Allergan株を約10％保有）と協調していたヴァレント（カナダ）のCEO、Pearson氏が成功したかに見えた。11月17日（2016）、伏兵アクタビス（アイルランド）にしてやられた。立役者は、Chief chairman、Paul Bisaro氏である。5.5bnポンド（約10兆円）でアクタビスを買収した氏は、7月にはフォレストを約3兆円で買収、そして今回は約8兆円での買収である。人いわく、彼は機を見るに敏な経営者だと。社交的には、シャイな人物だという。彼こそ、Thanks for Nothingを実行した人である（後述）。

　ミシガン大学出の弁護士である彼は、製薬会社として大きくなったアクタビスを医薬のプロに任せる決断をする。すなわち買収したフォレストLaboのCEO、Brent Saunders氏をCEOに任命し、自らはExecutive Chairmanとなり会社全般を見ている。これは、前述のような欧州的Chairmanでもあると同時にThanks for Nothing（タイトルに拘らない）を実行したのである。

　それでは、何がこの成功をもたらしたのか。そもそもアラガンのCEO、David Pyott氏は、スコットランド出身の両親のもとに英国で生まれた。ありきたりの目薬会社だったアラガンを皺取り治療薬（Botox）により処方薬会社にまで育てた中興の祖である（1998〜2014）。彼の穏やかな口ぶり、そして丁寧な応対は生き馬の目を抜く米国では異質だった。筆者は2001年、彼のオフィスで小一時間話したことがある。

　また、ここでBisaro氏の作戦が冴える。CEOでアイルランド出身のBrent Saunders氏にスコットランド出身のDavid Pyott氏と接触するよう指示を出したのだ。共通の文化的バックグラウンドが急速に親密さを増し、11月17日の発表となった次第である。これこそ、Bisaro氏の買収金の決断"Thanks for Nothing of Dead Money"とスコット魂のDavid Pyott氏の"Thanks for Nothing of Valeant"という3人6脚の賜物である。成功を祈ってやまない。

period when Merger & Acquisition related corporate tax payments were discussed. An example of an inversion can be seen in the Pfizer situation. If Pfizer had been successful in its bid to acquire AstraZeneca, it could have reincorporated in Britain and paid substantially lower corporate taxes.(AstraZeneca had a significant presence in both Sweden and Britain.) AbbVie's attempt to acquire Shire met with a setback due to a reinterpretation of the tax rules regarding inversions.

Finally, attention was mounting on the Allergan acquisition, where the activist hedge fund manager William Ackman(holding an estimated 10% of Allergan stock) teamed up with Valeant's(Canada) CEO, J. Michael Pearson, to launch a hostile takeover, and it looked like they would succeed. However, on November 17, 2014 there was an ambush made by Actavis(Ireland). The leading player behind this was Actavis Board Chairman, Paul Bisaro. As CEO of Watson Pharmaceuticals, he had acquired Actavis for $5.5 billion(estimated 600 billion yen) in November 2012, and in July 2014 he purchased Forest Laboratories for an estimated $25 billion(about 3 trillion yen). He then succeeded in purchasing Allergan for an estimated $66 billion(about 7 trillion yen). According to some individuals, as soon as he recognized an opportunity, he was quick to act. Socially, it was said that he was a shy individual. His actions were in line with 'Thanks for Nothing', which I will endeavor to explain in the following text.

Bisaro, an attorney, graduated from the University of Michigan in 1983. Following the acquisition of Forest Laboratories, he made the decision to allow the pharmaceutical professionals to run what had become a large pharmaceutical corporation: Actavis. In short, he appointed acquired Forest Laboratories CEO, Brent Saunders, as CEO and President of Actavis, while he took the title of Executive Chairman of the Board to oversee the firm in general. His management style represents what I mentioned earlier, both the European-style Chairman and a 'Thanks for Nothing-no concern for a title' attitude.

What brought on this successful acquisition of Allergan? To start with, Allergan's Chairman and CEO, David Pyott, hails from Scotland, while both of his parents were born in the UK. Allergan was a typical eye medicine manufacturer until he built the firm into a prescription pharmaceutical manufacturer with the development of the blockbuster wrinkle treatment Botox(1998-2014). His calm, quiet manner of speech and courteous actions were unusual within the cut-throat corporate US business environment. In 2001, I stopped by his office and spoke with him for about an hour.

Here again, Bisaro's sharp strategy is evident. He instructed CEO Brent Saun-

Chapter I Thanks for Nothing ● —— 39

ders, who is from Ireland, to approach David Pyott, who is from Scotland. With their shared cultural background, a close relationship soon developed, thus resulting in the November 17th announcement. This is an excellent example of Bisaro's acquisition price decision of 'Thanks for Nothing of Dead Money' and David Pyott's 'Thanks for Nothing of Valeant'. The successful acquisition was the result of three remarkable individuals. I will continue to pray for their success.

第2話

Thanks for NothingとG-Zero

ユーラシア・グループ（Eurasia Group）代表のイアン・ブレマー（Ian Bremmer）氏によるG-Zeroという言葉は、当時（2012）新鮮な感じがした。同時に世界はそれ程までに、混迷しているのかと不安も感じた。これは、ノーベル平和賞を授与された米国オバマ大統領の"戦争はもうできない"という外交政策の曖昧さ（Constructive ambiguity）がもたらした結果かと思われる。オバマ大統領のIS・Levantに対する対応には彼の決意を感じるが。

なお、イアン・ブレマー氏については、日経新聞が定期的に取り上げており（2014年6月23日、12月24日）、一読をお薦めしたい。

医薬品業界を眺めてみると、G-Zeroではなく、米国の一人勝ちの状況が続いている—Thanks for Nothing of others—自信満々他国なんか気にしない。何故、そうなのかを考えてみたい。米国はなんだかんだ言っても、マクロ的には豊かな国なのである。今話題のピケティ氏の言う富裕層が多く、彼らは自らの健康のためなら費用を惜しまない。そしてそれを医療保険会社が有効活用する仕組みが存在する。結果として、他の国では当たり前の統制薬価がなく、メーカーが決めるメーカー希望価格というPricingが存在するのは、ご承知のことである。もちろん、オバマ大統領の"Affordable Care"では、かなりのカットが義務付けられている（Plan D）。このメーカーの仕切るPricingに対する当局の風当たりは強く、英国のNICE的風は、米国にも吹くであろう。しかし、筆者はこのPricingこそ米国のBreakthrough（革新）やInnovation（変革）をもたらしていると考えている。なぜなら、米国大手の医薬品会社は変わり身が早い。アウトソーシングできる部門は切り離し、物取りはエクスター

Narrative 2
Thanks for Nothing and G-Zero

The concept of G-Zero by Ian Bremmer of the Eurasia Group describes the position that in international politics Western influence has declined, resulting in a lack of global leadership. In 2012, when I first encountered the G-Zero concept, it was a refreshing experience. At the same time, I was uneasy to learn of the existing global sense of uncertainty. This state of global uncertainty may be the result of constructive ambiguity of foreign affairs policy, as reflected in a sentence in US President Obama's Nobel Peace Prize acceptance speech where he said "And within America, there has long been a tension between those who describe themselves as realists or idealists." If we reflect on how President Obama responded to ISIS-Levant issues, we see that his resolve was evident. Ian Bremmer has been covered periodically by the Nikkei newspaper(For example, June 23, 2014 and December 24, 2014) I would like to suggest that the articles be read.

Ian Bremmer
イアン・ブレマー氏

When viewing the pharmaceutical industry, it is not in a G-Zero state. The US continues to be the leader-'Thanks for Nothing of others'. The US pharmaceutical industry is brimming with confidence, in spite of the progress of pharmaceutical companies in other countries. I would like to reflect on why this is the case. All things said, the US, on a macro level, is a wealthy nation. According to 'Capital' author Thomas Piketty, a large number of the ultra-wealthy reside in the US, and these individuals have no reservations about spending money when it comes to sustaining or improving their health. In addition, an established structure allows health insurance corporations to benefit from this. As a result, the absence of regulated drug pricing, which has become standard in most countries, allows manufacturers to set the suggested retail price. Of course under President Obama's "Affordable Care Act", also known as 'Obama Care', significant mandatory price reductions are required(as seen in Plan D). Pressure is being applied by the responsible government entity to stop pric-

ナル・リサーチと称して投資家に早変わりしている。生き馬の目を抜くとはこのことか。Thanks for Nothing of Others' Eyes。おー、こわーこれはジョークです。

　それでは、Pricingに絡み世界の話題になっているGilead社のC型肝炎の特効薬Harvoniの開発を眺めてみたい。Harvoniの高額なメーカー希望価格をめぐり、いわゆる米国の統制不可能な薬価システムの典型と言われている。しかし、私見であるが、このHarvoniは94％の確率でC型肝炎患者を死から救うといわれる。数週間の延命のために数十万円の費用が掛かるというのとは、訳が違う。

　まさにThanks for Nothing of C-deaths、C型肝炎による死亡がなくなるありがたさよ。米国製薬大手のリスクをかけた研究開発 (投資家としての顔) と成果に対する投資家 (株主) の期待に応えるための薬価体制 (Premium Pricing Model) をどう維持するかという問題である。これと同じ現象は、日本でも起きている。新薬創出・適用外薬解消等促進加算 (Premium Maintenace Pricing) である。Tufts Center for the Study of Drug Developmentによると、主要な欧米製薬企業においては2003年に＄803milだった1品目当たりのR＆D費が今や＄2.6bn (約3千億円) になっており、こうした状況を考慮すると宣なるかなである。

注) 第1話で触れたサノフィのCEOには、フランス人であるオリヴィエ・ブランデイクール氏 (独バイエルのヘルスケアーAGChi会長兼CEO) が4月2日に任命されるという。よくバイエルのマーリィェン・デッカー氏が手離したものだと思っている。

ing being controlled by manufacturers. A US version of UK's NICE may be in the making. However, I believe that it is this pricing mechanism that supports the US pharmaceutical industry's Breakthroughs and Innovation. The reason for this is that major US pharmaceutical corporations are quick to change. Divisional operations are outsourced and procurement is referred to as external research, but in reality these corporations become investors. This is the real cut-throat competition. Thanks for Nothing of Others' Eyes.

I would like to look at the development of Gilead's hepatitis C miracle drug Harvoni, which has become a pricing topic globally. Debate over the high suggested manufacturer's price of Harvoni is a typical example of the US drug pricing system that cannot be regulated. Harvoni has delivered a 94% rate of saving patients with hepatitis C from death, and it is my personal opinion that this cannot be compared to the several thousand dollars spent on extending one's life for a few weeks. Thanks for Nothing of hepatitis C-fatalities. We should all be grateful if there were no further deaths from hepatitis C.

The issue is how to maintain the 'Premium Pricing Model' which factors in the R&D risks taken by major US pharmaceutical manufacturers(as investors) and the expectations of investors(stockholders) toward the results. The same phenomenon is occurring in Japan with the Premium Maintenance Pricing. According to the Tufts Center for the Study of Drug Development, the R&D cost of one product at major European and American pharmaceutical manufacturers in 2003 was $803 million, now it is at $2.6 billion. Taking this reality into consideration, perhaps what we are seeing in US drug prices is inevitable.

NOTE : In the first topic, on April 2015, Sanofi appointed Olivier Brandicourt as CEO. Brandicourt was Chairman and CEO of Germany's Bayer Healthcare AG. I am surprised that Bayer's Marijn Dekkers let him go.

第3話

Breakthroughと Innovationは違う

　ところで、中国では Thanks for Nothingの意味するところを"空霊"と言うらしい。なかなか味のある漢字である。突っ込んで考えたくなるが、それはさておき。

　科学技術分野で Breakthrough（ブレークスルー）とは、どのような時に使うのだろうかと考えてみた。あの成層圏を飛び出して宇宙に飛び出した時のような感じが浮かんできた。Innovation（イノベーション）は、筆者にはブレークスルーには届かないが、家のリフォームに通じる Incremental breakthrough（少しずつブレークスルーしていく）という感じがする。すなわち、次元は変わるが、医薬品で言えば First in Class と Best in Class のような感じか。

　このところバイオ医薬の世界は、そのブレークスルーをめぐり、細胞関連のベンチャー主導で買収に鎬を削っている。しかも3〜4兆円と従来では考えられなかった規模の案件が並ぶ。今まさに抗がん剤の研究がガラッと変わりつつある。

　A．まず、がん免疫療法（Immunocancer Therapies）である。免疫システムを道具として使う。がん細胞が、敵（抗がん剤）から身を守るために着ている見えないマントを見破ることで、がんを征圧しようとする方法である。簡単にいうとがん細胞を外から（制がん剤）攻めるのではなく、がん細胞内の免疫システムを変えることで、がん細胞を自死させるのである。この分野の初期のリーダーは、米国のメルクとブリストル・マイヤーズ スクイブ（BMS）の2社である。がん細胞の Programmed cell death receptor という受容体（PD-1、死に至る段取り）を見破って結合することで、がん細胞を死に追いやる。それが、オプジーボという名の

46 ──── ●第1章　Thanks for Nothing

Narrative 3

Breakthrough is Different from Innovation

It so happens that in China, characters written as "Air Spirit" is their expression of 'Thanks for Nothing'. Quite an interesting choice of characters, for the character for 'air' can also represent 'void' or 'empty'. Although I would like to think about this further, I will move on for now.

Let us ponder on the circumstances in which the word 'Breakthrough' is used in the science/technology field. The example of shooting out of the stratosphere and into outer space comes to mind. Personally, I think 'Innovation' falls short of a 'Breakthrough', and can be thought of as 'incremental breakthroughs'(i.e., steadily making breakthroughs). This can be experienced when renovations are being done to a home. In short, although the magnitude changes, in pharmaceuticals it can be seen as the difference between 'First in Class' and 'Best in Class'.

In the biopharmaceutical sector, this breakthrough factor has become the focal point in the furiously competitive buyout strategies led by cellular related ventures. In addition, transactions on a scale of $27-36 billion(3~4 trillion yen), which were unheard of in the past, have become much more frequent. We may be experiencing a total transformation of cancer drug research. I would like to consider two different strategies: Cancer Immunotherapy and Adoptive Cell Therapies.

Cancer immunotherapy involves the utilization of the immune system to fight cancer. This treatment method entails detecting and penetrating the protective cloak worn by cancer cells to prevent detection by the 'enemy'(anti-cancer drugs), and then conquering the cancer. Simply put, instead of attempting to attack the cancer cells from the outside with toxic anti-cancer drugs, the cancer cell's defense system is altered to set in motion a self-destruction of the cancer cell. Leaders within this area are the two firms US Merck and Bristol Meyer Squibb(BMS). The programmed cell death protein(PD-1) is a receptor on the cell surface. It has the capability to remove the two proteins(PD-L1 and PD-L2) that bind specifically to PD-1, and thus limit the immune cell's ability to attack cancer cells. This capability can be undone by an anti-PD-1 antibody. The mechanism of the new breakthrough drug Opdivo is based upon this approach. The EU approved it in April 2016. An illustrated process was pub-

Chapter Ⅰ Thanks for Nothing ●   47

新薬（ブレークスルー）である。EUで2016年4月に承認を得た。このプロセスを5月6日のFinancial Timesが図解しているので、ご覧になられることをお薦めする。最近、この分野のバイオベンチャーをめぐり、かまびすしい。独メルク、ロシュと続いている。その市場は10年内に4兆円に拡大するともいわれており、益々ヒートアップしている分野でもある。

　B．次にアドプティブ（養子）免疫細胞療法（Adoptive Cell Therapies）である。患者の免疫細胞を取り出してリエンジニアリングにより抗原受容体を持つキメラT-細胞にして元の患者に養子よろしく戻してやるという方法である。Adoptiveとは、粋な名づけで、誰か専門家が良い日本名を考えてくれるでしょう。

　こうしてブレークスルーに成功した暁にはどうなるのか、見てみたい。代表的なバイオ医薬ベンチャーの売上高を5年前と比べると、Gilead 3.5倍、Amgen 2.5倍、Biogen 3.3倍、Celgene 3.3倍、そしてRegeneronはなんと21倍。このようなベンチャーが続々出てきても、その陰には敗者累々…

　第2話では、欧州の大手製薬企業の会長のリーダーシップ・権限拡張に触れたが、今月、5月には、英国最大GSKの会長にSir Philip Hampton氏の着任が発表された。氏は、スコットランド中銀の辣腕で知られた前総裁である。CEO兼社長のSir Andrew Wittyも、業績回復に向けNovartis社とのスワップなどの新しい方策により、医薬品・ワクチン・コンシューマープロダクトに絞り注力している。ここ1〜2年が勝負か。

Cancer cell　　　Straight punch!　　　Baby gang

lished in the May 6, 2016 edition of the Financial Times; I suggest that this be referred to. Recently, the environment surrounding bio-ventures of this sector has become boisterous. Germany's Merck and Roche have also followed the trend. It is said that within 10 years, the market size for cancer immunotherapy drugs will expand to an estimated $35 billion(about 4 trillion yen), furthering the current intense interest toward this sector.

The second strategy I would like to discuss is Adoptive Cell Therapies. The therapy involves the process of removing immune system derived cells(T cells) from the patient or another individual, genetically modifying them into antigen receptor Chimera T-cells, and transferring them to the patient. Using the term Adoptive to name this therapy is fetching, and I am confident that a specialist will think of a similarly appealing Japanese name.

I look forward to seeing what will occur in the event the breakthroughs succeed. Dramatic increases have been seen when comparing current sales with the sales from five years ago of typical pharmaceutical ventures. Examples of these dramatic increases include 3.5 times at Gilead, 2.5 times at Amgen, 3.3 times at Biogen, 3.3 times at Celgene, and an amazing 21 times at Regeneron. Although there is a succession of successful ventures, in the shadows are numerous failures.

In the First Topic, I discussed the leadership and expansion of authority of the chairman of a leading European pharmaceutical corporation. In September 2014, it was announced that Sir Philip Hampton was appointed as Chairman of GlaxoSmithKline(GSK), Britain's largest pharmaceutical corporation. Sir Hampton, the former Chairman of The Royal Bank of Scotland, is noted for his astute management ability. In addition, to improve business performance, GSK's CEO and President, Sir Andrew Witty, has shown unorthodox new business methods, such as conducting swaps with Novartis, and concentrating upon pharmaceuticals, vaccines, and commercial products. The next year or two will be decisive in determining whether or not these two individuals will be successful in guiding the company forward.

第4話

黒田日銀総裁と異次元

　間違っても、黒田日銀総裁も異次元も要らないというのではない。

　黒田東彦日銀総裁は、今や世界のクロダとして、EU連銀総裁ドラギー(Mario Draghi)、米連銀総裁イエレン(Janet Yellen)そして英中銀総裁カーニー(Mark Carney)と並んで世界の金融政策に最も影響のある4人の1人になった。

　黒田氏は、2013年3月に日銀総裁に任命された時、自らを無にして——空霊：Nothing for Thanks——異次元という言葉を選んだに違いない。

　筆者は、第3話でブレークスルー(breakthrough)を成層圏を飛び出し地球の引力から離れることだといった。黒田氏の異次元とは、このbreakthroughを意図したに違いない。すなわち、Breakthrough QQE(Quantitative-Qualitative Easing：質的・量的金融緩和)だったのだ(幸い、当時の英訳を知らない)。

　黒田氏の1発目のバズーカ砲：異次元緩和は、2013年3月31日に鳴り響き、瞬く間に株価上昇と円安を導き、失われた10年といわれた日本経済に明るい見通しを示した。

　また昨年(2014)、株価が低迷すると、まったく予期せぬ第2のバズーカ砲を10月31日に打ち上げ世界をアッと言わせた。まさに世界のクロダの面目躍如だ。これは米連銀のイエレン女史をも出し抜くものだった。欧米の株価も上がり非常に高く評価されている。

　第2の緩和とともに円安が進む様子に、牽制球を投げ周りを煙に巻いている。しかし、素人の筆者は、120円対USドルはあり得ると、3年くらい前から実体験をもとに言ってきたので、あまり驚かない。120円

50 ——●第1章　Thanks for Nothing

Narrative 4

Bank of Japan's Governor Kuroda and Another Dimension

In this topic, I would like to discuss Bank of Japan's Governor Haruhiko Kuroda and his concept of another dimension. Don't be mistaken, I am not saying that there is no need for Governor Kuroda or another dimension. He is now on a global platform. With European Bank President, Mario Draghi, US Federal Reserve System Chairman, Janet Yellen, and Governor of the Bank of England, Mark Carney, he has become one of the four most influential people in global financial policy. When Mr. Kuroda was appointed Governor of the Bank of Japan in March 2013, he probably selected the term 'Empty Spirit'(Thanks for Nothing) to define another dimension to express his mental being.

Within the Third Topic I compared the term breakthrough to shooting out of the earth's gravitational pull into outer space. If I am not mistaken, Kuroda's other dimension was intended as a breakthrough. In short, the Breakthrough was the Quantitative-Qualitative Monetary Easing Policy.

Mr. Kuroda's first bazooka blast, Monetary Easing of Another Dimension, was heard on March 31, 2013. It immediately brought about a rise in the stock market and a lower of yen, and reflected positively on the Japanese economy from its lost decade of recession.

In 2014, when stock prices were hovering at a low level, Kuroda fired a totally unexpected bazooka shot on October 31 which surprised the world. He increased stimulus spending because economic growth and inflation were not increasing as expected. This was in line with the character of the global Kuroda. This move surprised the Federal Reserve's Ms. Yellen. However, Western stock prices rose, and thus Kuroda's strategy was very highly appraised.

Seeing that the second Monetary Easing Policy was lowering the value of the yen, Kuroda started tweaking the Policy and was deluding the public. However, although I am an amateur in economic matters, because I had been saying for several years that, through personal experience, I felt that 120 yen to the US dollar was possible, I am not surprised by Kuroda's actions. I believe that 120 yen to the US dollar is still a high rate, and that even 160 yen to the US dollar would be appropriate. The Japanese are

Chapter I Thanks for Nothing ● —— **51**

ではまだ円高で、160円くらいでもよいと思っている。日本人は知恵があるから、160円になってもトータルバランスは取るはずで、大丈夫である。

　一人勝ちに見えるクロダに比べ、ほかの3人は、それぞれ頭が痛い。ドラギーは、EUのデフレだけではなく、ギリシャ問題（もういい加減にしたら…）、スペイン問題と多事多難だ。しかし彼の頑固そうな面構えは、頼もしい。英中銀のカーニーもカナダ中銀総裁から三顧の礼をもって英銀総裁に迎えられた（前任者の倍の給与）。予期しなかったスコットランズの独立と対応に奔走した。切れ者に期待。

　一方、イエレンにとっては嬉しい悲鳴とも取れる利上げの話で、記者会見をしては周りの反応（Chemistry）を探っている。ほぼ連日、各国の新聞が彼女の記者会見を取り上げており、何といっても"USドルは強いねー"というところですか。

　また黒田氏は類推（analogy）も得意だ。最近では、"ピーターパンは、自分が飛べると信じているから飛べる。飛べるかどうか疑った瞬間に永遠に飛べなくなってしまう"という。おそらく黒田氏は、自ら飛べると信じているからこそ躊躇なく決断ができるのだろう。黒田氏は超自信家だ。小気味が良い。

　そのような黒田氏にも周囲が心配することが出てきた。中国のAIIB（アジアインフラ投資銀行）である。黒田氏は、チャンスと思っているかもしれない。AIIBの総裁（金立群・元中国財務次官）がアジアインフラ投資銀行総裁として登場すると新たな調整が必要となるであろう。いずれは、日本も加わることで情報を得ることの方がメリットがあるのでは。

雪の東京大学赤門
The University of Tokyo Akamon in snow

52 ──── ●第1章　Thanks for Nothing

wise; they will most likely take the total program from Kuroda, and it should be alright.

Although it looked like Kuroda was the lone winner, the other three were respectively facing painful issues. Draghi had to deal with a number of critical events, including the EU deflation, the Greece government-debt crisis(enough already), and the Great Spanish Depression. Although faced with these issues, his determined countenance emanated a sense of resolve. The Bank of England's Carney, who was coaxed out of his position as Governor of the Bank of Canada(by doubled compensation), was kept busy by the unexpected move regarding Scotland's independence. There are always expectations placed on an able leader.

On the other hand, for Yellen, the story surrounding the rise in US interest rates could be compared to her positive assessment of the US economy, which she announced during a press conference as a way of measuring the reaction to her announcement. Almost on a daily basis, newspapers around the world reported on her press conference. At the end of the day, it all could be summed up with the comment, "The US Dollar is Strong".

Further insight into Kuroda's thinking can be gained by looking at his triumphant analogy when he stated that "Peter Pan flies because he believes he can fly. The instant he questions this, he never will be able to fly again."(sic) Presumably Kuroda believes he can fly; this is probably why he can make critical decisions without hesitating. Kuroda is extremely self-confident and bold.

Even for Kuroda there is a development that has those surrounding him worried. It involves China's Asian Infrastructure Investment Bank(AIIB). There is a possibility that Kuroda believes it to be an opportunity for Japan to join this institution. The Governor of AIIB is Jin Liqun, former China Vice Minister of Finance. However, if there are intentions for him to become the governor of the Asia Union, it will probably be necessary to initiate new coordination efforts between Japan and AIIB. Ultimately, Japan joining the AIIB will have the merit of gathering intelligence and information.

第5話

人財の引き抜きの表・裏

　新聞が2015年6月25日一斉に"武田：寝耳に水"と報じた。武田薬品工業のCFOであるフランソワーザヴィエル・ロジェ氏（François-Xavier Roger）が6月26日付けで退任すると。引き抜いたが、引き抜かれた。ある意味で武田もグローバル企業になった証しでもある。この先の成長が続けられるなら、本物である。成長を祈ってやまない。

　これは、常にトップを目指して全力を尽くすロジェ氏の選択であり、誰も止めることはできない。武田も目的地へ向かうマイルストーンだったのである。考えれば、時価総額約5兆円の武田から約30兆円のネスレ社（スイス）のCFOは、魅力のある地位である。氏に自信があるからできることだ。ネスレのCEO ポール・バルキー氏（Paul Bulcke）も良い手を打ったものである。

　グローバルには、エグゼクティブの引き抜きはロジェ氏に限ったことではない。ただ言えることは、お金、地位そしてお金・地位の両方が絡む時がある。

　最近、地位をめぐる驚きの人事があった。かのカラヤンの創立になるベルリン・フィルハーモニク（Berin Philpahamonic）の常任指揮者に選ばれたキリル・ペトレンコ氏（Kirill Petrenko）である。氏はロシアのシベリヤで生まれたが、両親と共に10代でオーストリアの移民となる。最近では、ベルリン・オペラ・ハウスの音楽ディレクターも務め（2007〜2012）、ベルリン・フィルは多様化と若返りを同時に果たしたことになる。

　お金・地位を同時に得た人もいる。ソノトバンクの孫氏の後継者に任命されたニケシュ・アローラ氏（Nikesh Arora）である。報酬は約165億

Narrative 5

Executive Pipeline: the Front and Back of Headhunting

©The Granger Collection/amanaimages

On June 25, 2015, in unison, Japanese newspapers reported "Takeda: Out of the Blue". They were referring to the decision by Takeda Pharmaceutical Company Limited's CFO, François-Xavier Roger, to resign as of June 26. It was a matter of Mr. Roger being pulled in to Takeda only to be pulled out by Nestlé. In a way it reflected that Takeda had become a global corporation in that a company the size of Nestlé was interested in its CFO. If Takeda continues to develop and grow, it will be proof that they are the real thing. I pray for their success.

Herbert von Karajan (1908-1989), Austrian orchestral conductor
ヘルベルト・フォン・カラヤン

As an individual who constantly aims for the top, the choice was Mr. Roger's, and nobody had the right to interfere. For Takeda, the event was a milestone toward their ultimate destination. If we think about it, becoming the CFO of Swiss giant Nestlé, with a 2015 market value of approximately $265 billion(30 trillion yen), was a far more attractive position than staying on with Takeda, whose market value was an estimated $43 billion(5 trillion yen). Mr. Roger possessed the confidence needed to make the move. Nestlé's CEO Paul Bulcke made a good deal.

Globally, the process of attracting superior and able executives is certainly not limited to Mr. Roger. One thing is for certain, it involves the elements of money or prestige, or both. For example, there was a surprising personnel affairs move in June 2015. The prestigious Berlin Philharmonic, which was conducted by Herbert von Karajan for 35 years, announced the election of Kirill Petrenko as its chief conductor, replacing Sir Simon Rattle. Although Mr. Petrenko was born in Siberia, Russia, he immigrated to Austria with his parents when he was in his teens. He is currently the music director of the Bavarian Opera House, and is scheduled to take on the position at the Berlin Philharmonic for the 2019-2020 season. The selection of Mr. Petrenko reflects the orchestra's successful attempt to rejuvenate and diversify.

円という。年俸と契約金の関係が不明なので、コメントは避け、2015年の総収入開示を待ちたい。公表された例を1つ挙げてみたい。銀行業界で話題の多いJPMorgan Chase の頭取 ジェミエー・ダモン氏 (Jamie Dimon) である。基本給は約200万ドル、ストック・オプション他約800万ドル、そして現金約1700万ドルで、総収入は約2700万ドル。約32億円である。一方、中央銀総裁の給与は、紙一枚の薄さである。これを何と見るか、人それぞれで結構です。

さて今回触れたかった人物は、第1話で触れ、2014年10月に突然解任されたサノフィ社の前CEO クリス・ヴィーバッハー氏 (Chris Viebacher) である。9カ月の沈黙を破りヘルスケア事業への復帰を公表した。氏は、前セローノ社のオーナーであるエルネスト・ベルタレリ氏 (Ernesto Bertarelli) と組んで新構想の会社を創るという。ベルタレリ氏といえば、イタリア生まれの在スイスの企業家にして祖父セロノ氏 (Dr. Suren M. Serono) 創立のセローノ社のオーナーでもある。V氏・B氏2人が組めたということは、両氏にとって大満足なのではないだろうか。両者の類まれな才能を生かして創る新構想の会社とは、バイオテックだけでなく医療機器・その技術に基づくものになるという。これこそ、奇しくも欧州の大手バイオ医薬会社が目指している多様化ではないか。V氏がサノフィの新路線をこのように考えていたのではないだろうか。しかも新会社は、ジュネーブに本拠地を置くという。自らの夢を現実のものにする。しかし、一泡吹かせたいのは人情である。目を離せないし、成功を祈ってやまない。

As executives move between corporations, there are those who simultaneously gain both money and status. As an example, there is Nikesh Arora, who was appointed President and Chief Operating Officer of Japan's Softbank Corporation in September 2014, and was first in line to succeed Softbank's Mr. Son as CEO. His pay package for moving to Softbank was said to be $135 million(16.5 billion yen), comprising $16.4 million(2 billion yen) in stock and the remainder in a signing bonus. This was a substantial increase from his pay in 2012 of $51 million in cash and stock as the Head of Global Sales at Google. The following year, his pay at Softbank was $73 million(8 billion yen) making him the third highest paid executive in the world. It is interesting to note that Arora resigned from Softbank less than 2 years after joining the Company due to a disagreement with Son over when Arora would replace Son as CEO.

I will like to bring up another example that has been publicly disclosed. It involves Jamie Dimon, the Chairman and CEO of JP Morgan Chase, a company which never fails to provide topics for discussion within the banking sector. In 2015, his compensation package included a salary of $1.5 million, a cash bonus of $5 million, and a stock award worth $20.5 million, totaling $27 million. This is approximately 3.1 billion yen. On the other hand, the salary of the Chairman of the US Federal Reserve is as thin as a sheet of paper in comparison. How this is viewed is totally upon the individual.

I will like to touch upon an individual that I referred to within the First Topic of this series, Chris Viehbacher, who was abruptly relieved of his post as CEO at Sanofi in 2014. After breaking a silence period of about 9 months, an announcement was made of his return to the healthcare industry. Mr. Viehbacher joined with former Serono CEO, Ernesto Bertarelli, to establish a company, Gurnet Point Capital, based on a new concept. It is a hybrid of venture capital and private equity strategies with a long-term investment focus. Mr. Bertarelli, is the Italian-born Swiss entrepreneur whose grandfather, Pietro Bertarelli, joined Serono when it was founded in 1906. Ernesto succeeded his father, Fabio, as CEO in 1996, and was CEO when it was sold to Merck KGaA of Germany in 2007. After the deal, Bertarelli was reported to have a fortune of close to $15 billion. Upon hearing that Mr. V and Mr. B are collaborating, it must surely mean that they are both extremely confident. Both gentlemen possess unique capabilities that are surely being reflected in this new company they are endeavoring to establish, which will not only specialize in biotech, but also medical devices, and products developed from these technologies. This diversity is exactly what large European biopharmaceutical corporations are aiming to achieve. It is very pos-

カラヤンは将に王将である
Karajan is King

sible that Mr. V was envisioning this new path for Sanofi. While Mr. V and Gurnet Point Capital are located in Cambridge, Massachusetts, USA, they are backed by Waypoint Capital(the Bertarelli family's investment group), which is headquartered in Geneva. Their dreams appear to be becoming a reality. I will pray for their success.

第6話
何も無いのが一番

　今回は、Thanks for Nothing の裏側から、パラドックス風に眺めてみたい。"何も無い"ということが、最も大切な時があるということである。

　この第6話を書き始めた夜（2015年7月22日）、インターネット上で、長年の我が愛読紙フィナンシャル・タイムズ（FT）がこれまた愛読紙日経新聞によって買収との報道が流れているではないか。翌日の日経もFT買収を一面で大きく報じている。7月24日のFTも、一面トップで127年の歴史に終止符を打つと伝えている。まあ一日本にとっては、快挙であり日経新聞に拍手を送りたい。FTの親会社であるピアソン（Pearson）の前CEOマージョリエ・スカルヂノ（Marjorie Scardino）氏が、私を屍にして現CEOジョン・ファレン（John Fallen）がピアソン、すなわちFTを売ってしまったとの嘆き節も、今は空しい。

　しかし、日経もFTの編集権は尊重するというし、FTも不公平なく（without fear or favour）、新しい未来を築く決意を述べている。日経・FT両者の発展を祈って止まない。

　さてさて、序曲が長くなってしまった。本題に戻りたい。"無いのが一番"の例を挙げたい。7月19日の日経新聞"そこが知りたい"に登場した日本たばこ（JT）の社長曰く"たばこで世界一目指す"。たばこを吸うかどうかは、個人の問題で自由である。筆者も1980年まで愛煙家であったが、外資系に移り意外にもアッサリと禁煙することになった。JTの社長の立場としては、そう言わざるを得ないのか、お気の毒である。しかし、日本医師会は2005年5月31日に政府に要望書を提出し、2008年9月17日には禁煙に関する声明文を出している。生活習慣から考えるがん予防を説いた資料"たばことがん"の中で示されている"たばこによ

60 ──── ●第1章　Thanks for Nothing

Narrative 6

Nothing is the Best

In this topic, I would like to take a separate view of the underside of 'Thanks for Nothing'. There is a time when "Possessing Nothing" may be the most important factor.

On the night of July 22, 2015 as I was working in my office, I noticed that over the internet, reports were coming in about the buy-out of the Financial Times(FT), which I had enjoyed reading for many years, by another much-loved media group, the Nikkei. The following day, the Nikkei largely reported its purchase of FT. On the front page of FT's July 24th issue, it reported that its 127 year history had come to an end. For Japan, it was a significant achievement; thus, I applauded the Nikkei. Marjorie Scardino, the former CEO of Pearson which owned the FT, had once stated "over my dead body" regarding a potential sale of FT. However, it became a reality under her successor, John Fallon. Her previous comments now sound barren.

Nikkei said it would respect the editorial independence of FT, and FT would report on the basis of fairness, without fear or favor. Tsuneo Kita, Chairman and CEO of Nikkei, commented that "Together, we will strive to contribute to the development of the global economy." I pray for the continued development of Nikkei and FT.

My prelude has become too long so let me return to the main topic. I offer smoking cigarettes as an example of "Nothing is the best". It is often said that whether you smoke or not is a matter of an individual's freedom of choice. I used to smoke until 1980, but after joining a foreign capital firm I easily quit. In the July 19th, 2015 issue of the Nikkei's column "I want to know that", Japan Tobacco's(JT) President stated, "We aim to become number one in the world with tobacco." For the President of JT, it was perhaps a statement that he could not avoid making, for which I express my sympathies. However, on May 31, 2005, The Japan Medical Association submitted a petition to the government regarding tobacco control, and on September 17, 2008 it put out a statement regarding non-smoking. When I read informational material on the relationship between lifestyle habits and cancer, and see phrases such as "Social Losses due to Tobacco" and "It's Never Too Late to Stop Smoking", I cannot help but question what the president of JT is aiming for. Even if they target a developing nation

Chapter I Thanks for Nothing ●——— 61

る社会的損失"や"遅すぎる禁煙は無い"との指摘を読むと、JT社長の目指すことは、いかがなものかと言わざるを得ない。たばこが普及していない途上国をターゲットにするのは、一時的に潤っても、その後始末(健康被害など)をどうするのだろうか。

　JTがそれを負担する心算なのだろうか。米国では、たばこ産業界が社会的損失を補うために、25年間25兆円(年1兆円)を支払っている。この現実を直視してほしい。

　裏の裏"これは本当に無くてよかったのか"の例を挙げたい。村上ファンドの村上世彰氏とホリエモンこと堀江貴文氏である。共にインサイダー・トレードによる証券法違反により逮捕され数年間服役した貴重な経験の持ち主である。最近、FTが村上氏の復活を大きく扱っている。村上氏の愛娘であるアヤ・ムラカミも南青山不動産・C&IホールディングスのCEOになるという。

　素人の筆者には解らないが、米国だったら日本と違って、両氏とも塀の外に落としたであろう。だから米国には、常に異次元(Breakthrough)の発想とテクノロジーが生まれるのである。

　もう1つ、NHKで日曜日夜11時から放送されていた"ダウントンアビー(Downton Abbey)"。約100年前(第一次世界戦争前後)の英国貴族社会を描いたものである。英国では視聴率40％とか、米国でも高い人気である。日本の"君の名は"みたいなものである。創作したガレス・ニーム(Gareth Neame)氏は、下僕部屋で電気冷蔵庫の購入が話題になった時、料理長のパットモアー夫人(Mrs. Pattmore)に"これを買うと誰かの仕事が要らなくなるから、買うのを止める"と言わせる台本を描いている。氏は、無尽だらけの貴族社会を皮肉ったのであろう。

where tobacco use is not widespread, they may profit for a period. But what about the aftermath(the health damage)? Does JT intend to compensate for the consequences of tobacco use? In the US, the tobacco industry has paid about 25 trillion yen over a period of 25 years(1 trillion yen per year) in compensation for tobacco-related damages. I want people to take a hard look at this reality.

I want to give an example of a double bluff, which is a situation in which a person tries to deceive another by telling them the truth while knowing they will assume it is a lie. It concerns Murakami Fund's Yoshiaki Murakami and Takafumi Horie(aka Horiemon). Both individuals were arrested for insider trading and found guilty. They thus possess the valuable experience of serving time in prison. In early 2015, FT reported a come-back by Mr. Murakami. Mr. Murakami's daughter, Aya Murakami, is the CEO of the investment firm C&I Holdings located in Minami Aoyama. In late 2015, both Yoshiaki and Aya Murakami were being investigated by the Securities and Exchange Surveillance Commission for suspected illegal activities.

Although I am an amateur and would not know precisely, unlike Japan, the US would probably just drop the two gentlemen outside of the fence. That is the reason why the US is in another dimension, constantly inspired(Breakthrough) and introducing new technology.

In another example of a double bluff, for several years at 11:00 every Sunday night Japan's largest broadcasting organization, NHK, broadcast "Downton Abbey". The show was set around 100 years ago(with the first episode set before WW1 and the last episode set in 1926) and evolved around an aristocratic British family. Audience ratings in the UK were said to be at 40%. Even in the US it was an extremely popular program, similar to Japan's popular animation film, "Kimi no Na Wa"(Your Name ?). The producer, Gareth Neame, reflected on how the characters were very much like us. For example, when the issue of whether a refrigerator was to be purchased for the kitchen, Mrs. Patmore(the cook) did not like the idea, because she saw it as something that would put someone out of a job. This was probably a sarcastic view of the aristocratic class.

第7話

無名の効用

　無名であることは具合の悪いこと（unjust）ではない。むしろ成長のためにはご利益（goriyaku・benefit）でもある。

　高い望みのある作家は、今は無名でも、秘かに己の成功のため自らを研いている。最近話題の芥川賞・直木賞のうち直木賞を目指す作家にその傾向が強いように見える。良いことである。高い望みを達成するまでには、人知れぬ個々の苦悩・葛藤があると思う。このような情況を、心理学では防衛規制（Defence of Mechanism）という。心理治療・療法士であるナオミ・シラガイ（Naomi Shragai）によれば、自らの情況を把握できていれば何とかなるという。そうはいかない強いストレスの場合、2つの対処法があるという。1つ目は、心理学でいう自助（self-help）である。誰かがいった自分とはうまく付き合った方がいいよ、一生一緒だから──というところですか。あまり衝動的にならないことである。最近気になるのは、筆者にとって普通と思われる方が"うつ"の薬を処方されている場合が多いことである。筆者の著書『国際人になるためのInsight Track』の第2章 第16話で触れた瞑想（Meditation）を読んでいただくと良いのですが。

　2つ目は、外部からの助け（outside-help）である。専門医により"うつ"と診断された方の中でも組織で働いている方は、行政、同僚・上司そして隣り組などが、支援してくれる恵まれた方々である。個人で働いている場合は、家族の支援が必要であり、また、市町村の窓口に相談することをお勧めしたい。とにかく、独りであまり頑張らないことである。筆者は迷ったら、潜在意識に考えるのを任せて、ゆっくりすることにしている。目が覚めた時の最初の答えが正解、そして実行。単純である。

Narrative 7

The Benefits of Obscurity

Obscurity is not necessarily an inconvenience or an unjust status. On the contrary, it can be a benefit toward an individual's development and advancement.

An author with high aspirations, although unknown early in their career, is in all likelihood secretly honing him/herself toward success. In the talked about prestigious literary Akutagawa Award and Naoki Award, this trend is strongly evident in authors who aim for the Naoki Award, which I believe is a good thing. Those who strive to fulfill high aspirations will face numerous emotions, hardships, and obstacles in the process. They may use an unconscious psychological mechanism to lower the anxiety they experience in this situation. In the practice of psychology, this state is referred to as the Defense Mechanism. According to psychotherapist Naomi Shragai, if an individual can grasp his/her current situation and the unconscious forces that influence their decisions, they are likely to be alright. However, in cases of severe stress, there are two methods to overcome this. The first method is, in psychological terms, 'self-help' in which individuals work to change their habits and character traits to improve themselves. Someone once said, "It will be in your interest to stay on good terms with me, because we will be together forever." It may be better to be less impulsive and more thoughtful in your actions. Recently I have become concerned that an alarming number of people, whom I believe to be ordinary individuals, are being prescribed medication for depression. Within narrative 16 of my book "Insight Track" touch upon 'Meditation', which I would like to suggest be read.

The second method is to receive 'outside help'. According to specialists, those who are diagnosed with depression and are employed in an organization, benefit from the support of colleagues, superiors, and programs provided by the government. Those who are self-employed need the support of their family. I would like to advise these individuals, or family members, to visit their local government offices for information on the support programs. The important thing is not to try too hard. For example, I myself, when it is difficult to gather my thoughts, allow my subconscious to take over and relax. When I awaken, the first answer that pops into my head is the right one, which I act upon. It is simplicity.

さて、無名の効用をバイオ・医薬分野で眺めてみたい。まさにそのものズバリである。筆者は、米国バイオベンチャーの戦略アドバイザーとして現役である。そのバイオベンチャーのCEOであるギル・ヴァン・ボッケレン氏（Gil Van Bokkelen）たるや、八面六臂の活躍である。自ら異次元（Breakthrough）の科学技術を理解し、資金集めに奔走している。なぜ？今は無名でも、バイオベンチャーの成功例といわれるAmgen、CelgeneやBiogenになりたいからである。ここで重要なのは、基礎科学（CSO）・規制・臨床・予算管理（CFO）・IT・人事と採用に飛び切りの人材（COO）を配置していることである。幹部の異動がない——ガバナンスがしっかりしている証拠。すべての従業員が自らのミッションを理解している。すなわち、CEOは能力だけではない、部下から慕われるだけの信頼と心が必要なのだ。

　ところで、Risk-Parityという言葉をご存じだろうか。リスクをどのように配分するかということである。分散しすぎると戦線が拡大し、速度が出ず成果が出ない。一極集中の資金配分をすれば、プロジェクトが失敗すればすべて終わりである。CEOは、常に難しい選択を求められている。数多くのベンチャーが誕生しては、消えていく。広野の果ての月見草、ひとり咲くべき恋の夜に……咲けないのだ。蜻蛉の如し。

　このRisk-Parityの間違いをしたのは、最近の東芝であろう。畏友、三菱ケミカルホールディングス会長兼経済同友会代表幹事である小林喜光氏の社外取締役としての辣腕に期待したい。1年と時限を切ったのは、凄い。成功を祈ってやまない。

I would like to discuss how obscurity is beneficial in the biopharmaceutical sector because it is absolutely spot-on. Currently I am a strategy advisor for a US-based bio venture. The CEO of this firm, Dr.Gilvan Bokkelen is unbelievably task-oriented. He understands the potential of his breakthrough in scientific technology; thus he is looking for investors. Why? Because, although unknown now, their goal is to become a bio venture success similar to Amgen, Celgene, and Biogen. What becomes vital to achieve this goal are the basic science(driven by the Chief Science Officer - CSO), the regulatory/clinical trials/budget management(controlled by the Chief Financial Officer - CFO), the information technology(IT), and the personnel. It is crucial to secure the best possible human resources. In this company, there are no transfers among the executives, which is proof of sound governance. All employees are very aware of and understand their respective mission and goals. In short, it is not just a CEO's capabilities that are important, but the respect and trust that he/she garners from those who work for him/her are also important.

By the way, are you aware of the term 'Risk-Parity'? It is the practice of trying to equalize the risk in a financial portfolio by dividing the risk levels and asset distribution across a wide range of categories(e.g., stocks, bonds, and inflation hedges) within the portfolio. However, allocating funds into too many categories increases the necessity of continuous oversight and, depending upon the approach taken, does not yield beneficial results. If an over-concentration of funds is made into a specific category and the category fails, all is lost. In the same way, CEOs are constantly required to make difficult choices in trying to balance the risks in their companies. While some succeed, many fail. Countless venture companies are born and disappear. These companies are analogous to the lone evening primrose blooming in the fields, which is reminiscent of a promised night of romance that, alas, was not to be.

An example of mistaken Risk-Parity was recently made by Toshiba. Their purchase of Westinghouse Company, which subsequently filed for bankruptcy protection amid an accounting scandal, has put Toshiba in a very difficult financial position. A trusted friend, Mitsubishi Chemical Holdings Chairman and Chairman of the Association of Corporate Executives, Yoshimitsu Kobayashi, is an external board member of Toshiba. I anticipate his astute participation on the Board. A one year time limit has been established for Toshiba to strengthen its finances, which is amazing. I will continue to pray for his success.

第8話

無冠の帝王

ドン・キホーテ
Don Quijote
© scusi - Fotolia.com

　無冠の帝王、いいじゃないですか。裸の王様という言葉もあるし。他人（ヒト）は誰も気づいていないのに、自分が実はすべての決定権を握っている帝王であることを自覚しているなんて、格好いいじゃないですか。凄い体験をした人物を思い出し、彼こそこの稿にふさわしいと思い紹介します。
　その名は、オリバー・サックス（Oliver Sacks）。最近ニューヨーク（NY）で82歳で亡くなった精神内科医である。彼は1933年ロンドン北西部ユダヤ社会の裕福な医師の家に生まれ、オックスフォード大学で医学を修め医師となり米国に渡った。時に1960年。西海岸サンフランシスコやロサンゼルスで病院勤務の後、NYに移った。NYでの生活と神経精神医学に魅了され、以来生涯をNYで過ごした。なにゆえ、この様に彼の生い立ちを書いたかは、彼のユダヤ人としての特殊な悩みと葛藤に、後ほど触れるためである。
　まず、精神医学分野での先駆的活動に触れたい。当時"Sleepy Sickness"（眠り病）といわれる、今でいう"うつ病"があった。彼は患者の社会復帰のために新薬を開発しようとして、L-Dopa（L・ドーパ、現在の抗パーキンソン病薬）を患者に投与する新薬開発治験を行っている。もちろん周囲の協力があってのことであるが、凄い集中力とエネルギーである。患者は一時的に社会復帰ができても、再発する結果となった。しかし、当時L-Dopaに目を付けるなんて、なんとアンテロレノアー（企

Narrative 8
A King without a Crown

You may have heard of the tale of the 'Emperor's New Clothes.' There is also the phrase, 'A King without a Crown'. Although many do not realize it, there are those who aim for a position in which they have the final say in all decisive matters, literally becoming an emperor of sorts or a king without a crown. Why not? It reminds me of an amazing individual for whom this narrative is made for. I will introduce the individual.

His name is Oliver Sacks, a renowned neurologist, who passed away in August 2015 in New York at the age of 82. He was born in 1933 in the Jewish community of Cricklewood,(northwest) London, England. Both of his parents were physicians. Sacks received his medical degree from Queen's College, Oxford before moving to the US in 1960. After an internship in San Francisco and a residency in neurology and neuropathology at University of California, Los Angeles(UCLA), he moved to New York. He was fascinated with living in NY and with his work as a neurologist, and thus lived out his days in NY. Some may wonder why I am referring to the life of Oliver Sacks. It has to do with his fight with a specific anguish that afflicts the Jewish people, which I will touch upon later.

Hans Christian Andersen
(1805-1875)
ハンス・クリスチャン・アンデルセン

First, I would like to discuss a pioneering activity within the field of neurology. In the 1920s what was referred to as 'Sleeping Sickness' is actually an atypical form of encephalitis in which the disease attacks the brain. Sacks conducted research into a drug that would assist his patients' return to society. The drug was L-Dopa(currently used to treat Parkinson's disease). Of course he had cooperation and assistance from those around him, but I believe that he possessed unbelievable concentration and energy. Although his patients enjoyed a period of returning to society, it was only for a limited period of time. However, recognizing L-Dopa as a treatment for this disease - what an entrepreneurial spirit!

Now, returning to the anguish he suffered because he was Jewish. Normally the term Goyim(Goyim:for those who are non-Jews, please refer to Chapter 9 of my first

Chapter Ⅰ Thanks for Nothing

業家精神)なんだ！

　さて、彼にはユダヤ人であるが故の悩みと葛藤があった。通常のゴイム（Goyim：ユダヤ人にとっての異邦人）の中で暮らす生活環境の悩みと葛藤ではない。正統派のユダヤ人夫婦であった両親に、彼の真の心を打ち明けた時の両親の驚きと戸惑いは大変なことであったという。また、それはユダヤの教義にも反することであるので、彼は両親とユダヤの教義に自己をどのように律してきたのか。それにも耐えてきた集中力は、精神医学に対するそれとも共通するものである。彼自身は自らの生き方を貫き、彼自身がすべてを決める帝王であったことの証ではないかと思う。時代は移り、世界がそうだが、彼自身も同性愛者であること公にした。

　もう一例、無冠の帝王は誰だったのかを語りたい。中年以降では、知る人ぞ知るであるが、「007」のショーン・コネリーである。アンソニー・ホロヴィッツ（Anthony Horowitz）による"James Bond TRIGGER MORTIS"に詳しいが、ショーン・コネリー自身は、役柄の定着を気にして007の役を降りたいと頼んでも、ここまで人気が出るとシリーズものとして続けなくてはならなかった。銀幕での帝王は将にショーン・コネリーであったが、決定権を持っていた帝王は製作者だったというわけである。以降の彼の名作の数々と現在の演技は、帝王である。

"Lunch in Monaco、Dinner in Moscow"といわれて世界を飛び回っているダイヤモンドディーラーがいる。その名は、オデイト・マンソリ（Oded　Mansori）、アントワープに居を置く。はて、マンソリがダイヤをコントロールしていたのか、ダイヤが彼を支配していたのか。ダイヤである。ダイヤは、やはり宝石の帝王である。

series "The Ten Commandments of Becoming an Internationally Minded Person") would refer to those who live a lifestyle that is alien to the Jewish people. However, Oliver Sacks' parents were orthodox Jews. It is hard to imagine the surprise and confusion they experienced when they learned of his true feelings. In addition, since his personal preferences were against the Jewish faith and beliefs, he was not only defying his parents, but the Jewish faith as well. How did he impose the self-discipline to live his life according to his convictions? The concentration required to endure can perhaps be compared with or is similar to neurology. I believe that his conviction to live his own life demonstrates that he was an emperor who made his own decisions. With the passing of time and society's evolving to accept an individual's personal choices, he made public his homosexuality.

I would like to share another example about one who is a king without a crown. The individual I am referring to is Sean Connery of 007 fame. According to Anthony Horowitz, who is the author of the James Bond novel "TRIGGER MORTIS", Sean Connery himself wanted to avoid becoming stereotyped with the role of 007 and no longer wished to play the role. However, because the series was immensely popular, it was only natural that it would continue with him acting as Bond. As a general of the real emperors of the silver screen, Connery did not hold the right to decide. It was the true emperors, the producers, who held the power. In the end, the unforgettable films which followed his Bond films and his superior acting skills reflect that he is a true emperor.

A final example of a king without a crown is described in 'Lunch in Monaco, Dinner in Moscow.' It tells of a day in the life of a globe-trotting diamond dealer. That diamond dealer's name is Oded Mansori, who resides in Antwerp. Let us take a moment to consider the situation: does Mansori control the diamonds, or do the diamonds control Mansori? It is the diamonds. The diamonds are King!

Chapter I Thanks for Nothing ● —— 71

第9話

小さく考える！

　本シリーズの第2話でG-Zeroを取り上げたのをご記憶であろうか。中東シリアの現政権をめぐる駆け引きに端を発したパリ(仏)の更なるテロ殺人。欧米の主要各国と中東の盟主の鳩首協議も役に立たないという。この混沌はどうしようもないと嘆くが(Nothing works)、どのような事態にも必ず解はあるというのが筆者の基本である。時間の制約はあっても。

　そろそろ、小さく考えてみようではありませんか(Think Small)。資本主義下のマーケットは、すべて証拠があっての話である(Evidence Based：EB)。しかし、バイオ医薬業界にしろ、ホテル業界にしろ、幻想に踊らされている感じがする。本当にエビデンスに基づいているのだろうか。大きく考える(Think Big)と長期化して往々にして失敗している。時の流れに勝てない。

　バイオ医薬業界のグローバルM＆Aを見ていると、おい、大丈夫かいと声をかけたくなる。バイオベンチャーでは、Valeant (CEO, J. Machael (Mike) Pearson) とActavis (現Allergan、CEO, Brenton L. Saunders) が小回りが利くベンチャーよろしく自由自在に動き回っている。一方、大手のPfizerやGSKは巨体を持て余して喉が渇いているのがよく解る。

　ValeantのCEOは、カナダ生まれの大男でマッケンジーで鍛えた根っからのM＆A男である。バンバンM＆Aを繰り返し、次週には製品の値上げ(60％)を断行するというタフガイである。

　それに対して空売りを仕掛けられた株価は250ドルから一気に50ドルに急降下。仕掛けたのは、アンドルー・レフト(Andrew Left)である。辣腕の投資家ビル・アックマン(Bill Ackman)ですら、あいた口が塞が

Narrative 9
Think Small!

You may recall that within the Second Topic of this series, I brought up the issue of Ground Zero. The murderous terrorist attack committed in Paris(France) in 2015 was the result of dealings surrounding the government within Middle Eastern Syria and Iraq. Talks involving key western nations and the leaders of the Middle East appear to be useless. Although there are those who lament that 'Nothing Works' in stopping this chaotic situation, I fundamentally believe that no matter what the circumstances, there is a solution, even when there is a time restriction. I would suggest that maybe we should start to 'Think Small'. In a market under capitalism everything is said to be 'Evidence Based.' However, be it the biopharmaceutical industry or the hotel industry, I feel that manipulation through illusion exists. I would ask, "Is every decision really based on evidence?" 'Thinking Big' and prolongation of the status quo more often than not fails. We cannot win against the current of the times if we do not pursue alternate solutions.

A Colt with big head thinks things right
仔馬は穢れなきものを見る

When we look at the global mergers & acquisitions in the biopharmaceutical industry, there are times when I would like to say, "Hey, are you really sure about this?" In the bio-venture sector, J. Michael(Mike) Pearson, the CEO of Valeant Pharmaceuticals until April 2016, and Brenton L. Saunders, the CEO of Actavis(now Allergan), have been able to smoothly guide their companies' paths in the pharmaceutical industry. On the other hand, large corporations such as Pfizer and GSK find that their humongous size is a hindrance in pursuing their plans.

Pearson, a massive gentleman born in Canada, began his career as a consultant at McKinsey & Company. He became a true M&A man, becoming a Director in the firm. He was a truly vigorous man whose aggressive tactics were credited with the financial success of Valeant. While in the process of conducting multiple M&A transactions, he would deliver strong growth in product sales.

らないといった具合である。さて、彼の運命は今月後半 (2016) に開かれる上院の薬価についての公聴会で、どのように正当化するのかが注目である。差しは得意だが、公聴会は苦手という……はたして。

さて、大手の話に戻そう。昨年のAZ買収に失敗したPfizerが、その根付いたPfizer-Modelの追求を止めることは無いと信じていたが、今度こそは成功するのではないかと思っている。Pfizer CEOイヤン・リードは、今は米国籍であるが、スコットランドに生まれ穏やかな人といわれる。ロンドン大学インペリアル・カレッジでエンジニアリングを修め、のちに公認会計士になり1978年よりPfizerに在籍。対照的な人物であるAllergan (アイルランド・ダブリン市) CEOソウンダー (元フォレスト・ラボCEO) との差しの話も進んでいるようだし、イヤン・リード後のファイザーCEOも視野に入り、ソウンダー (B. Saunders) としては満足であろう。

この合併が成立すると、次はGSKあたりを狙うかもしれずバイオ医薬業界はコモディティの時代に突入し、新薬創生はベンチャーに投資して賄うのか。まったくの異次元の世界になるのか。

しかし、ちょっと気になる点がある。R&Dの人が見切りを付けて去っていくであろう、ベンチャーあたりに。そして納税国がアイルランドになることで210億ドルの節税に対する米国の政策を跳ね返せるのか、大変興味がある。ちなみに合併不成立の時に支払うブレークフィーがたったの4億ドルといわれている。ひびの入ったカップで苦いティーを飲んでいる2人は見たくない。

However, in 2015/2016 Valeant's stock price drastically dropped by more than 90%. Much of the decline was due to a short selling of the stock which was initiated by the activist short-seller Andrew Left. Even Bill Ackman, the shrewd activist investor who owned about 31 million shares of Valeant stock, was struck speechless. Pearson's fate was determined by the outcome of findings of the Senate Special Committee on Aging, which was probing the soaring prices of prescription drugs. The Committee ultimately ordered his removal as CEO of Valeant in April, 2016.

Now, I would like to return to the topic of large corporations. As I discussed in the First Topic, in 2014, Pfizer failed in its attempt to acquire AstraZeneca. I was convinced that they would continue to pursue the established Pfizer Model of acquiring rival companies. Pfizer's CEO, Ian Read, a Scottish-born American, is said to be a genial man. He received a bachelor's degree in Chemical Engineering from Imperial College London, later becoming a chartered accountant, and starting with Pfizer in 1978. A contrasting individual is Allergan(Dublin, Ireland) CEO, Brent Saunders(former CEO and President of Forest Laboratories). In April 2016, Pfizer was in a position to purchase Allergan and it appeared that Saunders would eventually become Pfizer's CEO following Ian Read.

One of the drivers of the deal was that paying taxes in Ireland would have resulted in a tax saving of about 21 billion dollars. However, due to new rules from the US Department of Treasury which removed potential tax benefits, Pfizer and Allergan ended negotiations and Saunders remained at Allergan. Because the Treasury appeared willing to do almost anything to block the merger, Pfizer's Board felt that they had to stop the deal even though it had agreed to pay a break-free penalty of up to 400 million dollars.

After the negotiations with Allergan were ended, there were news reports that Pfizer's next target was GSK. It appears that the biopharmaceutical industry may be entering an age where it is a commodity, and developing a new drug will be through investing in a venture. Drug development could also be through a totally different dimension. However, a point that concerns me about this model is that those who are responsible for R&D will give up, leave the firm, and maybe join ventures.

第10話
慈善事業の今昔

　さて慈善事業を眺めてみたいと考えたのは、慈善事業といっても、その動機は何なのだろうと思ったからである。そう、慈善事業にも目的がある筈である。どのような？これは事業費を享受する側で決まるのである。

　たとえば、マリア・テレサ（Maria Teresa）、公園、教育機関、老人ホームなどの慈善事業への寄付であれば、善意の寄付となる。しかし、大統領選の政党への寄付となると趣が変わってくる。

　最近の驚くべき真（まこと）の慈善事業の例を挙げてみたい。2015年7月4日に、サウジアラビア国王子（前国王の甥）アルワリード（Alwaleed）とその王妃アメーラ（Ameera）がその生涯を通して3200億ドルを主にサウジ国の慈善事業に寄付をすると公表。また2015年12月2日には、マーク　ザッカーバーグ（Mark Zuckerberg）と妻の（Doctress）プリシラ・チャン（Priscilla Chan）が愛娘マキシム（Maxim）の誕生を祝って、フェイスブックの株式99％（現在価値で4500億ドル）を、慈善事業に寄付をしていくと発表した。それも生涯を通してである。金額の大きさに驚いたが、その動機となった人物がいた。

　その人こそ、ともすると我々が世界一の金持ちだから寄付は当たり前だと思っていた、ビル＆メリンダ・ゲイツ（Bill & Merinda）である。毎年400億ドルを寄付している彼に学んだという。我々も少額でもそうしたいものである。

　また別の観点から。筆者がまだ若かった頃、尊敬と憧れとでも言おうか、その生い立ちと苦労の果ての成功に魅せられた人物が2人いた。その一人は、『国際人になるためのInsight Track』の第1章第14話で取り

Narrative 10
Philanthropy – Past and Present

St. Maria Teresa
聖人となったマリア・テレサ

The reason I thought of reflecting on philanthropy is to try to elucidate what motivates individuals or corporations to be philanthropic. Yes, there must be an objective or aim for a philanthropic project. What would it be? This is often decided by those who receive the funding.

For example, Maria Teresa, Grand Duchess of Luxembourg; educational institutions; and elderly care facilities are goodwill philanthropic causes. However, in a presidential election campaign, donating to a specific political party changes the character of monetary contributions so that they are not considered philanthropy.

I wish to introduce examples of surprising genuine philanthropic causes. On July 4, 2015, Saudi Arabian Prince Alwaleed bin Talal(nephew of the former King) and his then wife, Princess Ameera, announced that through the Alwaleed Philanthropies organization they would donate 32 billion dollars(all of his wealth) to charity. On December 1, 2015, Mark Zuckerberg and his wife, Priscilla Chan, in celebration of the birth of their daughter, Maxima, announced they would eventually give 99% of their FaceBook shares(estimated worth at the time was about 45 billion dollars) to the Chan-Zuckerberg Initiative. This is to be carried out over the course of their lives. The sheer size of the sum is astonishing, but it is also fascinating that there was one couple who seemed to provide the motivation. That couple is one of wealthiest in the world, who we would naturally assume would donate to a cause, Bill & Melinda Gates. We can all learn from their practice of making annual endowments amounting to about 4 billion dollars. Even if the sum is small, we should also follow suit.

Now, from a different perspective, when I was young, there were two individuals whom I respected and idolized for the success they had achieved, in spite of their upbringing and the hardships they had faced. One of them is mentioned within the

上げた世界の新聞王となったニューズ・コーポレーションのルパート・マードック(オーストラリア)である。今、裁判で苦労しているが。もう一人は、今も輝いているジョージ・ソロス(George Soros)。ハンガリー生まれのユダヤ(隠れ:父親は姓をScwartzからSorosに変えたほど)の投資家にして慈善事業家(現在、米国／ハンガリー国籍)である。ご存じの方も多いのでは。

一躍世界の注目を浴びたのは、ロンドンで育てられた彼が、1992年英国銀行を相手に100億ドルを空売りし、英銀の政策決定を右往左往させ、しかも10億ドルの鞘を得たという事件(?)である。もちろん、異論があってもおかしくないが、彼にもそれなりの理由があったはずである。

ともあれ彼の最も大きい功績は、自らが苦しんだ世界:共産主義の息の詰まる社会に対して行った大きな基金・慈善事業であろう。現在までに浄財110億ドルを、アフリカ、中東ヨーロッパ、中国、アジア、米国などに注いでいる。

彼の信条は、Concept of Frexibility:因果の回り合わせ——原因と結果が双方向性をもち、均衡と不均衡の中で、どのようにバランスを取っていくのか見抜いて投資そして浄財を配分していくのかを自らの鋭い勘と分析力、そして内助の功で決めているのである、多分。彼は1960年に結婚をしてから離婚を2回して、現在は3度目の結婚をTamiko Boldon(2013年、42歳年下)としてラブラブである。最後に、彼女は母親が日本人、そして父親が米国人で日米のバイカルチャーであることを加えたい。

余談ではあるが、第9話で触れたヴァリアント社CEOピアソン氏。公聴会は苦手といわれていたが、その前に重症肺炎で3か月の長期入院。3か月限定のCEO代理を任命する始末。ご意見番の張本氏なら、カッーッ!

Fourteenth Topic of my former book ; Insight Track for Internationally, that person is the media mogul Rupert Murdoch who owns News Corporation, and who was on trial as recently as 2015 for a wire-tapping scandal.

The other individual is the ever intense George Soros. He was born in Hungary to a non-observant Jewish family, who were uncomfortable with their roots. His father changed their name from the Jewish Schwartz to Soros. George Soros is a Hungarian-American investor and philanthropist who is known to many due to his high profile investments and deals in currency speculation.

He became famous overnight because of one of these deals. Although he was raised in London and attended the London School of Economics, in 1992 he became known as "The Man Who Broke the Bank of England" because of his short sale of 10 billion US dollars' worth of Pound sterling, and in the process making a profit estimated to be over 1 billion dollars. Of course, there may be those who hold another opinion of his actions, but he must have had his reasons.

Aside from this, Soros has a far greater achievement, which was his role in the transition of Eastern Europe from communism to capitalism by the significant donations he made. Up to the present, he has donated 12 billion US dollars to Africa, Eastern Europe, China, Asia, and the U.S. to reduce poverty and increase transparency.

He developed the concept of reflexivity, in which the biases of individuals enter into market transactions, potentially changing the fundamentals of the economy. He further proposed that changed fundamentals lead to the interactivity of cause and effect and the equilibrium and disequilibrium conditions, resulting in boom and bust cycles. I assume that he keenly measures and balances investments and the distribution of donations to be made. In his personal life, he has been married three times and divorced twice. In 2013, he married his third and current wife, Tamiko Bolton, who is 42 years his junior. She is the daughter of a Japanese-American nurse and a retired naval commander.

On another subject, within the Ninth Topic of this book, I mentioned Valeant's CEO, J. Michael Pearson. It has been reported that he disliked the Congressional Hearings, but before he was able to testify to the Committee, he was hospitalized with severe pneumonia for three months, making it necessary for Valeant's Board of Directors to appoint a proxy Office of the CEO for a term of three months. The woes of Valeant!

第11話
2016年米国大統領選挙の台風の目

　まだ向こう正面というのに、第3コーナーを回った感じの米国大統領選。見物する側としては、これほどスリリングなことはないが、世界の潮目が変わる中、米国の潮目もターニングを迎えたのか。米国の潮の流れを読むには、英国、EU、アジアだけでも日・中・韓そしてASEAN他、中東そしてスカンジナビアなどとも関連が深く、地球規模で見ないと簡単に占うことはできない。そんな米国大統領選の行方を、その影響をもろに受ける日本の潮の流れも見ながら、素人の筆者が切ってみたい。

　筆者には、台風の目となるのは前NY市長ブルームバーグ（M.B.Bloomberg）氏ではないかと思える。民主党（～2001）から共和党（2001～2007）、そして現在は独立（民主・共和に属さない無所属）であるが、2001年から2013年まで3期連続でNY市長を務めた。2000年初め頃のNY市は、犯罪数の増加と環境悪化の只中であり、マンハッタンに足を踏み入れた時の異様な雰囲気は忘れられない。しかし、行くたびにキレイになっていくマンハッタンに驚きを禁じ得なかった。氏が自ら創設のブルーグバーグL.P.を離れ、そのビジネス成功の体験をNY市で実験をしたのだ。保有する資産400億ドルを見れば、腕は確かなのがお分かりになるだろう。その彼が米国大統領になったら、米国が良い方向に変わるのは間違いないであろう。何といってもいまだに世界の中心は米国である。そのような立ち位置での、ブルームバーグ氏への期待は大きい。

　氏が立候補するケースを想定してみたい。①共和指名トランプ氏――民主指名サンダース氏なら、確実に立候補し100％の当選を期する。②共和指名トランプ氏――民主クリントン氏の場合、クリントン氏圧勝と

Narrative 11

2016 U.S. Presidential Election - The Eye of the Storm

Although they were still running on the far side of the track, the candidates of the 2016 U.S. presidential election seemed to be running down the home stretch early in the campaign. For those of us who are viewers, nothing compares to the excitement in an environment in which the tides are changing. It looked as though the U.S. had come to a turning point. To read the tidal changes in the U.S.at this time, it became evident that it involved looking at countries such as the U.K. and the E.U. It also involved looking in the Asian region at Japan, China, Korea, and the Association of Southeast Asian Nations(ASEAN), and in the Middle East and Scandinavia, which are all deeply related. It became obvious that the election had to be viewed on a global scale if one were going to try to predict the outcome. Japan would be directly impacted by the results of the U.S. presidential election. While much of the impact is yet to be felt, the manner in which the U.S. has interacted with North Korea has had a large influence on Japan, and will continue to do so. Although I am an amateur at political predictions, I would like to share with you the analysis I made regarding the tidal changes of 2016 presidential election.

I believed that the eye of the storm would be former New York Mayor, Michael Rubens "Mike" Bloomberg. He was a Democrat before 2001, a Republican from 2001 to about 2007, and an Independent from 2007 to the present. From 2001 to 2013, he served 3 consecutive terms as Mayor of New York City. In the early 2000's New York City was in the middle of an increase in crime and the deterioration of the environment. I will not forget the strange atmosphere when I first stepped into Manhanttan. However, each time I visited, Manhanttan had become cleaner and more inviting. I just could not help but be surprised. Bloomberg had left the firm he founded, Bloomberg L.P., and applied his experience of succeeding in business to the problems in New York City. Looking at his massive personal net worth of 40 billion dollars, it was easy to assume that he was good at what he did. If he became President of the United States, it seemed evident to me that the U.S. would pursue a sound and favorable path. It also seemed to me that the center of the world lay with the U.S. because of its global financial and political presence. In that respect, expectations toward

Chapter I Thanks for Nothing ● ——— **81**

読めば、出ない。しかし両氏伯仲なら出馬。当然当選を期する。

　噂によると、ブルームバーグL.Pでは、2017年から8年間はボスがいないという状況を想定し、新CEO、新COOなどすでに決めたというので、立候補の可能性は高く、米国史上初のユダヤ系大統領誕生となるのか、個人的にも非常に関心が高い。英国では、ヴィクトリア朝の大物政治家としてベンジャミン・ディズレーリ（スペイン系セファルディム）が2期にわたり英国首相（1868、1874～80）を務めている。

　興味深いことに、2月24日のフィナンシャルタイムズに、元英国首相ブレア（Blair、労働党）が米国大統領選についてコメントしている。すなわち、15年の英国総選挙で同じ労働党党首を左寄り政策と批判したように、米国の民主党候補者サンダース氏の左寄り政策をリスクのある政策と批判しているのである。トランプ氏は論外とも。

　ここでちょっと変わった視点を通して、この選挙を眺めてみたい。その視点とは、本シリーズ第10話で触れたジョージ・ソロス氏の目である。ソロス氏自身、そのConcept of Frexibility（因果の廻り合わせ）の論理ですでに新大統領については、織り込み済みかもしれないが、問題は彼がその資産をどこに投資するかである。中国経済のハードランディングに触れるソロス氏に対し、何度も対決姿勢を崩さない中国政府との確執の中で、ソロス氏がどう出るのかで大変なことになる。どうぞ米国新大統領に祝砲を！

キャンベラ素心会
Canberra Soshin club

Bloomberg were quite significant.

I would like to discuss a hypothesis regarding Bloomberg's candidacy as President. Senario 1. Republican nominee, Donald Trump. Democratic nominee, Bernie Saunders. Bloomberg would voice his candidacy with a very high possibility of winning. Senario 2. Republican nominee, Donald Trump. Democratic nominee, Hillary Clinton. If there was a high possibility of a landslide victory for Hillary Clinton, Bloomberg would not run. However, if Trump and Clinton appeared to be evenly matched, Bloomberg would run. Of course, I had high expectations for his election to the highest office of the United States. Ultimately, it appeared that Senario 2 would be the outcome of the election. Bloomberg announced that he would not run for president and endorsed Hillary Clinton.

It was rumored that at Bloomberg L.P., a simulation was made for the absence of its boss for 8 years beginning in 2017. Potential executives were designated for such positions as CEO and COO, reflecting a high possibility of his candidacy. If Bloomberg had decided to run for President, it would have been the first time two presidential candidates in the same election were of Jewish decent. Personally, I was extremely interested in this. In the United Kingdom during the Victorian era, the prominent politician Benjamin Disraeli(Sephardic Jew) served as Prime Minister twice, first in 1868, then again from about 1874 to about 1880.

What is also very interesting, is that in the February 24, 2016 issue of the Financial Times, former British Prime Minister Tony Blair(Labor Party) commented on the U.S. presidential elections. In short, he said that Bernie Saunders seemed to have leftist policy ideas very similar to those of Jereym Corbyn, the left-wing candidate who was elected Labour Party leader following Labour's defeat in the British general elections of 2015. Saunders probably should have contemplated the risks involved in taking a leftist position.

Here, I would like to endeavor to take a different view of the election. I would like to look at it from the point of view of Mr. George Soros, who I wrote about in the Tenth Topic of this series. Soros himself, with his Concept of Reflexivity(the relationship of cause and effect and its impact on the cycles in financial markets), probably narrowed in on the potential new President quite some time before the election. The more vital issue was where he would invest his vast assets. After becoming alarmed at the popularity of Trump, he poured millions of dollars into the campaigns of Hillary Clinton and other Democratic candidates. In the face of Mr. Soros's prediction of a hard landing for the Chinese economy, China continues to take a confrontational position. I wish the best of luck to the new President of the United States.

Chapter I Thanks for Nothing ● —— 83

第12話

読めなくなった欧米医薬品市場

　ノバルティスCEO、Joe Jimenezが嘆いて曰く"ホッケーステック型のような新薬販売はもう過去のものだ"と。健康保険会社(HMO)も、他の支払者(企業、納税者である患者)も財布の紐を締め始めた。たとえば、ノバルティスの新薬Entresto(心不全)は、ピーク年には50億ドルを期待しているが、何と発売第1四半期に、たったの0.17億ドルしか出なかったというのだ。どうしてこのような事態になったのか、背景を探りたい。

　まず、皆様ご高承のごとく、日本には世界に誇る国民皆保険という公的薬価がある。米国にはメーカー希望価格という価格があるが、これは私的な薬の値段である。再度取り上げることになるが(本シリーズ第9話)、バリアント(カナダ)のCEO Michael Pearsonが(結局取締役会から追放)、この米国の価格制度を悪用し金曜日に買収をし、翌月曜日には被買収会社の医薬価格を3〜5倍にして、HMOは供給を止められず、バリアントは荒稼ぎをするということを繰り返した。これで、医薬品市場は支払い側が躊躇し混乱した。供給側も支払い側もブレーキを踏んだのである。

　前Chairman、Daniel Vassella氏の呪縛から解かれたJoe Dimenez氏は、嘆きながらも着々と3分野(ワクチン、アニマル ヘルスとOver-the-Counter医薬)に収斂させ、より焦点の定まった組織の出船を果たした。興味のあるGSKとのワクチンとがん領域の交換という、相手GSKのCEO Sir Andrew(Witty)にとっても職を賭しての選択である。双方の成功を祈って止まない。

　さて、オバマ大統領・財務長官の突然の税制改革(Inversion:節税のために低税制の海外に納税(Domicil)することを阻止する)のためにあっ

Narrative 12

The Unreadable European Pharmaceutical Market

Novartis's CEO, Joe Jimenez, bemoaned the observation that "Hockey Stick sales patterns for new drugs are a thing of the past." Health Management Organizations(HMOs) along with other payers(corporations and tax-payers) are beginning to tighten their purse strings. For example, Novartis'new drug Entresto(a treatment for heart failure) was expected to earn $5 billion in a peak year. However, results of its first quarter of sales showed that sales were only $170,000($0.17million). Why did this occur? I would like to take a closer look into the background of what may have led to this mishap.

Firstly, as many of you are well aware, Japan boasts universal health insurance coverage that includes official, regulated drug prices. In the United States, manufacturers set the suggested retail price, which is a private drug pricing system or a market-based pricing system. In Topic Nine of this series, I discussed Valeant's(a Canadian company) CEO Michael Pearson, who was ultimately deposed of his position as CEO by Valeant's Board. He had exploited the US drug pricing system by buying the rights to older drugs or conducting a corporate buy-out one day and then raising the prices and selling the older drugs or the drugs of the acquired company at prices 3~5 times higher a few days later. HMOs were unable to terminate distribution of these drugs to patients because some patients' lives depended on them. This allowed Valeant to repeatedly rake in profits based solely on exorbitant price increases, resulting in payers becoming hesitant and confused. Both suppliers and payers applied the brakes and the Senate Special Committee on Aging held hearings to investigate the situation.

In dark......
暗闇……

さり退散したファイザーとアラガン (2015年11月24日) の現状が、また興味深い。

　合併後Ian Read氏の後継CEOを夢見ていたアラガンのCEO Brenton Saunders氏は、株価は急落し (23%)、立て直しに躍起になっている。新たなバイオ医薬のビジネスモデルといわれたSpeciality Pharma (特化医薬製品群に集中) が問われているということである。先ほどのバリアントのM.Peason氏やB.Saunders氏 (もちろん、Peasonと一緒にしては気の毒であるが) などが先駆者である。ここで違いを見せなくてはならないのが、Saunders氏である。彼に言わせると、社内研究からの新薬 (抗がん免疫治療関連) そしてM & A、所謂 "Open Science" に賭ける他はない。幸い中長期治験臨床製品が70ほどあるという。自社株買いもやるという。成功を祈りたい。

　一方、ファイザーは、5月18日にアナコールの買収 (52億ドル) を発表したが、まあ焼け石に水か。落ち目のGSKでも買収しないと。ファイザー社内ではIan Readの後継者に内定していたGeno Germanoは、合併が無くても、ファイザーから退任するという。この3月に東京で会う機会があり、他人 (ヒト) の話もよく聞く耳を持ち、医科学の知識も豊富で決断のできる大物の印象を受けた。それこそ、GSKのCEO Sir Andrew (Witty) が自ら探している後継者に指名されるかもしれない。そうなったら、ファイザーが食うのか、GSKが食うのか。生き馬の目を抜くこの世界、目が離せない。最近の情報では、GenoはGSKには行かず、自身の戦略会社を設立したようである。

Joe Jimenez, who has been released from the legacy of former Chairman Daniel Vasella, lamented the situation of dismantling parts of Novartis, but stoically proceeded to withdraw from three areas: vaccines, animal health, and Over-the-Counter(OTC) drugs, thus allowing a more focused organization to set sail. In 2014, Novartis sold its animal health business to Eli Lilly. In a complicated deal, Novartis obtained GSK's cancer drug business while GSK obtained Novartis's vaccines division and control of a joint venture involving OTC drugs. In making this deal, GSK's CEO Sir Andrew Witty put his job on the line. I prayed for an outcome that would be a success for both sides.

When President Obama's Treasury Secretary, Jacob Lew, suddenly announced new tax regulations to discourage inversions(the practice of moving corporate headquarters overseas after a merger to cut tax payments), it foiled the deal between Pfizer and Allergan(November 24, 2015). I would like to reflect on how this affected their situations.

If the merger had succeeded, Allergan's CEO Brenton Saunders had planned to succeed Pfizer's Ian Read as CEO of the combined company. However, when the merger failed, the Allergan stock price took a free-fall of about 23%, and Saunders had to frantically try to regain control. A new biopharmaceutical business model, the 'Specialty Pharma' which entailed developing high cost, high complexity specialized drugs, was being scrutinized. The previously mentioned CEO of Valeant, M. Pearson, and B. Saunders were two of the pioneers of this model. Of course, it is unfair to place Saunders with Pearson because their business models to become 'Specialty Pharmas' were so different. It is here that I would like to briefly describe the difference between them. Mr. Saunders said that they believe strongly in innovation and R&D, and that they have invested heavily in both. He further said that they have sustainable growth in the areas they focus on. When they pursue acquisitions, they rely on "Open Science" and growth assets, not mature assets. He stated that they have a social responsibility to price their drugs responsibly.(Matthew Herper, Forbes, Pharma & Healthcare, April 6, 2016) Luckily, it was said that there were 70 products in Allergan's mid- to long-term clinical trial pipeline. It was also said that Allergan intended to buy back their company's stock. I prayed for their success.

On the other hand, although Pfizer on May 17, 2016 announced that it would acquire Anacor for $5.2 billion, it may just have been a token move. There was some speculation that Pfizer would bring more value to shareholders in the company if the company was broken up. But to do so, it would have needed new drugs to assure it prospered. They may have had to acquire the declining GSK. In September 2016,

花を咲かせよう　もう一度！
Hope, flowery again!

Pfizer announced that would not break up. Internally at Pfizer, Geno Germano, who was slated to succeed Ian Read, said that even without a merger, he would leave Pfizer. I had the chance to meet him in Tokyo in March 2016, and had the impression that he is a good listener, knowledgeable in medical science, and can make difficult decisions, all of which are elements of a superb leader. There was some speculation that he might have been named the successor CEO at GSK that current CEO Sir Andrew Witty was personally searching for. In that scenario, would Pfizer be the predator, or GSK? In the dog-eat-dog environment of this industry, one cannot be complacent. Recent information revealed that Geno decided not to join GSK and established his own strategic consulting firm.

第13話
落としどころが見えた脱ヨーロッパ

　欧米というとヨーロッパ（ドイツ、フランス、イタリア他）と米国となるのが普通かもしれない。しかし、筆者にとっては、欧がロンドンになるのである。若い頃見た現エリザベス女王の戴冠式の写真などの影響かもしれない。そんな訳で、"英国びいき/Angrophile"なのである。

　それはともかくとして、自信満々のカメロン前英国首相による国民投票（2016年6月23日）の結果、Brexit（脱EU）派が、55.3％対44.7％の大差で逆転勝利した。驚きであった。また意外に早く、離脱派のライバル、アンドレア・リードソン女史（Andrea Leadsom）の脱落により、テレサ・メイ女史（Theresa May）が7月13日英国首相に選ばれた。首相になるや、豹変した。"Brexit is Brexit /脱EUありき"。したたかである。ライバル脱落前には、早めに解散をして国民投票を行いEU残留を目指すような発言をしていたが、どうしてどうして……。ここは、じっくり2～3年をかけてEU（ドイツ、フランス他）と交渉し、EU側から、残ってほしいというシグナルを待つのではないかという成り行きに、筆者は賭けたい。また7月14日（木）に首相官邸（Number 10 Downing Street）に入るや、数時間後にはオズボーン蔵相（George Osborne）を解任。外相には離脱派のボリス・ジョンソン氏（Boris Johnson）を任命、多難なEUとの交渉に充てるという何とも巧妙な決断。舌を巻く。

　この辺で、夫君フイリップ・メイ氏（Philip May）とのなれ初めに触れたい。共にオックスフォード大学出身、1976年に知り合い1980年に結婚という40年に及ぶおしどり夫婦である。ただ残念なのは、子宝に恵まれなかったこととも言っている。

　さて脱EUにより、世界の経済が後退するのではないかという懸念が

90 ───●第1章　Thanks for Nothing

Narrative 13

Recognizing the Common Ground of Brexit

ⓒZUMA Press/amanaimages

The Japanese characters representing the western hemisphere are naturally taken as Europe(Germany, France, Italy, etc.) and the United States. However, for me, when I think of Europe, London comes to mind. This is probably influenced by the coronation photograph of the current Queen Elizabeth II that I saw when I was young. That is why I am what is referred to as an "Anglophile"(an individual who favors or admires England).

Mr. Cameron, too confident!
自信満々だったカメロン前英国首相

Putting that aside, the overly confident former British Prime Minister Cameron decided to hold a referendum to determine whether the UK would remain in the European Union(EU) or leave it(informally known as Brexit), which was held on June 23, 2016. The results were surprising in that 51.9% voted in favor of Brexit vs. 48.1% voted in favor of remaining in the EU. This was a turnabout victory by a slim margin. Early in the aftermath of the referendum, Cameron announced that he would resign as Prime Minister. In the campaign to choose his replacement, Leave campaign rival Andrea Leadsom suddenly withdrew from the race, which led to Theresa May being elected on July 13th as England's Prime Minister.

Prior to her rival's withdrawal, May mentioned her intentions to call for an early dissolution and prepare for another referendum that would enable England to remain in the EU. Soon after becoming Prime Minister, there was a sudden change of attitude. Although there was a petition with more than 4 million signatures to hold a second referendum on Brexit, it was rejected by the government. "Brexit means Brexit" she said quite shrewdly. After her election, she said that she would not trigger Article 50(the article that governs withdrawal from the EU in the Treaty on European Union) until a unified, UK-wide approach was established. Intentions appear to be to conduct exit negotiations with members of the EU(Germany, France, etc.) over a span of 2-3 years, while waiting for some sign from the EU that they wish for England to re-

紙上をにぎわしているが、時間と空間を無くしたITがある。筆者は、専門家ではないがあまり心配をしていない。

　このあたりで、バイオ医薬品業界に与えるインパクトについて私見を述べたい。EUの行政センターのあるベルギー・ブリュッセルからEMA（European Medicines Agency：ヨーロッパ医薬品庁）がロンドンに移行してすでに21年（1995年〜）が経つ。地球上に人間が住む限り、病気は発生し患者が生まれる。二重手間を取ることがあってはならない。世界の各国が協調して、例えばICH（日米EU医薬品規制調和国際会議）が音頭をとって直ちに動けば大丈夫である。

　さて、ちょっと違う視点で、脱EUを見てみたい。ファッション界の皇帝、狐の毛皮をかぶった狼といわれるLVMHのバーナード・アーノード（Barnard Arnaud）（2012年10月8日〈通巻971号P.32〉）は、英国のファッション界にとっては、Brexitは厄介なことになるという。2015年でも英国ファッション界は28bnポンド（約4兆円）の売上と88万人の従業員を支えている。だからこそ、国民投票の前に残留の大々的なキャンペーンを張ったのにともいう。ただ英国・フランス・イタリアのファッション関係者は共通の理念と利害で絆を築いてきた。脱EU後も、バラバラにならないよう、皇帝アーノルドに力を発揮してもらいたいものである。

　最後になるが、英国がEU離脱を正式に通達した段階で、EU各国の理解と結束を目的に2009年に成立したリスボン協定（Lisbon Treaty）の50条の1.〜5.に沿って解決して行かなければならないという関門がある。ボリス・ジョンソン氏にとって楽ではない仕事である。メイ宰相曰く（？）、まず汗をかきなさい。

main in the EU. This is something I would like to see occur. However, the leadership in the EU appears to be firm in the position that exit negotiations should proceed. In addition, on Thursday, July 14th, a few hours after officially arriving at the Prime Minister's residence(Number 10 Downing Street), Ms. May relieved George Osborne of his position as Chancellor of the Exchequer and replaced him with Philip Hammond. She appointed Boris Johnson as Secretary of State for Foreign and Commonwealth Affairs, making him responsible for the trouble-filled Brexit negotiations. This was an ingenious decision because he was a prominent figure in the Leave EU campaign. It left me speechless with admiration.

It is here that I would like to touch upon the Prime Minister's husband, Philip May. They are both graduates of Oxford University, meeting in 1976 and marrying in 1980; they have been happily together for the past 40 years. In perhaps the only unfortunate element of this union, May has shared her regret that they were not able to have children.

Around the time of the referendum, there were concerns being voiced in the news that Britain's leaving the EU would bring about a regression to the global economy. However, although I am not an expert, I am not that concerned because of information technology(IT), which has obliterated the boundaries of time and space.

At this point, allow me to share my personal observation of the potential impact to the biopharmaceutical industry. The administrative center of the EU is located in Brussels, Belgium, from which the EMA(European Medicines Agency) had re-located to London 22 years ago(1995). As long as there is human life on this planet, there will be patients who fall prey to a disease or ailment. There should never be a duplication of a process or work in order to focus resources on treatments and cures for patients. To obtain this, a global cooperation of nations is necessary. For example, the ICH(Japan/U.S./EU International Council for Harmonization) could take the lead in the transition of Britain's exit from the EU, and by acting immediately would help bring stability to the industry.

Allow me to present a different view of Britain leaving the EU. The ruler of the fashion world, who is often referred to as the wolf wearing a fox's fur, is LVMH's Bernard Arnault.(volume 971, P.32 of October 8, 2012) He has stated that within the English fashion industry, Brexit will bring about problems. In 2015, the English fashion industry made 28 billion pounds(estimated 4 trillion yen)and employed 880,000 people. This is the reason that before the referendum, the fashion industry conducted a huge campaign for Britain to stay in the EU. However, those who represent the English, French, and Italian fashion industries have created a bond, sharing mutual

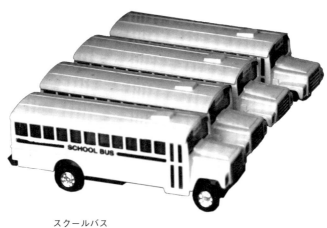

スクールバス
School bus

94 ──●第1章　Thanks for Nothing

principles and interests. After the decision for Britain to leave the EU becomes a reality, I look forward to the ruling emperor Arnault exerting his powers to ensure that this bond is not broken.

In closing, when England officially notifies the EU of its intentions to leave the Union, a hurdle they will face is that resolutions are to be made in line with Article 50, Clauses 1~5 of the 2009 Lisbon Treaty, the treaty ensuring that nations of the EU share an understanding and are united. It will prove to be a difficult task for Boris Johnson to negotiate Britain's exit.

第14話

"To think is to Dream：考えるということは、夢の中に夢を追うことである"

ⓒArchivio GBB/ CONTRASTO/
amanaimages

ウオルター・ベンジャミン氏
Walter Benjamin

　最近、"To think is to Dream"という言葉に出会った。誰が言ったのか調べたら、かの有名な哲学者、作家そして翻訳家ドイツ系ユダヤ人（アシケナージ）ウオルター・ベンジャミン（Walter Benjamin　1892〜1940）であった。彼は、独自の夢を追い続け、天命の終わりは自死であった。48歳であった。自死で思い出したのが、ほぼ同世代の72歳で自死した川端康成（1899〜1972）である。

　1892年に生を受けたウオルターは、ドイツ、フランス、ポルトガルに滞在し米国ビザを取得（1940）するも、スペイン系警察からフランスに追放されパリへと帰国。ナチに追われ転々とした。しかし、パレスチナ（後に1948年のイスラエル建国の地）には行っていない。単なるシオニズムとは違うのである。そこに彼の夢を見つけることは無いと判断したのだろう。一方1968年ノーベル文学賞授賞式で"美しい日本"と賛美した祖国を持つ川端とはあまりにも対照的といえる。

　自死を選んだ心の奥底には芸術家・哲学者としての共通の何かがあったのではないかと思わざるを得ない。この2人の生きてきた環境、結婚、仕事（小説家、哲学者、評論家）、自死に至る過程などを、素人である筆者が、考えてみるのも少しは意義がある。素人の目は、うそを付けないから。

　まず共に女性には魅力のある人であろうことは想像できる。川端の人を射るあの大きな眼そして豊かな髪、端正な顔立ちと、ウオルターの端

Narrative 14

To Think is to Dream: To Think is to Pursue the Dream within the Dream

Recently I have come in contact with the phrase, "To think is to Dream." I looked into whom this phrase is attributed to and discovered that it was the renowned German jewish(Ashkenazi) philosopher, author, and translator, Walter Benjamin(1892 – 1940). Throughout his lifetime he had relentlessly pursued his dream. However, his life fatefully ended with suicide. His suicide brought back the memory of a Japanese novelist of roughly the same generation, Yasunari Kawabata(1899 – 1972), who committed suicide at the age of 72.

Yasunari Kawabata received the Nobel Prize for literature (1968)
川端康成は1968年にノーベル文学賞を受賞した

Born in 1892, Walter resided in Germany, France, and Portugal, although while trying to obtain a U.S. visa in 1940, he was deported to Paris by the Spanish police. Pursued by the Nazis, he moved from place to place. However, he did not go to Palestine, which later became the State of Israel in 1948. It is not a simple matter of Zionism. It can be concluded that he did not find his dream there. On the other hand, it is a stark comparison to Yasunari Kawabata, who in his acceptance speech for the 1968 Nobel Prize for Literature, praised his homeland as "the beautiful Japan".

I cannot escape from the assumption that there must be something in common deep down inside the hearts of artists and philosophers who choose to end their own lives. I would like to examine the process of how these two individuals arrived at suicide by looking at the environment in which they lived, including their marriages and professions(novelist, philosopher, and critic). I may be an amateur, but I believe that there is, to some extent, meaning to think about the matter. An amateur's eye cannot lie.

It is easy to imagine that both gentlemen were attractive to women. Kawabata had large piercing eyes, a full head of hair, and clear-cut features. Walter had handsome features and a countenance which conveyed an individual in breathtakingly deep concentration or thought. A woman could find him very attractive if she were subjected

正な、そして思いつめ息が詰まりそうな面影は共に譲れない魅力であろう。ジッと見つめられると、女性は……。しかし結婚という枠をはめると、両者は対照的だ。川端の旧制一高時の初恋は有名な話である（東京ステーションギャラリー"川端康成コレクション　伝統とモダニズム" 2016年4月23日～6月19日）。一方ウオルターの結婚は、何と5回に及ぶ。女性は不器用なウオルターを見ていられず世話をしたくなり、真面目なウオルターは、結婚という形で報いる。ウオルターの目が別の女性に移ると、妻とは別れて新たな結婚を繰り返す。別れた妻は、日本の流行歌ではないが"別れても好きな人"としてそのまま消えていく。それを繰り返していく。モスクワでは、女優の恋人もいた。何とも羨ましい男である。

　生活という面では、ウオルターは貧乏であった。最初の結婚では息子までもうけたが、家族を支え切れず両親のもとに帰ったほどである。そして離婚（1930）。川端は、川端コレクションでも有名であるが、ロダンの本物（"女の手"）を含むそのコレクションは素晴らしい。

　仕事という面では、小説家・評論家である川端とは、かなり違う。彼は、翻訳という仕事をしている。ドイツ語からフランス語への翻訳である。人の役に立ちたいというのも、彼の真面目な夢であったのであろう。

　夢の実現を求め続けた彼は、この世で夢の実現は無理だと観念した時のためにモルヒネ錠を持ち歩いていた。そして米国への出国を妨害された1940年9月25日、遂に実行に移す。地上の夢の実現をメシアと共に実現しようと安らぎを感じていたのかもしれない。

　川端の場合、"美しい日本"を十分満喫した、そろそろ別の世界を覗いてみるかと、ふと思ったのかもしれない。

みんなと一緒の"ぬくもり"が……
"Warmth" with everyone……

to this gaze. However, when put in the context of marriage, the two are in conflict. Kawabata's first love during his high school years was famous(Tokyo Station Gallery [Yasunari Kawabata Collection, Tradition and Modernism] held during April 23rd ~ June 19th, 2016). On the other hand, Walter was married an amazing five times. This is probably partially the result of women who felt a desire to look after the awkward Walter, and the conscientious Walter's desire to express his feelings in the form of marriage. When Walter's gaze moved on to another woman, he divorced his wife and married the other woman, a process which was repeated multiple times. The wives who were divorced simply disappeared, much like the words in a popular Japanese song which state, "departed but still loved". While in Moscow, he had a lover who was an actress. He was a man you just could not hate.

In terms of their living situations, Walter was impoverished. In his first marriage he and his wife had a son. To support his family he had to return home and live with his parents. Then he was divorced in 1930. Kawabata, on the other hand, was famous. He assembled the superb Kawabata Collection of art which included an authentic Rodin(Woman's Hand).

In the area of their professions, there was a significant difference between Kawabata who was a novelist and critic and Walter who was a translator and writer. He specialized in translating German texts to French. He wanted to be useful to people, perhaps that was the dream of a conscientious man.

In pursuing his quest to have his dream become a reality, he met many great German artists and intellectuals. With the rise of Hitler and anti-Semitism, he was pursued by the Nazis across Europe. He may have become resigned to the fact that his dream would not become a reality in this world, so he had taken to carrying morphine tablets. Then on September 25, 1940, when his departure to the United States was obstructed, he moved into action and committed suicide by taking an overdose of morphine tablets. Perhaps he sought the comfort of pursuing his dream with the Messiah.

In the case of Kawabata, after enjoying a full life in "the beautiful Japan", perhaps he felt that it was time to take a glimpse of another world.

Chapter Ⅰ Thanks for Nothing ●────── 99

第15話

"質より量"、それとも"量より質"

　今、日本時間の2016年11月8日（火曜日）の午後である。米国大統領選が米国時間明日11月8日に開始される。開始時刻は午前6時といわれているが、各州まちまちということである。開票は同日午後6時といわれている。

　ここのところ、ロシア大統領プーチン氏の間接的介入、FBIまで巻き込まれるという混戦ぶりである。どちらが勝利しても、米国ドルの優位は変わらないし、世界のリーダーとしての重みも変わらないと、筆者は思っている。

　2人の候補者を量か質で見るならば、"量より質"に当てはまるのは、ヒラリー・クリントン氏である。何もしなかった30年と言われても、ファースト・レディ、国務長官、上院議員として活躍した実績はご立派である。

　一方、"質より量"に当てはまるのは、ドナルド・トランプ氏である。選挙戦における物量作戦がそのものである。しかし、彼の"量"は彼の"質"によるものである。氏は、ペンシルベニア大学の有名なウォートン・スクールのMBA首席修了者である。彼の子供たちも優秀であることは、ヒラリーもディベート中に触れている。

　そして迎えた日本時間11月9日（水曜日）そして翌10日（木曜日）、何人かの方から直接間接"言った通りトランプが勝ちましたね！"と声をかけられた。

　実は、10月15日に行われた東大ホーム・カミング・デーの東大薬友会総会前の役員会などで、ステルス・トランプ（Stealth Trump：筆者造語）の多さを実感していた。低所得者層のブルーカラー族にとっては、

100————●第1章　Thanks for Nothing

Narrative 15
"Quality over Quantity" or it is "Quantity over Quality"

I would like to discuss the United States(US) Presidential election of 2016. The election was held on November 8th. It was said that in some states the election would start at 6:00am. However, depending upon the state, the start time could differ, and 6:00am on the west coast is 9:00am on the east coast. It was an unusual election in that Russian President Putin's indirect intervention into the election reached the extent so that the FBI became involved, resulting in heightened confusion. I believed that whichever side won, it would not alter the dominance of the US dollar in world markets, and it would not change the weight of the US as a global leader.

We should look at the quantity and quality of the two candidates in this election. The phrase "Quality over Quantity" fit Hillary Clinton, the Democratic Party candidate. Although it was said that she did not do anything for 30 years, she was the First Lady, Secretary of State, and Senator, reflecting her outstanding achievements.

On the other hand, "Quantity over Quality" fit Donald Trump, the Republican Party candidate. His presidential election campaign strategy depended upon his abundance of resources and material. Mr. Trump earned a bachelor degree in economics from the Wharton School of the University of Pennsylvania. His children are recognized for their academic excellence, which was noted by Hillary during a pre-election debate.

At the end of the fateful day of November 8 and the early hours of November 9, it became clear that Trump had won the election.

To tell the truth, October 15th was the University of Tokyo's Home Coming Day. During a gathering of officials before the general assembly meeting of the Alumni Association of Pharmaceutical Sciences at the University of Tokyo, I understood

Imaging of late daughter: Yoko
次女・陽子のイメージ

Chapter Ⅰ Thanks for Nothing ● 101

Change（変化）を約束しながら、Change（変化）できないオバマ政権からのChange（変化）を求める心理があったのである。そして、11月8日に黙々とオバマ政権からのChange（変化）を求めたのだ。

筆者が冗談交じりに言っていることは、トランプ氏は選挙中とまったく逆の政策を1月21日から実行すると考えていれば、そう予測不能でもないと。まー、TPP、対メキシコ壁は別としても。

さて、トランプ氏になれば減税策によってほとんどのブルーカラー族は税を払わなくて済むが、彼らが求めたのは、Change（変化）をもたらす政権ができたという"心の安らぎ"なのであると、筆者は思っている。

だからこそ、トランプ氏はChange（変化）をもたらさなくてはならないのである。

その中心になるのが、長女イヴァンカ（Ivanka）の夫、ジャレド・クッシュナー（Jared Kushner）と言われている。ハーバード大学卒の弁護士でMBA（NY大）。とにかく交渉事のプロと言われ、イヴァンカをユダヤ教に改宗させたほどの腕前。また家族を大切にし、脱税で服役中の父親を大切に守ったのも、事実である。いよいよ義父であるトランプ氏に仕え、ホワイトハウスのコントロールタワーになるのは、間違いない。

結局のところ、この米国大統領選挙で勝利したのはプーチン氏で、負けたのはオバマ氏と言われる始末。面白いことに、プーチン氏もトランプ氏も共に実存主義（サルトル）だから、馬が合うのかもしれない。トランプ氏には、勝利者であることを自覚して納得の行くChange（変化）を期待して筆をおきたい。

ボンアート素心会
Bon-Art Soshin club

ボンアートのピアニスト
Pianists at Bon-Art

the reality of just how many 'Stealth Trumps'(my coined phrase) existed. Although the Obama Administration promised 'Change' to the low-income blue collar working class, this promised 'Change' was not delivered. However, the working class's psychological desire for 'Change' remained strong, and this was one of the issues that Trump successfully used during the campaign. Half joking, I said that if Trump, beginning on January 21st, the first day of his administration, was going to take an absolutely opposite policy direction from what he promised during his campaign, then predictions of what would happen may be totally impossible. Well, perhaps the issues of the Trans-Pacific Partnership(TPP – which Trump pulled the United States out of after only three days into his administration) and the wall bordering Mexico may be excluded from this outlook.

After Mr. Trump was elected, he continued to talk about his policy of tax reduction, stating that the majority of the blue collar class would see a reduction in their taxes. I believe that the blue collar workers probably experienced a "Spiritual Calm" with an administration that talked about 'Change'. However, the tax reform bill currently before the U.S. Congress raises taxes for the poor and middle class and lowers them for the rich and corporations. Because of this, nearly 60% of Americans disapprove of the bill. This is exactly why Mr. Trump must bring about the 'Change' he promised during the campaign.

It was said that a central role player in the Trump administration would be his daughter Ivanka's husband, Jared Kushner. He graduated from Harvard University with an A.B. and New York University with a M.B.A. He is said to be a professional negotiator; converting Ivanka to the Jewish faith is one example which reflects his ability. He has shown how he strongly values the family, which is evident in his care toward his father who is serving a jail sentence for tax evasion. While at the beginning of the Trump administration, he had a prominent role within the White House serving his father-in-law, Mr. Trump. However, it is said that his role was being diminished.

Ultimately, the victor of the 2016 American presidential election campaign was Mr. Putin, and the loser was Mr. Obama. It is rather interesting that both Mr. Putin and Mr. Trump are existentialist, so they must get along. I do hope that Mr. Trump will become aware that he is a victor and proceed in bringing about a 'Change' that will satisfy his followers and all Americans, although one year into his term, this has not happened.

Chapter I Thanks for Nothing ●──── 103

第16話

Money for Nothing：
ユートピアなんてあるの？

　人間働かなくて食べていける環境なんてあり得ない。どこかの国の
トップ（国王、大統領などなど）や貴族といった人々は、自ら、またはそ
の祖先が必死に働いたお蔭でそうなったのであろう。もちろん、平気で
粛清を繰り返すどこかのトップは、ユートピアどころか、誰も信じられ
ない不安に怯える地獄の生活である。

　歴史的にはユートピア（Utopia）の作家であるトーマス・モア氏
（Thomas More、1478～1535）が、その中で最低収入の必要性について
書いている。非常に現実的な方である。また最低収入を保証すること
（guaranteed minimum income）を提唱したのは、スペイン生まれのヨハ
ンネス・ルドヴィカス（Johannes Ludovicus）である。

　2016年OECD統計によると、最低収入のトップはスイスで日本はな
んと20位である。日本の福祉は、医療を含めて、世界一である。統計
の基準が違うのであろう。

　さて米国新大統領がトランプ氏に決まり、税制改革に乗り出すと約束
している。従来共和党の税制改革のチャンピオンは、2012年に共和党
のロムニー氏が大統領選挙に出馬した際、副大統領候補としていたポー
ル・ライアン氏であった。氏は、現在下院議長の要職にある。下院議長
は、大統領、副大統領に次ぐ3番目の要職である。ライアン氏は、オバ
マ政権の税制を"破たんした税制（a broken tax system）"として改革に乗
り出していた。すなわちオバマ税制の法人税率（35％）そして海外収入
に対する税率（39％）の削減など。

　最近の例では、米国製薬企業ファイザー（Pfizer）がアイルランド企業
であるアラガン（Allergan）と対等合併し、本社をアイルランド（法人税

104──●第1章　Thanks for Nothing

Narrative 16

Money for Nothing:
Why is there a Utopia?

There is no such thing as an environment in which humans can eat without working. Leaders(kings or presidents) and those who can be referred to as the aristocracy of some countries are in that privileged position because either they, or their ancestors, toiled desperately to attain that position. Of course, there are rulers and leaders who repeatedly purge their country of people they do not trust. This is far from Utopia for both the ruler and the citizens in which they are not able to trust anyone. Their lives become a living hell filled with uncertainty and suspicion.

Historically, in the book 'Utopia', the writer Sir Thomas More(1478 – 1535) stressed the importance of a minimum income. He was an extremely realistic individual. It was the Spanish-born, Johannes Ludovicus Vives, who advocated the guaranteed minimum income.

According to 2016 OECD statistics, the country with the highest minimum income is Switzerland. Japan is an unbelievable 20th. This is surprising to me because Japan's social welfare system, including healthcare, is the best in the world. One would have to look at the criteria for determining these statistics to understand what these rankings mean.

As I discussed in the fifteenth topic, Mr. Trump became America's new President in the 2016 election. He promised to reform the U.S. tax system. Up until Trump became involved, the Republican Party's tax reform champion was Paul Ryan, the 2012 Republican vice presidential candidate and running mate of presidential nominee Mitt Romney. Currently, Ryan is the Speaker of the United States House of Representatives, an important position which is third in succession to become president after the President and Vice President. Mr. Ryan has referred to the Obama Administration's tax system as "a broken tax system", and has undertaken to reform it. He ultimately wants to reduce the corporate tax rate(currently 35%) and the overseas income tax rate(currently 39%) of Obama's tax system.

For example, in an effort to lower its corporate taxes, American pharmaceutical manufacturer Pfizer had tried to conduct an equal merger with the Irish corporation Allergan, and move its headquarters to Ireland where the corporate tax rate is 12.5%.

率12.5％）に移し、節税を図ろうとしたが、オバマ政権に逆転され、アッサリ降参。この辺りは共和党は法人税を下げることで解決するのだろう。

　2016年11月8日次期米国大統領にトランプ氏が決まり、2017年2月21日に就任する。以来変身を続けるトランプ氏は11月11日金曜日、声高らかに＄1 tn財政投資（100兆円超）を公表した。法人税率は15％減額して20％にすると。法人税率を下げれば、税収は減り財政は苦しくなるはずだ。財政投資により企業業績が減額以上に上昇し税収が増えるというのか。レーガン大統領の時のドル高・株高の財政赤字にならないよう願いたいものだ。

　つい先日、日経新聞に日本におけるトランプ氏の人気調査の結果があり、否定的が66％と出ていた。米国での調査なら解るが、トランプ氏にとっては痛くも痒くもない話である。誰が調査したのか知らないが。トランプ氏の公共投資（＄1 tn）は、日本企業にとってもチャンスであるはずなのに。

　一方、中国ではトランプ氏は歓迎されているという。お金もうけ好きな中国人と馬が合うのだろうと（伊藤忠商事社長岡藤正広氏・日経新聞）。

　最後に"Money for Nothing"に戻って、本当のユートピアに住んでいる人が一人おります。それは、トランプ氏と現夫人との間にいつも立っている三男のバロン君である（Barron Trump、10歳）。とんでもない、バロン君は早くも将来の大統領候補として帝王学を学んでいる！って。将来が楽しみな若者の一人である。日本にも多くの優秀な若者がいる。

However, Pfizer and Allergan quickly surrendered this plan when the Obama Administration turned the tables with new tax regulations that made this move unprofitable. These issues should be resolved if the Republican party succeeds with the lowering of corporate taxes.

Mr. Trump was elected the next President of the United States on November 8, 2016, and he was inaugurated on January 20, 2017. However, on November 11th Mr. Trump, who continually undergoes transformations, emphatically announced that he will make a fiscal investment of $1 trillion(100 trillion yen) in public spending. He also said that he would reduce the corporate tax rate from 35% to 20%. One might ask if reducing corporate taxes would result in an overall tax revenue decrease, making the state of America's finances difficult. The logic seems to be that through new corporate financial investments, the U.S. economy would grow, which would provide an increase in tax revenue. I do hope that this does not evoke the days of the Reagan Presidency, when the dollar and stock prices were high, and the finances were in the red.

The Nikkei newspaper 'Japan Times' recently(October 30, 2017) reported the results of a Pew Research Center popularity poll of Mr. Trump within Japan in which only 24% of Japanese thought Trump would do the right thing in world affairs. This might carry more weight if it were a research study conducted in the United States; however, for Mr. Trump it has absolutely no relevance. Mr. Trump's promised public investment of $1 trillion is a chance for Japanese corporations to profit as well.

On the other hand, Mr. Trump seems to be welcomed by China. It has been suggested that it is probably the result of the fact that the Chinese like making money, so they should get along with him(Itochu Corporation President Masahiro Nagaoka/ Nikkei Newspaper).

Lastly, returning to "Money for Nothing", there really is an individual who resides in Utopia. This individual is Barron Trump who is Mr. Trump's third son and his current wife's first and only child. It is rumored that Master Barron is being prepared to be a presidential candidate by receiving leadership education. His future is something we all look forward to. It should be noted that there are a significant number of excellent young Japanese children being groomed in this same way, as well.

Chapter I   Thanks for Nothing ●——107

第17話
トランプ政権下のバイオ医薬産業

　一言でいうなら、トンネルの先に光が見えている情景である。

　株価の上昇が期待されるのは、バイオ医薬と銀行株と言われる。処方薬の値段に切り込むことを強調していたクリントン氏が当選したらと、陰で気をもんでいたバイオ医薬関係者は、ホッとしているに違いない。

　一方で、Obama Affordable Care (オバマ皆保険、2010年3月23日 連邦法令として成立) が消えるのは、筆者は残念である。議会で反対意見が出たのは、連邦法令のため、違反者に対して罰則を設けたことなど皆保険を推進するあまり、少し無理があったかもしれない。

　トランプ氏もさるもの、この4年 Obama Care の廃案に熱中していたトム・プライス氏 (Tom Price、下院議員・整形外科医) を保険社会福祉省長官 (Secretary of Health and Human services ／ HHS) にノミネートした。どのような対抗案を出すのか。この選択は、オバマ皆保険を一端元に戻して、新たに健康福祉政策を立案することである。当然ながら、下院議員であるプライス氏は、下院議長のポール・ライアン氏と相談しながら、トランプ―ライアン―プライスの線で進めるだろう。政府が国民に求めるのではなく、米国人一人ひとりが自分が望む保険を購入できるようにするのだと言っている。

　トランプ氏に触れると、どうも脇道に振れてしまうが、2016年12月2日(金曜日)に蔡英文(女史)台湾総統と電話会議をしたという。外交音痴と言う専門家もいるが、習政権をこんなにも揺さぶれる米国大統領がいただろうか。G-ゼロ (米ユーラシア代表、イアン・ブレマー氏が提唱したリーダーなき世界) はもちろん、G2 (習近平―オバマ) なんて考えもしないだろうし、中東も含め今までと違う形態の世界のリーダーを期

Narrative 17
The Biopharmaceutical Industry under the Trump Administration

For the biopharmaceutical industry, a light can be seen at the end of the tunnel. It is said that the stock prices that are expected to rise under the Trump administration are those of biopharmaceutical companies and banks. If Clinton had won, her emphasis on cutting prices of prescription drugs would have become a reality. Now those related to the biopharmaceutical industry have probably let out a sigh of relief.

On the other hand, I am concerned that the Affordable Care Act, informally known as Obamacare which was signed into law on March 23, 2010, will disappear. The Republicans in Congress oppose the Act due to the fact that it is a federal statute which contains a penalty for those who do not have health insurance. It seems that efforts to push the Affordable Care Act through Congress caused some unreasonable opposition to develop.

Mr. Trump is shrewd; he nominated Tom Price, former member of the House of Representatives and orthopedic surgeon, as his Secretary of Health and Human Services. For the past 4 years Price has been determined to see Obamacare scrapped. The Republicans have tried to replace Obamacare but they have not been able to develop a counter proposal that is acceptable. One choice may be to reinstate the provisions of the Affordable Care Act and then to draw up a new bill of healthcare and welfare policy. Of course, Price, while holding discussions with House Speaker Paul Ryan, will try to proceed in a strategy sequence of Trump to Ryan to Price. What is being said by the Republicans is that it is not for the government to demand from its people, but for Americans one-by-one to individually select and purchase an insurance plan of their choice.

It is glowing!
陽が昇る！

待したい。

　保険社会福祉政策を推し進めるトランプ氏にとって、バイオ医薬業界の成長は欠かせない。ワールド・バンク（WBG）やワールド・ヘルス（WHO）などが奨めるアンメットの3大医薬品（結核、マラリア、エイズ）に加えて、アルツハイマー病医薬品の開発には、産官学の国家プロジェクトが必要である。アルツハイマー（AR）はアミロイドと呼ばれる斑点（Plauque）を対象とした臨床試験の失敗が続いている。イーライリリーは、数十億ドル（数千億円）を臨床に投資し、失った。同社のマーケット価値の損失は1兆円にもなるという。失敗の責任が会社や当局にあるのではない、ここまで長寿化した人間の生命との戦いなのだ。がんもARも成人病となってしまった。もはや、リスク管理が民間の域を超えている。がん領域のPDkm-1のようなブレークスルーが出てくれることを祈りたい。たとえば、別のターゲットとしてタウ（Tau）を対象としてみるとか。新しいトランプ氏の10億ドル投資のバイオ医薬領域への高い配分に期待したい。

　バイオ医薬産業には、利益への税の支払い国（domicile）の問題がある。トランプ氏は、米国に戻せば税の特例で15％（？）を考えている。そのままなら、通常の法人税（35％）を考えていると思われる。筆者は、海外に蓄積された利益を早く国内に戻し、米国内の研究開発投資に当ててほしいと思っている。

ＭＣ東京素心会
MC Tokyo Soshin club

110 ──── ●第1章　Thanks for Nothing

Although it might seem that I am going off on a tangent, on Friday, December 2, 2016 Mr. Trump had a telephone conference with the President of the Republic of China(Taiwan) Tsai Ing-wen. It was said that this act could cause a major break with China because the U.S. had severed its ties with Taiwan in 1979 when it recognized the People's Republic of China. Although some experts state that he has no sense of diplomacy, there has yet to be an American President that has shaken China's Xi Administration to this extent. G-Zero(discussed in the Second Topic of this book) is a term and concept introduced by the American president of the Eurasia Group, Ian Bremmer, who describes a world without leaders. Of course, Bremmer would not think of a G2 structure(Xi Jinping – Trump). By including the Middle East and other important countries, I have expectations toward a different type of global leadership.

For the insurance and social welfare policy that Mr. Trump is backing, it will be essential to have the biopharmaceutical industry grow. In addition to the three major unmet medical needs(tuberculosis, malaria, and AIDS) that the World Bank Group(WBG)and the World Health Organization(WHO)encourage development of drugs to treat, drugs for the treatment of Alzheimer's disease are also in great demand. Such Alzheimer's drugs require the establishment of a national project, involving representatives of the biopharmaceutical industry, government, and academia. Alzheimer's(AR) clinical trials involving a plaque named amyloid have continued to fail. Although Eli Lilly invested several billion dollars into AR clinical trials, their trials also failed. Lilly's market value loss was said to be nearly $10 billion. The responsibility of failure does not lie with the corporation or the federal agency, for it was a very complex battle against the longevity of the human lifespan. Cancer and AR have become adult lifestyle diseases; taking risk management beyond the limitations of private, non-government endeavors. For AR treatments, I pray for the appearance of a breakthrough such as PD-1 is in cancer research. For example, AR research could target tau proteins. I would like to hope that a substantial share of Trump's promised investment of $1 trillion be allocated to the field of biopharmaceutical research.

The biopharmaceutical industry has issues with the country(domicile) in which they pay the taxes on their profits. Mr. Trump seems to be thinking that if these companies return the profits to the U.S. he will allow taxation at a 20% tax rate. However, if they continue to leave the profits abroad, he is considering the retention of the current corporate tax of 35%. Personally, I would like to see the profits that are accumulated abroad be returned domestically, to be utilized for America's research and development investments.

Chapter I　Thanks for Nothing

第18話

君、ワシントンDCに来ないか！

2017年初春（はつはる）の夢物語。それは、米国大統領トランプ氏が、北朝鮮第一書記金正恩（キムジョンウン）氏に向かって言うセリフである。"君、ワシントンDCに来ないか！"そして、キムジョンウン氏答えて曰く、"了解、参りましょう"。世界は意表を突かれ大騒ぎ、キムジョンウン氏は、万が一のこともなく身の安全を保障されて渡米することになる。そして会談の結論は、原発関連ハードはすべて、国際原子力機関（IAEA）の監視のもとに解体・破棄する。その代わり、キムジョンウン体制の維持に米国も同調する。

G8の中で、北朝鮮と国交を持って大使館をお互いの首都に開設しているのは、英国・イタリア・ドイツ・ロシア・カナダの5か国である^(注)。日本・米国・フランスは国交がない。前述のごとく進展すれば、日本との懸案（拉致など）もすべて解決する。世にいう"近江の三方よし"ではないが、"米国・日本・北朝鮮そしてグローバル世界の四方よし"ではないですか。まさに初春の夢であるが、夢が正夢になることがあるのも、この世である。

2016年の年末に日本の安倍首相が、ハワイの真珠湾を米国大統領オバマ氏と共に訪問した。日米関係（安保条約など）の重要性を再確認し、さらに深化させた訪問は、成功であった。ただ、謝罪の言葉がなかったことに日米両国がそれぞれコメントしていた。筆者は、謝罪の言葉があってもよかったのではないかと、考えている。明らかに宣戦布告前の奇襲だったのだから。

当時、政府とは別に、開戦阻止に向けて外務省関係者も日英同盟の英国や、日ソ不可侵条約のソ連を通して鋭意努力していたのも事実である。

112———●第1章　Thanks for Nothing

Narrative 18
You, Why Don't You Come to Washington DC!

ⒸUPI/amanaimages

This is a tale of a 2017 New Years dream. It is about U.S. President Trump telling North Korean First Chairman Kim Jong-un, "You, Why Don't You Come to Washington DC?" To this, Kim Jong-un responds, "I agree, I will go." The World, being caught by surprise, would be in an uproar. Kim Jong-un, while taking precautions for his safety, would travel to the United States under heavy security. The negotiations at the conference result in North Korea agreeing to dismantle and destroy all of its nuclear power-related hardware under the supervision of the International Atomic Energy Agency(IAEA). In return, the United States would acknowledge the preservation of the Kim regime.

US President Donald Trump
ドナルド・トランプ米国大統領

While North Korea has diplomatic relations with 162 countries(OECD data), within the G8, five countries(England, Italy, Germany, Russia, and Canada) have diplomatic relations with them. They maintain embassies in the North Korean capital while hosting a North Korean embassy in their own capital. Japan, the United States, and France do not have diplomatic relations with North Korea. If progress were made as described above, all pending issues between North Korea and Japan(including abductions, among others) would be resolved. Although it is not like the television show "The Omi Three Sides Good", would it not be "Good for the United States, Japan, North Korea, and the World," making it favorable for all sides. It may only be the New Years dream of a leader, but sometimes, the dream may become reality. That is how it can be in this world.

At the end of 2016, Japan's Prime Minister Abe made a visit to Hawaii's Pearl Harbor with President Obama. It was a successful visit that reconfirmed the importance of Japan/US relations, and reflected a new heightened positive relationship. However, the absence of words of apology was pointed out by both countries. Personally, I think that words of apology could have been included in the speech. It is

Chapter Ⅰ Thanks for Nothing ● 113

開戦を心配していた関係者（日米を問わず）は、ヒョッとしたらという夢を見ていた人もいたかもしれない。

　筆者が言いたいのは、駐米日本大使館の武官山本五十六大将（1884〜1943）が、1912〜1925年の武官補佐を含め1925〜1928年と武官として、まだ28〜44歳という若さで当時の米国に滞在した体験は、日本国にとっても貴重であったということである。その体験から、米国の国力が日本国の20倍であることを知っていた山本五十六大将は、最も開戦に反対だったといわれる。なのに、なぜ奇襲攻撃・敗戦というプロセスを選ばざるを得なかったのか。結論は、1943年4月18日、連合艦隊司令長官山本五十六大将の撃墜死である。これは、近いであろう敗戦の責任を取る自決飛行であった。

　この時であれば、米国も何らかの休戦（日本国敗戦という言葉を使わなくても）に応じたのではないかと、筆者は考えている。残念である。

　話を表題に戻そう。四方よしと前述したが、そうなることでいったい誰が困るのだろうか。残った唯一の共産党政権である中国であろう。しかし、朝鮮半島が核なしの状況になれば、経済的発展は目に見えている。中国にとっても悪い話では無いはずである。北朝鮮の経済の面倒を見なくて済むし。ロシアの地位は相対的に上がり、朝鮮半島との経済協力も進み、日本との領土交渉も余裕が出てくる可能性がある。

　2017年の初春の夢である。夢を語るのは楽しい、努力次第で夢が現実になることがあるから。

注：筆者も知らなかったが、北朝鮮は162カ国との外交関係があるという（OECDデータ）。

clearly evident that it was a surprise attack, made before the declaration of war.

At the time, apart from the military, the fact remains that ardent efforts were being made to avoid the outbreak of war on several fronts, including by the personnel of the Ministry of Foreign Affairs, in England by the Anglo-Japanese Alliance, and in the Soviet Union by the Russo-Japan Neutrality Pact. Perhaps those who sincerely feared the outbreak of war,(regardless of whether they were Americans or Japanese) were perhaps dreaming, "What if?" In addition, Captain Isoroku Yamamoto(1884 – 1943) was the assistant military attaché at the Japanese Embassy in the United States during the years 1912 to 1925, and was the military attaché from 1925 to 1928. At the relatively young age of 28 ~ 44, he resided and worked in the United States, which was important to Japan during the war. From that experience, Commander Isoroku Yamamoto, being fully aware that the national strength of the United States was about 20 times larger than that of Japan, was strongly opposed to the outbreak of war. It is difficult to understand the reasons for the choice to launch a surprise attack, which led to the outbreak of war and ultimately the defeat of Japan. Another outcome was that on April 18, 1943 the Commander-in-Chief of the Combined Fleet, Isoroku Yamamoto, was shot down and killed. This was a suicide flight in which he took responsibility for recent defeats in battle.

I believe that during this period, the United States was probably prepared to respond to a truce, although the nation of Japan avoids using the word defeat. It is such a shame that such a truce did not happen.

However, now let us return to the title subject. Although I previously mentioned that all sides are good, one could wonder if there is a side that would be distressed if the New Years dream became a reality. Perhaps it would be the only remaining communist party regime: China. However, if the denuclearization of the Korean peninsula were to happen, the economic growth potential is evident. This should not be a bad scenario for China. They would no longer have to support North Korea's economy. The standing of Russia would become relatively better. Finally, with economic assistance for the North Korean peninsula advancing, there may be a possibility of conducting territorial negotiations with Japan.

This is the New Years dream of 2017. Talking about such a dream is enjoyable because, depending upon the effort put into making it a reality, this dream could come true.

Note : I was not aware of the fact that North Korea has diplomatic relations with 162 countries(OECD data).

第19話
難病と予防

　皆様ご承知のごとく、1980年(昭和55年)代初め、ヒト免疫不全ウイルス(Human immunodeficiency virus、HIV)によるAIDsと呼ばれる不治の病が世界を震撼させた。米国映画俳優ロック・ハドソン(Rock Hudson、米国映画、ジャイアンツでジェームス・ディーン、エリザベス・テイラーと共演、1925年〜1985年10月2日、59歳で終焉)や現マリインスキー・バレエ団(ペテルスブルグ)に属していたルドルフ・ヌレエフ(Rudolf K. Nureyev、1961年英国公演中に亡命し、英国ロイヤル・バレエのゲストとなり、マーゴ・フォンテーンと組み、伝説のペアとまで言われた。その後、オーストリア(Austria)に国籍移動。1993年1月6日終焉)。その死は共に前述のAIDsによるものであった。後に、共に同性愛者であったことがわかった。現在は同性愛者は堂々と宣言し、人々も気にしない世の中になったが、当時は違っていた。特にヌレエフについては、筆者は、1983年だったと思うが、西ベルリンのベルリン・シンフォニー(Berliner Symphonie)で日本の森下洋子との共演:眠れる森の美女を見る機会があり、懐かしい限りである。冥福を祈りたい。

　このAIDsであるが、AIDs薬の単独治療でなく投与前診断によりAIDs薬の数種類のカクテルを投与することで、AIDsはもう怖くなくなった。ただし、感染の可能性のある人は、毎年の検査が不可欠である。

　また、米国のギリアド社(Gilead)は、新しい発想(Breakthrough)のAIDs薬を開発した。ツルバダ(Truvada)と呼ばれる。これはAIDsの予防薬である。たとえれば、AIDsに感染してはいないものの、感染のリスクの高い人用の薬(AIDs-Negative、PrEPという新しいカテゴリーに入る唯一のAIDs薬)である。現に名前を公表して服用している同性愛

Narrative 19

Incurable Disease and Prevention

As everyone is probable aware, in the early 1980s, news of an incurable disease, AIDS, which is caused by the human immunodeficiency virus, HIV, shook the world. The American film actor, Rock Hudson(1925 - October 2, 1985), who co-starred with James Dean and Elizabeth Taylor in the film 'Giants', passed away at the age of 59. Russian ballet dancer Rudolf K. Nureyev(who was with the Mariinsky Ballet Company in Saint Petersburg) was allowed to participate in a tour in Paris and London in 1961. As the Company was leaving Paris for a performance in London, he defected. He became a guest artist at the United Kingdom's The Royal Ballet, partnering with Margot Fonteyn. They became known as a legendary pair. Later, with Margo Fonteyn, he transferred his citizenship to Austria. He died on January 6, 1993. The cause of death of both Nureyev and Hudson was due to the aforementioned AIDS disease. Later, it was discovered that both individuals were homosexuals. Today, homosexual individuals proudly declare their sexual identity, and society has become much more tolerant. However, in the past, this was not the case, especially Nureyev. I personally had the opportunity in 1983 to see his performance at the Berliner Symphonie in West Berlin. He partnered with the Japanese performer Yoko Morishita in Sleeping Beauty, which brings back memories. I pray for the solace of his soul.

Regarding AIDS, treating this disease is not done independently, but through pre-medication diagnosis, a change in lifestyle, and a cocktail of drugs. With this regime, AIDS is no longer a life-threatening disease. However, individuals who may become infected should receive an examination every year. In addition, the American firm Gilead has developed a breakthrough drug in the fight against AIDS. It is called Truvada. It is an AIDS prevention drug which is used for pre-exposure prophylaxis(PrEP). For example, an individual who is not infected with AIDS, but is a member of a high-risk group, can take this drug and it will provide protection from HIV. This is the only AIDS medication of this new category. Currently, in America, there is a homosexual physician who has disclosed his name and the fact that he is taking this medication. This forthrightness can be seen as typically American. Depending upon how widespread the practice of PrEP becomes, it is said that there may be a

Chapter I Thanks for Nothing ●——— **117**

者の医師が、米国にいる。いかにも米国らしい。このPrEPの普及次第で、AIDsが消える世界になるとまで言われている画期的予防薬である。しかし、世界の70％のAIDs患者が、アフリカのサハラ砂漠以南に生活しているのを考えると、まだまだ献身的な努力が必要であることを痛感せざるを得ない。

　日本に目を向けてみよう。広い意味での予防を考えると、前述のAIDsのごとく、感染症に対しては予防が可能であっても、人間の寿命が延びたために起こる成人病は予防できるのか。日本では、今やがんやアルツハイマー型認知症も成人病と化してしまった。成人病とは、約50％の人が罹患する病気という。がんもアルツハイマー型認知症も、高齢化と共に、終焉を迎えるまでに50％の人が罹患する。やさしい経済学（日経新聞）によると、予防医療も一時的には効果があっても、老後の医療費・介護費は確実にかかるという。

　どうするのか。国民皆保険を維持するために、あるレベルの収入のある人（家族）は、先発品を調剤してもらう場合、後発品または後続品との差額を個人負担とする位のことをすべきである。議員立法でもよいので、早急に政府が手を打つべきである。英国のNICE（英国国立医療技術評価機構）のような医療費削減の波は、すでに日本にも来ている。民間企業も、政府の政策実施に協力して先手を打った方が良いのではないか、と筆者は思っている。

神戸三宮素心会
Kobe Sannomiya Soshin club

day when AIDS disappears from the face of the earth. This is a truly amazing preventive drug. However, with the knowledge that 70% of the world's AIDS patients live in sub-Saharan Africa, I cannot help but strongly feel that devoted efforts are necessary to accomplish it.

Let us now look at Japan and further prevention of diseases. Although it is often possible to prevent infectious diseases as with the aforementioned AIDS, when thinking of prevention on a wide scale, I wonder if it is possible to prevent lifestyle diseases that occur with the lengthening of the lifespan of humans. In Japan, cancer and Alzheimer's-related dementia have become lifestyle diseases. Lifestyle disease refers to a disease that is associated with the way a person lives and is contracted by 50% of the population. Due to the aging population in Japan, 50% of those who pass away will have contracted cancer or Alzheimer's-related dementia. According to the "Simple Economics"(Nikkei Newspaper), although preventive medicine will have a temporary effect, medical and nursing care costs of the elderly are inevitable.

What can be done. To maintain universal care for drugs, those families who have a certain level of income should pay at least the difference between the drug's generic version and the branded version if they select to take the branded version of the drug. It can be established by a lawmaker-initiated legislation; the government should act upon this immediately. Just as in the U.K. with the establishment of the National Institute for Health and Care Excellence(NICE), the waves of healthcare reduction have already reached Japan. I believe that private corporations can take the initiative by providing cooperation with the government in establishing such policies.

第20話
独創か提携か

　独創という言葉は好きである。バイオ医薬にとって不可欠のスタンスだから。しかしバイオ医薬企業にとって、製造の工程をすべて自社で行うのは人・設備の面で効率が良くない。幸いにして、中間体製造を専門とする会社が存在する。有能な化学者・抗体専門家などを抱え、注文に応じて中間体を提供して、効率の良い経営をしている会社がある。

　一方で車産業では、いまだにドイツ社は、その部品は会社特有の部品を作り寡占化の利益を得ている。日本のトヨタは、いわゆる系列といわれるトヨタにのみ納める下請けを育成し、成功している。たとえば、鉄板は配分よろしく鉄鋼メーカー(複数社)に発注している。このような系列化に風穴を開けたのが、カルロス・ゴーン氏 (Carlos Ghosn) である。氏のここまで成功した経歴はちょうど本年 (2016) 1月の日経新聞"私の履歴書"に掲載されたので、それを読んでいただくのが一番と思われる。しかし、氏の実像は写真に写った表情とは違って、どうもかなり優しい方らしい。筆者にもレバノン出身の友人 (American University of Beirut医学部卒) がいるが、良き時代のレバノンは欧州の文化と米国文化の穏やかな街であったらしい。話を戻して、ゴーン氏の一番良質

竹はまっすぐに伸びる……
Bamboo means Straight forward......

Narrative 20

Originality or Collaboration

I like the word 'Originality' for it is an indispensable stance within the biopharmaceutical industry. However, for a biopharmaceutical corporation, it is often inefficient to conduct the entire manufacturing process individually because of the personnel and facilities requirements. Luckily, there exist specialized intermediate manufacturing companies. They employ capable scientists, anti-body specialists, and technicians who perform the manufacturing responsibilities. They also provide managers, which fosters management efficiency in both companies.

On the other hand, in the automotive industry, German companies still focus upon manufacturing their own unique auto parts, which allows them to dominate the market and make a substantial profit. In the case of Toyota(Japan), the car manufacturer has succeeded in developing a group of sub-contractors who only deliver to Toyota. For instance, they place a favorable allotment of sheet metal orders to iron makers, spread across a number of companies. The individual who refused to participate in this system was Carlos Ghosn, a Brazilian-Lebanese-French businessman who was Chairman of Nissan Motors. He eliminated Nissan's web of parts suppliers who had holdings in Nissan. A report of his successful career was timely published in the January 2017 edition of the Nikkei Newspaper's "My Resume." I think it would be best if this were to be read. However, it seems that his actual temperament is different from what is reflected in the photograph; it is said he is quite kind. I myself have a friend who is also Lebanese(graduate of the medical department, American University of Beirut). In the prior good days of Lebanon, it is said to have been a quiet and calm city, reflecting the influence of Europe and America. Returning to the story, Mr. Ghosn's ruthless strategy was to procure the best quality parts at the lowest price regardless of prior relationships, which allowed the company to achieve it business target. While the targeted value is not strategy, the manner of achieving it is. I approve of what Mr. Ghosn mentions as his position, that it is not M&A, but cooperation that achieves success. In addition, Mr. Ghosn's aggressive strategy has provided Japan's steel manufacturers a method of conducting structural reform and reorganization, resulting in a complete revamping of the industry(according to my Lebanese friend who

Chapter Ⅰ Thanks for Nothing ●———121

で一番安いものを調達するという非情な戦略が、業務目標値達成に役に立ったのである。目標値は、戦略ではない。氏が述べているM＆Aでなく提携という方針は賛成である。さらに氏の派生効果は、日本の鉄鋼メーカーの構造改革と再編という体質改善の変革をもたらしたことであるという（鉄鋼業界の筆者友人）。

　ゴーン氏の提携に比して、バイオ医薬産業において売上げトップクラスのある米国企業が、飽きもせずM＆Aを繰り返しては相手の社名を消していくやり方を、筆者は問題視してきた。大きくなり過ぎ動きが鈍くなって、ブレークスルーの自社製品の出ない会社は、もう消えていくしかないのではないかとも思う。動きがとれなくなった丹波竜のようである。ドンドン、バイオ・ベンチャーがブレークスルーの新薬を開発してバイオ医薬企業に衣替えしていく。下剋上、戦国時代である。

　この辺で、第1章第20話も終わりに近づいたので、筆者の暮らしに、太陽をあててみる機会をいただければ、幸いである。最近、“現役中から2地域居住”を推奨している（日経新聞）。自称現役の筆者も、“2地域居住とプラス・アルファ”を楽しんでいる。通常は我孫子市——かつて北の鎌倉と呼ばれ、白樺派の文豪が住んだ街である。JRの駅が6つもある、交通の便が良いところでもある。湖北台に住んで、多くの心優しい人々の中で、幸せである。そしてほぼ毎日、東京の研究室に通う。週末は、坂東市——東に筑波山を望み、西は坂東太郎（利根川）に接する関東平野の典型的なところである。8代将軍徳川吉宗による享保の新田開発に参加し、努力した約300年（1726年）にわたる住まいがあり、いまは衣替えして素心館として存在している。そこでは、高校時代の友達が押し寄せワイワイやっている。3年前に家内を天にお返ししたが、その寂しさを癒してくれる。感謝である。そして会議出席のため、米国中心であるが年に3〜4回海外に行く。これがプラス・アルファである。有難いことである。

is in the steel industry).

I would like to compare Mr. Ghosn's philosophy of cooperation with what often occurs in the biopharmaceutical industry. I have often said that the biopharmaceutical industry's top-class-in-sales American corporations continue their course of repetitious M&A deals, erasing the names of acquired firms. I believe that corporations that have become too big and cumbersome, which are no longer capable of developing breakthrough drugs in-house, are destined to disappear. This is similar to an immobile dinosaur. Smaller bioventures are churning out breakthroughs and developing new drugs, while changing into biopharmaceutical companies. These new companies are overthrowing former superior companies. It is an age of warring states.

At this stage where Chapter 1 is close to an end, I would enjoy the opportunity to share my lifestyle with you. Recently, the Nikkei Newspaper recommended reading, "While Active Residing in 2 Regions". As a self-styled active individual, I am enjoying "Residing in 2 Regions plus Alpha". I am usually in Abiko City, which was once referred to as the Kamakura of the north. It is a city in which a great man of letters of the White Birch School had resided. Because there are six Japan railway stations, it is a location where transportation is convenient. Living in Kohokudai, I am surrounded by many warm hearted individuals, and I am happy. In the afternoons, I go to the laboratory in Tokyo. I often spend weekends in Bando City where Mt. Tsukuba can be viewed in the east, and an absolute model form of the Kanto Plains border, Bando Taro(Tone River), can be seen toward the west. Here, individuals participate in the development of new rice paddy fields, which were introduced by the 8th Shogun, Yoshimune Tokugawa. The house, which was built roughly 300 years ago(1726), now has changed into the So Shin Kan. It was here that during my high school years, friends would arrive in rowdy groups. Three years ago, my wife returned to heaven; this house softens the loneliness I feel. Then when I wish to participate in a conference, I travel overseas, mainly to the United States, 3 ~ 4 times a year. This is my 'plus Alpha', for which I am very grateful.

Chapter Ⅰ Thanks for Nothing ● —— 123

第2章

Changes in the Trend of Globalization

第1話
グローバリゼーションの中心になろう

　明治新政府（1868〜1912）は、直ちに"自らが欧米列強の仲間入り"を立国のスタンスとして欧米先進国に目を向け、それに追いつき追い越せを目標に掲げた。その達成のために、どのような戦略を実行したのだろうか。
　まず（1）教育である。明治4年（1871）には、欧米に習い文部省を設立した。翌年にはすべての国民が学べる初等教育用の学制を制定した。同時に教員養成のための師範学校を設立している。そして高等教育としては明治6年（1873）、江戸幕府の藩校を中心として大学・専門学校令を追加した。その後大学設置が拡大され、帝国大学のほかに、条件を満たした専門学校が大学となり、一橋大学、東京工業大学や明治大学、慶應義塾大学、早稲田大学などが設立された。
　何故筆者が教育制度に触れたかというと、この教育制度こそ今日の日本国の繁栄の基になったからである。世界で非識字率が一番低い国は、日本であることはよく知られている。さらに江戸幕府の藩校から優秀な人材を選び、先進国に派遣し先進技術の習得に当たらせた。医理系はドイツに、文系は英国にと…。漱石はそれとして、ドイツに派遣された医系の森鷗外、幸田露伴などは、本職のほか、作家としても花を咲かせた。
　阿波国（現徳島県）の藩医の子息であった長井長義（ながい・ながよし）は明治4年、ドイツのベルリン大学の有機化学者ヴィルヘルム・ホフマン（Wilhelm von Hofmann）の教室に入り、計13年をドイツで過ごすことになる。その間、学位（Doktor der Philosophie：Ph.D.）を授与され、そ

Narrative 1

Becoming the Center of Globalization

The stance of the newly formed government of the Meiji Era (1868~1912) in Japan was to endeavor to build the nation by immediately adopting the concept of; "Join the ranks of the western great powers." Emperor Meiji did this by focusing upon the advanced nations of the western hemisphere. The goal was to catch up to and overtake developments made by the advanced nations. To accomplish this goal, he executed whatever strategy was deemed necessary.

The Meiji government first addressed education. In the 4th year of Meiji (1871), by adopting ideas from the west (England), the Ministry of Education was established. In the following year, an educational system enabling the entire population to receive elementary level education was enacted. Simultaneously, a school to educate and train teachers was established. In the 6th year of the Meiji era (1873), a law to provide advanced higher education was instituted, which allowed educational institutions that were developed within various domains during the Edo Shogunate to evolve into universities and vocational institutions. This led to a growth in the number of universities that were established. In addition to the founding of Teikoku (Imperial) University, vocational learning institutions became universities, including Hitotsubashi University, Tokyo Institute of Technology, Meiji University, Keio University, and Waseda University.

I am discussing the Japanese educational system because it is precisely this educational system that is the source of what has brought about the prosperity that Japan enjoys today. It is well known that globally, Japan boasts the lowest illiteracy rate. Those who excelled in studies within Edo Shogunate domain schools were selected and sent to developed nations to study advanced technologies. Medicine and science was studied in Germany, and literature was studied in the UK. The renowned author Soseki Natsume studied in the UK; Ohgai Mori and Rohan Kohda studied medicine in Germany. Not only were these individuals respected within their professional fields, they went on to become outstanding and famous authors.

In the 4th year of Meiji (1871), Nagayoshi Nagai, the son of a domain physician of Awa no Kuni (present day Tokushima Prefecture), entered the class of Wilhelm

してドイツの旧家であるシューマッハ家の令嬢テレーゼと恋愛結婚している。日本に戻った明治17年（1884）、東京帝国大学医学部薬学科の教授となり、薬学科が日本の有機化学のメッカとなる基を築いたのである。エフェドリン（気管支拡張剤）なども発見して医療関係への貢献も大きかった偉人である。また、東京大学薬友会を創設し初代会長になられた。不肖筆者が現会長である。

　そして（2）富国である。欧米の列強が東アジアに進出するのに対抗して、明治政府の経済発展政策は、殖産興業と呼ばれていた。欧米から技術導入した鉄道、造船などのハード面と共に紡績、製糸などのソフト面を政府が資金提供などの後押しをした。世界遺産となった富岡製糸場は有名である。

　それから、（3）強兵である。徴兵制を創り20歳以上の男性が対象になったが、抜け穴もあったようである。しかし、一旦軍隊に入ると士族も平民も同じ扱いとなり、"民主主義"の始まりを見る思いがする。

　以上のごとく、明治政府は目標達成のための的確な政策を実行し、尊皇開国に成功したのである。

　そのような過程で、日本国はグローバル化してきたので、我々日本人は自らを外に向けて適応していくような傾向が強い。しかし、これからは日本の優れた技術、文化を学ぶ人々をヨーロッパ・北米・南米・アフリカ・スカンジナビア・アジアを問わず招き入れることを実行していくことである。一人ひとりが勇気をもって発言していくことである。今、米国大統領トランプ氏により世界の再編が進んでいるが、所詮一国では、生きていけない時が来ているのである。

知恵を出さなくちゃ
Let's think of new idea

von Hofmann of the University of Berlin to study organic chemistry. He spent a total of 13 years in Germany. During this time, he was awarded with the academic degree of Doktor der Philosophie (Ph.D.) and married Therese Schumacher, a member of an old and wealthy German family. After returning to Japan in the 17th year of Meiji (1884), Nagai became a Professor of Chemistry and Pharmaceutical Sciences at The Tokyo Imperial University, and established the study of pharmaceuticals as the Center of Japanese organic chemistry. In addition to discovering ephedrine (bronchodilator agent), his contributions to the medical field were significant, and he is remembered as Legend. He also founded and was the first Chairman of the University of Tokyo's Alumni Association, Pharmaceutical Sciences. This unworthy author is the current Chairman.

The Meiji government next focused on the nation's industrialization. To counter the powerful western nations' progression into eastern Asian, the Meiji government's economic development policy was to encourage the growth of new industries. To accomplish this, the government provided support in the form of funding for industries to adopt western technology, as seen, for example, in the 'hard' segments of railroads and shipbuilding, and the 'soft' segments of spinning and silk reeling. The Tomioka Silk Mill, which has been designated as a World Heritage Site, is a famous example.

The government also addressed Japan's military strength. A military draft system was implemented, and men over the age of 20 were subjected to this. However, it was later discovered that loop holes existed, and some men were able to avoid the draft. Once drafted into the military, it did not matter whether a draftee was a descendant of a samurai or a commoner, the treatment was the same. It would appear to be that this was the beginning of "Democracy" in Japan.

As noted above, the Meiji government designed and executed precise policies to achieve its goals, and thus successfully opened its borders to the world through a government led by the Emperor. Japan's globalization was established through this process, and we Japanese have developed a strong tendency to look at and adapt to outside influences. The future Japan should be a nation that proactively invites and accepts individuals from all nations, including Europe, North and South America, Africa, Scandinavia, and Asia, who endeavor to study and absorb Japan's superior technology and culture. One by one, individuals should possess the courage to speak out. Currently, through America's President Trump, reorganization on a global scale has begun. Alas, the time is coming when a nation can no longer survive alone.

第2話
日本は広いぞ、こちらに来ないか

日本がグローバリゼーションの中心に
Invite overseas to Japan

　豊田佐吉(とよださきち)氏は慶応3年(1867)に静岡県の山口村に生まれた。第一話で述べた明治政府による学制(明治5年(1872))に基づいて、初等教育を受けた第一世代の代表者でもある。ご高承の通り、氏は豊田自動織機の発明者である。改良を重ね、大正15年(1926)に豊田自動織機製作所を設立する。昭和4年(1929)には、三井物産の仲介で、特許権を英国プラット社(Pratt)に売却した。それが自動車開発資金となり、世界の自動車業界のトップメーカーである今日のトヨタ自動車になったと言われている。

　その佐吉翁が中国進出(上海)を決断した時(1918)、慎重論が多かった時に言った言葉が"障子を開けよ、外は広いぞ"だと言われている。何か身震いしそうな愉快な言葉ではないですか。

　しかし、翁にとっても苦しい時もあり、米国視察の最中ニューヨークで、後に三共株式会社の設立者になるアドレナリンの発明者・発見者(1900)である高峰譲吉氏に会い意気投合、激励され、勇を得て日本に帰ったという話を知り、感動を禁じ得なかった。その時の同行者が西川秋次氏という技術者(東京高等工業学校／現東工大卒業)だった。このことは、初等教育を受けた翁が発明の基本である技術にいかにこだわったかが解り、筆者にとっては本当に魅力のある身近な人に感じられて仕方

Narrative 2
Japan is Spacious, Why not Come Here?

Sakichi Toyoda was born in the 3rd year of Keio (1867) in Yamaguchi Village of Shizuoka Prefecture. As noted in Narrative 1 of this Chapter, in accordance with the Meiji government's implementation of an educational system in the 5th year of Meiji (1872), he represents the first generation to receive the elementary level of education. As many of you are aware, he invented the Toyoda automatic power loom. After making numerous modifications, in the 15th year of Taisho (1926) he established the Toyoda Automatic Loom Works. In the 4th year of Showa (1929), with the Mitsui Trading Company operating as intermediary, the firm was acquired by U.K.'s Pratt. The funds from this acquisition became the capital for the development of automobiles. Thus, one of the largest companies in the auto industry, Toyota Motors, was established.

Plum, symbolic flower of new year!
新年を飾る梅

When the venerable Sakichi decided to advance into China (Shanghai) in 1918, there were many who voiced concern on the risks of such an endeavor. It is claimed that he said, "Open the screen doors, it is vast and spacious outside." This episode makes one tremble with excitement at such a delightful phrase. It perfectly embodies what Toyota Motors is today. However, for this venerable man there were times of hardship and difficulties. While on an inspection tour in New York, he met Jokichi Takamine, who later founded Sankyo Pharmaceuticals, the discoverer and developer of the hormone adrenaline (1900). The two immediately hit it off, and during their meetings, it is said that Takamine encouraged Sakichi. Fortified from these discussions, he returned to Japan. One cannot help but be moved by this episode. Accompanying Sakichi on this tour was Akitsugu Nishikawa, a technical expert who was a graduate of a forerunner of the present Tokyo Institute of Technology. This provides an explanation for the fixation that Sakichi, who received elementary level education,

がない。

さて、翁の"障子を開けよ、外は広いぞ"を実行したのは、まさにトヨタ自動車そのものでもある。

でもこのあたりで、海外の人々・国々に向かって"日本は広いぞ、こちらに来ないか"と言ってみたい。土地の広さでない、心・技術・文化の広さだとメッセージしたい。今はやりの中国の人々による爆買いは、いただけないが。

カルチュラル・ヘリテージズ・ジャパンという特定非営利法人があるのをご存じだろうか（奈良市学園大和町5丁目60番地）。筆者の長年の友人である岩﨑泰人氏（一般財団法人国際医学情報センター、ディレクター）が理事長を務め、副理事長に千原國宏氏（奈良先端科学技術大学院大学名誉教授）並びに香川次朗氏（関西電力代表取締役副社長）がなられている。南都として、日本文化の起点ともいえる奈良を基点に豊かな文化遺産をデジタルアーカイブ化して、日本文化に魅せられた欧米の人々を古都奈良に呼び込もうというプロジェクトである。そのWEBサイトのWABISABI NARAは、趣旨に感動した筆者が提案し、受け入れられた名称である。特に現在取り組んでいるのは、奈良の海龍王寺のアーカイブ化である（http://nara-heritage-online.naist.jp/）。

一方で従来世界の各地から観光目的だけでなく、日本の文化を学びたいという人々が訪れる京都がある。しかも奈良の隣である。奈良と同じように文化遺産にも恵まれた京都では、さらに京大教授の若林靖永氏を中心に（日経新聞2017年2月27日）、観光マネジメント人材の育成に取り組んでいる。このような京都の成果を、例えば観光マネジメントの専門家を奈良に派遣してもらうとか、奈良からの人材を京都に受け入れて育てていただくとか、いろいろ交流の機会も現実化しそうな感じがする。

このような活動こそ、日本がグローバリゼーションの中心になる例である。

had toward the fact that technology was the foundation of invention. For me, I cannot help but feel a certain understanding toward the man.

At this time I would like to call out to foreigners and countries around the world that "Japan is vast and spacious, why not come here." It is not the vastness of the territory that I want to proclaim, but a message to convey the vastness of the spirit, technology, and culture of Japan. The current explosive shopping sprees of visiting Chinese is a sign that this is true.

You may be aware of the non-profit corporation Cultural Heritage Japan. (Gakuen Yamatocho, Nara City 5 Chome, 60 Banchi). My long-time friend, Mr. Yasuto Iwasaki (Director, International Medical Information Center) is Chairman of the Board. Vice Chairmen are Mr. Kunihiro Chihara (Professor Emeritus, Nara Institute of Science and Technology) and Mr. Jiro Kagawa (Kansai Electric Power, Representative Director, Vice President). In regards to the southern region, Nara is often referred to as the starting point of Japanese culture because it possesses an abundance of cultural heritage. The mission of this corporation is to digitally archive significant works of Japan's cultural heritage and to invite visitors from western countries who are attracted to Japanese culture to the ancient capital of Nara. Because I was extremely impressed with the project's objective, I suggested the name 'WABISABI NARA', which was accepted for their website. Currently, they are specifically involved in archiving Nara's Kai Ryu Oo Temple. (http://nara-heritage-online.naist.jp/)

On the other hand, many visitors from around the world who visit Japan, not for sightseeing, but to absorb or learn of Japan's culture, are traveling to Kyoto, which is located next to Nara. Similar to Nara, Kyoto is also blessed with an abundance of cultural heritage. Kyoto University Professor Wakabayashi has developed a tourism management course on this (February 27th – Nikkei Newspaper). It would be ideal to have an expert of tourism management graduate from Kyoto University's program and be assigned to Nara, or to have an individual from Nara go to Kyoto to receive training. There are several opportunities for interactions, which I feel will materialize. This is precisely the type of activity which is a fine example of how Japan can become a center of globalization.

Chapter Ⅱ　Changes in the Trend of Globalization ●———133

第3話

日本がトップ！
再生医療の科学・技術と規制

山中伸弥教授と近藤達也PMDA理事長
Shinya Yamanaka M.D., Ph.D. & Tatsuya Kondo M.D., Ph.D.
「医療タイムス No.2003」から転載

ご高承のとおり、2012年にiPSの作製で山中伸弥教授がノーベル生理学・医学賞を授賞して以来、日本の再生医療の基礎研究は、政府の支援と多くの理解ある協力者によりトップを維持している。さらに規制側の厚労省・医薬品医療機器総合機構（PMDA）がその科学技術の優位性を支援するため、科学技術側とシェイクハンドしたのである。この連携こそが世界トップを維持している基本である。世界で有名な再生医療等製品の条件付き承認である。しかし、創薬関連の応用になると日本も頑張っているが、ビッグな資金提供をする資産家の多い米国には要注意である。

本年（2017）3月13日（月曜日）から16日（木曜日）まで日本で開かれた米国BIOによるThe 2017 BIO Asia International Conferenceの折には、米国からの参加者が150名という有様で、日本からの参加者をはるかに凌駕した。特に3月13日に行われた米国BIOのVIP使節は、米国BIO自体の代表者Jim Greenwood（元上院議員）がリーダーとなり、バイオ関連会社の4人の代表者が加わり、日本政府関係：内閣府官房、厚生労働省、PMDAなどの幹部と面談をして、"日本の医療関係政策決定過程を学び、その透明性を訴える"ということであった。まず、厚労省の馬場成志政務官（参議院議員）を訪ね、30分という短い時間であったが、それぞれ

Narrative 3

Japan Leads! Regenerative Medical Science, Technology, and Regulations

As many are aware, ever since Professor Shinya Yamanaka was awarded the 2012 Nobel Prize in Physiology and Medicine for the production of iPS cells, Japan's basic research of regenerative medicine has received government funding and has sustained its position at the top of the field with the support and cooperation of many advocates. In addition, the regulatory arm, represented by the Ministry of Health, Labor and Welfare (MHLW) and the Pharmaceuticals and Medical Devices Agency (PMDA), has collaborated to support the superiority of this scientific technology. This cooperative linkage is the basis for sustaining the top position in the world. These are the terms of approval for the world's famous regenerative medical products. However, although Japan is placing efforts into drug discovery-related applications, it must be cautious of the U.S. which possesses numerous wealthy investors who invest substantial amounts of money and may be able to catch up to Japan.

This year (2017), from March 13th - 16th America's Biotechnology Innovation Organization (BIO) held 'The 2017 BIO Asia International Conference' in Japan. The number of participants from the U.S. was an astounding 150, far overwhelming the number of participants from Japan. On March 13th a BIO VIP delegation, led by the organization's representative Jim Greenwood (a former U.S. Senator) who was accompanied by four representatives of bio industry-related firms, had meetings with Japanese government officials. This delegation, the Cabinet Secretariat, and high-ranking officials of the MHLW and PMDA met to "Learn about how healthcare policies are established, in addition to requesting enhanced transparency of the process." First, a visit was made to the Hon. Mr. Seishi Baba, MHLW, Vice Minister Director General, (Upper House Member). Although the meeting was relatively short at approximately 30 minutes, I believe that both sides mutually perceived the other's case. The following day, Vice Minister Baba delivered an hour long key-note speech at the Conference on the Japanese government's healthcare policy.

Also on March 13th the delegation visited the MHLW's Pharmaceutical Safety and Environmental Health Bureau for an exchange of views with Bureau Chief, Director General Mr. Toshihiko Takeda and Councilor to Minister, HMLW, Mr. Kazuhiko

の主張は理解できたのではないかと思う。馬場政務官には、翌3月14日のキーノート・スピーカーとして日本政府の医療政策につき約1時間講演をいただいた。

13日10時半から厚労省医薬・生活衛生局に移り、武田俊彦局長並びに森和彦大臣官房審議官と意見の交換を行った。1時間半におよぶ会議中、"Zero-base"という言葉が武田局長から出た。この解釈をどの様に受け止めたかが、興味深かった。これからゼロベースで透明性が増すと喜んだ人と、今まで良かったこともゼロベースになってしまうのかと解釈した人がいた。これは、個々の企業の立場とその製品にもよるが、企業のインサイト・トラック（Insight Track）の力量がいかに優れているかが勝負である。昼食をはさみ、2時にPMDAの近藤達也理事長を訪ね、赤川理事（技監）他と面談をした。いつものように近藤理事長よりPMDAの理念とレギュラトリー・サイエンスの話があり、あくまで科学技術に基づいて審査をすることを強調され、米国使節側もPMDAの条件付き承認の実施に敬意を表した。これからもFDA（新長官にゴットリーブ氏決定）とEUと三極で規制の共通化に向け努力する旨、近藤理事長よりコメントがあり、和やかな会議であった。

最後に首相官邸に移り、多忙の菅内閣官房長官の代わりに長官室長の和泉雅彦氏と面談を行い、米国使節側から薬価改定問題に切り込んだ。穏やかな和泉氏は、書いたもので提出してほしいと言われ、必ず返事をするからと約束された。

もう一つ米国が興味を持つ重要なことは、日本政府が承認を下した再生医療関連2製品に付けた薬価（償還価格）である。共に1500万円前後という値段である。患者が少ないということもあるが。米国には、ご高承のとおり、医薬品には公定薬価というものがない。彼らにとっては、この薬価は、新規抗がん剤オプジーボも含めて、極めて魅力のあるものである。

Mori. During the hour and a half meeting, the phrase "Zero-base" was used by Bureau Chief Mr. Takeda. How this phrase was interpreted by the delegates is of some interest. There may be those who were happy to hear that 'Zero-base' meant that starting at that time there would be an increase in transparency. However, there were those who probably suspected that 'Zero-base' meant that what was transparent would no longer be so. Although this would depend upon the position of individual corporations and their products, the decisions would ultimately be based on the corporation's capability and superiority of its Insight Track. After lunch, a visit was made to the PMDA for a meeting with Chief Executive Dr. Tatsuya Kondo, Associate Chief Mr. Haruo Akagawa, and others. Chief Executive Kondo explained the governing principle of the PMDA and about regulatory science in which he stressed that reviews would be based on scientific technology. The American organizations have voiced respect toward the PMDA's term-attached approvals. Chief Executive Kondo commented that continued efforts would be made among the three agencies, the FDA (new Commissioner Dr. Gottlieb), and the EU to standardize regulations. This provided the representatives at the meeting with a measure of comfort.

The last stop was to the Prime Minister's official residence instead of visiting the extremely busy Chief Cabinet Secretariat Suga. Director Cabinet Secretariat Masahiko Izumi met with the delegation. The American delegates opened the meeting by introducing the price revision issue. The quiet mannered Mr. Izumi requested that a written document be submitted, and promised that a response would definitely be made.

Another important issue in which the American delegates were very interested was the drug price (reimbursement price) of two regenerative medical products that had received approval from the Japanese government. Both were priced at approximately 15 million yen. The number of patients who need these medications is limited. It is well known that the United States does not have an official drug pricing system; it operates on a market-based system. For these gentlemen, this particular drug price, including for the new cancer drug Opdivo, proved to be extremely attractive.

第4話

脱EU、英国テリーザ・メイ首相バズーカ発射!

　第1章第13話(落しどころが見えたBrexit)において脱EUについて触れた。筆者の考えは変わっていない。予告なしに、この3月29日(EU時間13時30分直前／ロンドン時間14時30分／日本時間22時30分)に英国首相テリーザ・メイ首相(Theresa May)が、駐EU英国大使ティム・バロー氏(Sir Tim Barrow)を通して、最終離脱に向けてEU条約第50条の交渉を始めるという書簡を、EU大統領ドナルド・トゥスク氏(Donald Tusk)に直接手渡した。いよいよ、離脱に向けて2年間の交渉が始まった。どちらの交渉力／インサイト・トラック(Insight Track)が優れているかを睨んで、定期的に本件に触れていきたいと考えている。

　ところで、いま英国では面白い調査結果が出ている。FTのクールなコラムニスト、アンジャナ・アフージャ女史(Anjana Ahuja)による"Regrets？"／"後悔してる？"である。彼女いわく、これは世論調査に対する懺悔であると。英国選挙研究機関による調査では、残留(Remain)に投票した人々が後悔しているということが判明しているという。また後悔ということは、強い感情の表れでもあるという。

　ともかく、英国首相は自ら残留派であったが国民投票結果の離脱を尊重して、前述のごとく行動を始めたのである。離脱派のメイ首相そしてフランスのマリーヌ・ル・ペン女史(Marine Le Pen)、そしてEU統括首相を自認するドイツのメルケル首相(Angela Merkel女史、通称首相であるがドイツではChancellorと呼ばれる)の3人の女性の戦いが見ものである。三人三様に問題を抱えている。メルケル首相は次の総選挙に勝てれば、EUは安泰である。筆者は勝ちに賭ける。ル・ペン女史は、"財政のモーツァルト／Mozart of finance"と呼ばれる強敵マクロン氏(Em-

138────●第2章　Changes in the Trend of Globalization

Narrative 4
Brexit, U.K. Prime Minister Theresa May Fires a Bazooka Shot!

ⓒZUMA Press/amanaimages

U.K. Prime Minister Theresa May
英国首相テリーザ・メイ首相

In Narrative 13 of Chapter I, entitled 'Thanks for Nothing, Recognizing the Common Ground of Brexit,' I touched upon the U.K.'s decision to leave the EU. My opinion has not changed. With no prior notification, on March 29, 2017 (EU time 13:30/London time 14:30/Japan time 22:30) U.K. Prime Minister Theresa May dispatched Sir Tim Barrow, U.K.'s Ambassador to the EU, to directly hand a letter to EU President Donald Tusk to initiate negotiations related to the finalization of withdrawal from the EU as stipulated in Article 50 of the EU treaty. Finally the two year negotiation process toward Brexit began. I would like to continue to observe, and periodically note, which side is superior in these negotiations (Insight Track).

I would like to refer here to the results of a very interesting survey which was conducted in the UK. A March 29, 2017 article by Financial Times (FT) columnist Anjana Ahuja entitled 'Regret is a fascinating and complex emotion' describes the survey and what it reflects. According to Ahuja, voters confessed regret for how they voted to pollsters of the public opinion survey. The British Election Study's survey revealed that some of those who voted to Remain regretted doing so, but more who voted to Leave regretted that vote. In addition, the article explains on how regret is an extremely strong emotion.

The fact of the matter is, although UK's Prime Minister was personally in favor of Remain, she had to respect and honor the referendum results to leave the EU. Thus, as aforementioned, she initiated the process to do so. Three exceptional women are involved in EU politics: UK's Prime Minister May, France's nationalist Marine Le Pen, and the acknowledged EU overseer German Chancellor Angela Merkel. How they interact will be fascinating to watch. The three respectively face individual issues. Chancellor Merkel won the 2017 general election, so the EU is secure. I, personally, thought she would win. Le Pen had to face a strong opponent, Emmanuel Macron, manuel Macron）の出現に、決選投票で勝っても、すぐに離脱ではなく国民投票を行った結果に沿って最終決定をすると述べている。これはかなりの軌道修正である。決選投票での勝利を意識した作戦である。メルケル首相やメイ首相と違ってル・ペン女史はまず選挙に勝たなくてはならない。まだ舞台に上がっていないのだ。

　こうしてみると三女傑のうちでは、選挙を控えているメルケル首相と比べても、メイ首相が好位置につけている。米国新大統領トランプ氏の就任後初めて会った外国首脳は、メイ首相であった。どうやらメイ首相は、故サッチャー英国首相（Margaret Thatcher、1979〜1990 Prime Minister、The Iron Lady）超えのチャンスを掴んだのではないかと思う。

　一方で英国では、トランプ大統領の英国訪問時に英国下院（Commons）における演説を拒否する動きがあるという何とも大人気の無い話が伝わってくる。まあそこは、サッチャー超えのメイ首相が何とかするであろうが、そうすべきである。つい先日ロンドンでテロに見舞われたメイ首相、両首脳にとって共通の安全・安心という世界の課題を十分時間をかけてご検討いただきたいものである。

　また離脱後の経済発展のシナリオや中東問題、特にイスラエルをめぐるイランとの調整なども、一方に偏らない両首脳の知恵に期待したいものである。

also known as the Mozart of finance, in the final election. She had stated her intention to hold a national referendum and, depending upon the outcome, remain or withdraw from the EU. This would have represented a significant change in direction for France. It represented a strategy that reflected her confidence in a victory in the final election. Le Pen's situation differed from that of Chancellor Merkel and Prime Minister May, in the fact that she had to win the election first. However, she conceded to Macron on May 7, 2017.

I would like to make an observation regarding these three extraordinary women. While Le Pen lost the 2017 election in France, Chancellor Merkel won the election in Germany. Prime Minister May appears to be holding a favorable position. She was the first head of state to meet with the new American President Trump. It would seem that Prime Minister May had secured a chance which surpassed those of the late British Prime Minister Margaret Thatcher (The Iron Lady, who held the office from 1979-1990).

On the other hand, there is a strong protest to President Trump's visit to the UK in the early part of 2018. I am sure that Prime Minister May will take care of the matter, which I believe she should. Just very recently Prime Minister May was faced with a terrorist attach which took place in London; both leaders mutually face the global issue of security and peace of mind, which should be considered with in-depth discussions. In addition, the economic development scenario after Britain leaves the EU and the Middle East issue, especially coordination in dealing with Iran in regard to Israel, remain to be resolved. We anticipate the balanced wisdom of the two heads of state will help lead to positive outcomes.

第5話
イノベーションへの道は、険しく一筋ではない

神のご加護も実力のうち……
God's protection is also inside of capability……

　IUPAC（国際純正・応用化学連合）の"化学と人の健康"（2017年3月31日）の役員会と第253回米国化学会（4月2日〜6日）に出席するためサンフランシスコに来ている。今回の米国化学会の受賞者の一人、長年の仲間だったイヴォンヌ・マーチン博士（Mrs）の受賞講演の演題が、"Nonlinear to Innovation"（イノベーションへの道は、険しく一筋ではない）だった。「書いたものを読んでも、他人（ヒト）が信じていると言っても、信じてはいけない」とも諭していた。これは、筆者がオーストラリア国立大で師匠のアルマレゴ博士からよく言われた"Independent Thinker"と同じである。今回目立った専門的な化学技術については、紙面の都合で割愛したい。有名教授や有名グループの最後の謝辞（Acknowledgements）のリストが100人を超えることが、しばしばあった。すなわち、100人を超える研究グループの指導者（オーケストラの指揮者）が中心人物ということである。この中から第一バイオリンや第二バイオリンが独立して新しい研究グループを創生していくのである。いかにもアメリカらしい。そうしてノーベル賞に近づいていく。

　さて日本では、まだ講座制が残っており教授の獲得予算で仕事をしていると、准教授や助教といえどもなかなか自由がないのではないだろうか。杞憂ですか。筑波大学の学群制度が広がらないのは、何故でしょうか。

Narrative 5

The Road to Innovation Is Rough and Nonlinear

I attended the International Union of Pure and Applied Chemistry (IUPAC)'s "Chemistry and Human Health" Board meeting and participated in the 253rd American Chemical Society meeting (San Francisco, CA, USA, March 31 – April 6, 2017). One of the recipients of the 2017 National Awards was a long-time associate, Mrs. Yvonne Martin, whose acceptance lecture was entitled "Nonlinear to Innovation" (the road to innovation is rough and nonlinear). She advised, "Even if you read it in a written document, and other individuals state that they believe it, do not believe it." This is the same concept of the "Independent Thinker", conveyed to me by my mentor at the Australian National University, Professor Armarego. This time, with consideration to page space, I have decided to avoid going into the technical specifics on scientific technology. There were often instances when the list of acknowledgements of renowned professors and reputable groups exceeded 100. This reflects that the group leader (similar to an orchestra conductor) is the central figure of a research group of over 100 individuals. From within this group, or orchestra, it is foreseeable that the first or second violinist would become independent and create a new research group. This is very American. It is through this process that researchers move closer to winning the Nobel Prize.

In Japan, the university system remains and professors must work within the budgets that they have procured. Thus, although an individual may become an associate professor or assistant professor, they still find that they have limited freedom. Although it is a needless concern, it seems that Tsukuba University's cluster of colleges does not seem to grow.

Another individual, a professor at Columbia University, spoke on the industry-government-academia collaboration success factor. He said that the keys to success were 1. Complementary relationships, 2. Keeping it loose, 3. Appraisal of outcomes, and 4. Patience. He made these points while including jokes, which brought about laughs from the audience and made the speech interesting. Lastly, he talked about COD:Cash on Delivery (payments are made when the results are delivered).

Let us look at an example of success in an industry-government-academia col-

Chapter II Changes in the Trend of Globalization ● ——— 143

もう一人、コロンビア大学の教授が産官学のコラボレーション成功ファクターを述べていた。まず、①Complementary relationships（補完的関係）、②Keeping it loose（ゆとりのある連携）、③Appraisal of outcomes（結果の検証は厳しく）、④Patience（忍耐も必要）が成功の鍵かなということを、冗談を交えて笑わせながら面白く話していた。そして最後にCOD：Cash on Delivery（着払い――結果が出たら払ってやるよ）。

　日本における産官学の成功例を探してみたい。大手企業のそれよりも、身近な提携の成功例を述べたい。その一つが福島県の東北協同乳業と東京大学大学院薬学系研究科の関水和久教授（現名誉教授）が協働で研究開発を行った"研Q室のヨーグルト85グラム"である。関水氏は、同研究室でキウイフルーツの果皮から分離発見した"乳酸菌11／19-B1株"を使い、東北協同乳業とヨーグルトに仕上げたのが、研Q室ヨーグルトである。両者は製品化にも成功し2015年4月17日に発売した。キウイの果皮からとれた乳酸菌という、何か爽やかな感じがして、従来のヨーグルトと比べて付加価値がついた感じがする。東北乳業は、売上げの一部を福島県の教育活動支援などに寄付をしているとのことである。一方、関水研究室は1つ売れるごとに1円のCOD（着払い）を受けるという。聞くところによると、このヨーグルトは便秘によく効くことがクチコミで伝わり、女性に人気とか。両者の成功を祈りたい。また関水教授はユニークな発想の持ち主で、ゲノム創薬研究所を立ち上げ、カイコの免疫特性を活用した研究も進めていると聞く。

　良い機会なので、関水教授の天命に触れたい。氏は中学生の時、クラスメートの父親（病院長）に、自分は将来こういうことをやりたいと相談をしたという。するとその病院長は、それなら東京大学の薬学部に行くのが一番良いとアドバイスしてくれたという。そうしようと関水少年は決心して、今日までの研究生活の軌跡を辿ったというのである。いまだに少年の関水氏に声援を送りたい。

laboration. Instead of discussing a large corporation, I would like to talk about a collaborative success that is more familiar. It is the collaborative research conducted between Tohoku-Kyodo-Nyugyo (Tohoku Dairy Cooperative) and the Graduate School of Pharmaceutical Sciences at The University of Tokyo, led by Professor Kazuhisa Sekimizu (now professor emeritus). During the project "Research Laboratory Yogurt 85 grams," Professor Sekimizu discovered the "Lactic Acid Bacterium 11/19-B1 strain" which resulted from a separation process of kiwi fruit peel. The Tohoku Dairy Cooperative produced yogurt from this strain, which came to be known as the Research Kiwi Yogurt (Ken-Q- Yogurt). Together the Tohoku Dairy Cooperative and the University succeeded in developing a commercial product, which was announced on April 17, 2015. Lactic Acid Bacteria were isolated from the peel of a kiwi fruit; the concept has a refreshing feel. Compared to the conventional yogurt of what we are used to, there is also a sense of added value. A portion of the sales of Tohoku Diary Cooperative is donated to the Fukushima Prefecture's educational support program. On the other hand, the Sekimizu Research Laboratory receives COD of 1 yen for each yogurt sold. Rumor has it that this yogurt is effective in relieving irregularity, and through word-of-mouth, it has become popular among individuals who need this benefit. I pray that both parties will be blessed with success. In addition, Professor Sekimizu possesses the ability to come up with unique ideas. He established a genome drug development research laboratory in which he is pursuing the study of how to utilize the specific quality of immunity among silk worms.

This is a perfect opportunity to touch upon Professor Sekimizu's destiny. While he was in junior high school, he decided to ask advice from his classmate's father who was the head of a hospital, on what he intended to do in the future. It was during this talk that this head of a hospital advised that it would be best if he attended the Graduate School of Pharmaceutical Sciences at The University of Tokyo. This cemented the young Sekimizu's resolution. Even today, he continues to follow the path of research. I want to send a shout of encouragement to the still young Professor Sekimizu.

Chapter II   Changes in the Trend of Globalization ●────145

第6話
習政権下の中国バイオ医薬研究開発力を診る

　中国のTPPへの多様な分野への参加意思はかなり強い。なかでも中国のバイオ医薬の新薬開発力は恐るべきものがある。

　実例を挙げたいと思う。香港バイオベンチャーで、ロンドンAIM市場および米国ナスダック上場のChi-Med（ハチソン・チャイナ・メディテック）は、医薬品並びに健康関連製品を研究開発し、製造し、販売をする会社であり、がん並びに自己免疫疾患の画期的新薬に注力している。中華人民共和国・香港を拠点とするコングロマリット：Hutchison Healthcare Holding limitedの傘下にある。

　例えば、製品候補としてFruquintinib（大腸がん治療薬）をE.Lilly（E.リリー）と中国で共同開発中である。両社の発表によると、中国での第3相プラセボ対照比較試験（FRESCO試験、h＝416）において好結果を得たようである。中国FDA（CFDA）への新薬申請（NDA）は本年（2017）半ばを予定しているという。そしてSulfatinib（腫瘍血管免疫阻害剤）を開発しており、第3相試験が2つ進行中という。これらの情報はすべて公開されている。中国における科学分野の情報開示はかなり進んでいることがおわかりいただけると思う。

　そして、知る人ぞ知るWuXi AppTec（ウー・シー／薬明功徳、NYSE上場）がある。その事業開発担当・広報担当VPであるHui Cai（フイ・カイ）PhD、MBAとは知り合いである。また創立者（4人）の一人であり、

陽が昇る！
It is glowing!

Narrative 6:

Examining China's Biopharmaceutical Research and Development Strength under the Xi Administration

China has a strong determination in placing strategic footholds within multiple sectors of the Trans-Pacific Partnership (TPP) negotiations. One sector that stands out is China's formidable strength in the development of new biopharmaceuticals.

I will illustrate an example. The Hong Kong venture, Chi-Med (Hutchison China Meditech), which is listed on both London's AIM and America's NASDAQ stock exchanges, is a firm which conducts research and development, manufacturing, and sales of pharmaceuticals and health-related products. The firm focuses on groundbreaking new drugs to treat cancer and autoimmune disorders. The firm is a subsidiary of Hutchison Healthcare Holding Limited, a conglomerate based in The People's Republic of China and Hong Kong.

Chi-Med conducted the research and development of a drug candidate Fruquintinib (colorectal cancer therapy) in conjunction with Eli Lilly in China. According to announcements made by both firms, the placebo-controlled Phase III trial (FRESCO trial; 416 patients) was conducted in China and showed favorable results. Chi-Med submitted a new drug application (NDA) to China's FDA (CFDA) in June, 2017, and it was given priority review status because of its substantial clinical value. In addition, Chi-Med is also developing Sulfatinib (advanced solid tumor cancer therapy) which is in the process of two Phase III trials. All findings and information pertaining to these drug candidates have been made public. This is evidence of China's advancement in regards to scientific sector information disclosure.

Many in the industry are well aware of WuXi Apptec (listed on the New York Stock Exchange (NYSE)). I happen to have the pleasure of knowing their VP of Corporate Development/Public Relations, Dr. Hui Cai, PhD, MBA. She is one of the four founders of the firm. The current Chairman and CEO, Dr. Ge Li, is a friend from his days at Mitsubishi Corporation in the U.S. Also formerly of Mitsubishi Corporation is my friend Mr. Akira Niwayama, who is a statistician. It is indeed a small world. According to Dr. Li, when the firm was founded in December, 2000, it was only a one room laboratory. They have since expanded into a firm that employs 7,000 researchers in a 3 million square foot complex that contains both laboratory and manufacturing

Chapter II　Changes in the Trend of Globalization ●──147

現Chairman and CEOであるDr.Ge Liは、元三菱商事の筆者の友人である庭山明氏の米国三菱時代の友人である。統計学者と聞いている。世の中狭いものである。Li氏によると、2000年12月に4人の創立者と実験室1部屋で発足したが、今では7000人の研究者と300万平方フィートの研究室と製造設備をもつまでに発展したという。2013年から毎年WuXi Global Forumを開催しており、2017年はサンフランシスコで1月10日に第5回目が開かれた。

　また製造物責任については、最近の中国における食品による被害に対しては、かなり厳しい処置をとっているのは、ご承知の通りである。

　このように見てくると、中国のバイオ医薬における新薬のR&Dは、知的財産権の保護（紙面の都合上次回取り上げることにする）や製造物責任などに囲まれ、順調に進むと判断したい。

　日中間の新しい動きに注目したい。ミレイユ・ギリングスCEO（Mireille Gillings）が率いる中国発のバイオベンチャー"HUYAバイオサイエンス／HUYA Bioscience"である。すでに中国で、末梢性T細胞リンパ腫（PTCL）の適応で新薬承認を得ている経口ヒストン脱アセチル化酵素（HDAC）阻害剤HBI-8000について、日本での臨床治験を開始したという。CFDAではこのような科学的レベルの新薬審査ができるのである。また新薬開発では、日本企業もそうであるように、通常欧米での臨床を先行させ、続いてアジアでの臨床を行うが、このベンチャーは（アジアの一環である）中国で臨床治験を先行させ承認を得てから、日本で臨床治験を行うという。アジア先行という新手を繰り出したのである。

　日中韓における臨床治験データをASEAN諸国での承認に利用するのであれば初めてだと思う。このデータをどう使って米国FDAやEUにチャレンジするのか、興味深い（thrilling！）。

早く卵を産みたいね
Let's lay eggs

facilities. Every year since 2013, the WuXi Global Forum has been held. On January 10, 2017, the 5th Forum was held in San Francisco, California.

In regards to responsible manufacturing, recent food damage incidents in China have led to severe measures to prevent this from happening, as has been reported in the news.

In summary, I believe that China's biopharmaceutical new drug R&D, although challenged with intellectual property protection (which I will write about later) and responsible manufacturing issues, will progress smoothly.

I would like to focus upon new developments between Japan and China. A Chinese bio venture, HUYA Bioscience whose CEO is Mireille Gillings, is proceeding with an interesting plan for drug development. The firm's oral class histone deacetylase (HDAC) inhibitor, HBI-8000, is a therapy for Peripheral T-cell lymphoma (PTCL). It has already received approval in China, and is now being studied in clinical trials in Japan and the US. The CFDA is capable of conducting new drug examinations on a scientific level. Traditionally, firms in China and Japan have conducted new drug development clinical trials in Europe and the US, followed by clinical trials conducted in Asia. However, HUYA began its drug development process by conducting clinical trials in China as part of its Asia plan. After receiving marketing approval in China, it then initiated clinical trials in Japan. By pursuing approval in Asia first, HUYA has introduced a new approach. If Japanese, Chinese, and Korean clinical trial data are utilized in the approval process within ASEAN nations, I believe that it will be a first. It is thrilling to imagine how they will work with the US FDA and EU EMA with these Asian data.

第7話
知的財産権、今昔

©The Granger Collection/amanaimages

相対性理論のアルバート・アインシュタインノーベル物理学賞（1921）
Albert Einstein of Relativity Theory won the Nobel Prize in Physics in 1921

　WIPO（The World Intellectual Property Organization：世界知的所有権機関）が国際機関としてスイスのジュネーブにある。最近発表された調査－国際特許の発明者の住所調査によると、日本の東京－横浜地区が世界トップだったという。中国の深圳－香港が2番だと伝えている。WIPOのランキング10位に大阪－神戸－京都、名古屋が入り、日本はイノベーション・パワーとしてあり続けているという。

　一方、筆者が現役だったころは、先発明主義か先出願主義かが関心事であった。日本・欧州の先出願主義に対し、米国の特許法が先発明主義であったからである。その対策のため、実験ノートはすべて本人がサインをして、研究所が保管していたのを思い出し懐かしい。しかし、米国も後発医薬品会社対策として先出願主義に変わろうとする議論が長く続いてきた。FDA承認または申請中の医薬品につき、後発品メーカーが、その発明は不十分であるとクレームをつけ、後発医薬品の開発をするからである。FDAへの申請・審査は特許とは関係なく、進むのである。米国議会（下院／上院）は先出願主義への移行を承認し、2011年9月16日オバマ大統領が法案に署名をして成立した。移行への施行日は2013年3月16日とした。

　米国の先発明主義は、個人の発明に重きを置く発想から来ていると言われている。これに関連するのか、日本では製品がマーケットで化けた

Narrative 7

Intellectual Property – Past and Present

WIPO (The World Intellectual Property Organization), as an international institution, is based in Geneva, Switzerland. According to a recently disclosed report regarding where inventors who applied for international patents resided, it was found that Tokyo and the Yokohama area of Japan were at the top globally. In second place were China's Shenzhen and Hong Kong. Major Japanese cities such as Osaka, Kobe, Kyoto, and Nagoya were 10th in the WIPO ranking, reflecting that Japan continues to be an innovation power-house.

I would now like to discuss inventorship in regards to the patent process. When I was employed, there was an interest as to whether a patent should be awarded based on the first-to-invent principle or the first-to-file principle. Japan and Europe operated on the principle of 'first-to-file', while the United States patent law was centered upon the 'first-to-invent' principle. In order to prove that an individual was the first to invent, measures had to be taken to ensure that there was sufficient evidence to support the research process. Thus, all research notes were signed by the individual conducting the research, and these notes were stored within the laboratory. Recalling this process brings back memories. However, as a measure against generic drug manufacturers in the U.S., there was an on-going lengthy debate about transitioning to the 'first-to-file' principle. This debate began when generic manufacturers claimed that there were inadequacies in the support of inventorship of pharmaceuticals in applications that had received FDA approval or had been submitted for approval. These manufacturers initiated generic drug development programs based on these claims. Since FDA review proceeds without regard to patent status, this method opened the path for generic manufacturers to submit an application to the FDA. The United States Congress (Senate and House of Representatives) approved the transition to the 'first-to-file' principle, and the Bill was signed into law by President Obama on September 16, 2011. Enforcement of this Bill commenced on March 16, 2013.

It has been said that America's 'first-to-invent' principle originated from the desire to place value on the individual's idea. In relation to this, legal cases have been seen in Japan when a product is extremely successful in the market. An employee re-

Chapter Ⅱ   Changes in the Trend of Globalization ●———151

場合、発明者としての自らの取り分を寄こせという訴訟をする従業員が出てきた。しかし、その発明は、働いている職場の施設と研究費を使って初めて達成できたのであって、職務特許といわれる所以である。

このきっかけとなったのは、青色発光ダイオードの中村修二氏の訴訟に始まる。氏は（米国籍）、カリフォルニア大学サンタバーバラ校教授としての生活になじみ、米国的発想から来ているのかもしれない。中村教授は、青色発光ダイオードの発明の対価として、前に勤めていた日亜化学工業に200億円の支払いを求めて裁判を起こした。一審の東京地裁は請求どおりの支払いを日亜化学工業に命じた。筆者は、ビックリしたのをよく覚えている。現実には、2005年1月11日に8億4,391万円の支払いで和解した。中村教授はノーベル物理学賞を受賞し、米国で益々研究にのめり込んでいる。

米国会社勤務の経験のある筆者は、自分の会社でこのようなこと（訴訟など）を聞いたことが無い。入社の時に契約書（個人対会社）に、職務発明は会社に帰属する事項が入っているし、その職務発明がA製品として化けた場合、その発明者・関連者に、特別な名称、例えば、A－チャンピオンとか呼び、特別ボーナスを出すのである。収入が増えれば税金を支払うのは、彼女・彼である。

物凄いエネルギーを要する係争を避けるために、日本の企業はいろいろ工夫を凝らしている。発明者だけでなく製品化に協力した従業員も入れたグループに報奨金を提供するという方法である。良い方法だと思う。その金額は、会社の大きさ、製品の大きさにより多様性に富むものであろう。

もう一度、外に目を向けてみたい。米国では、バイオ医薬の研究が益々深化・進化し、莫大な研究投資を要するにいたった。その発明すなわち投資価値を守るため、先発明主義に戻るべきではないかということが語られている。目が離せない。一方のEUでは、統一特許が成立しようとしている。そこに英国のEU離脱が決まり、どうなるのか。これも目が離せない。

sponsible for inventing the product would sue the company in an effort to receive his/ her share of the profits. However, the invention or discovery was made while the inventor was employed by the firm, and was achieved by utilizing the research funds, instruments, and facilities financed by the company. This is the principle behind the concept of the 'job patent'.

The case which established the 'job patent' is the lawsuit by Mr. Shuji Nakamura, who discovered the blue light emitting diode (LED). Mr. Nakamura is a naturalized U.S. citizen and is a professor at the University of California, Santa Barbara. Residing in the U.S. had perhaps given him the idea to take legal action regarding his invention. Professor Nakamura, in trying to obtain compensation for discovering the blue light emitting diode, took Nichia Chemical Corporation, the firm he was employed by when he invented the LED, to court for 200 billion yen. The first trial held at the Tokyo District Court resulted in an order for Nichia Chemical Corporation to pay the full amount requested by the plaintiff. I remember being surprised. In the end, after an appeal process, a settlement was reached on January 11, 2005 and payment of over 800 million yen ($7.6 million, $1=\111) was made. Professor Nakamura received the 2014 Nobel Prize for physics and is dedicated to continuing his research endeavors in the U.S.

I have experienced being employed in U.S. corporations and have not heard of a lawsuit similar to the aforementioned. Upon joining the firm, I was required to sign a contract (individual versus company) which included a clause which stipulated that any on-the-job discovery would belong to the firm. Thus, if an on-the-job discovery or invention of product A became extremely successful in the market, the individual responsible for the invention/discovery and those who collaborated in its discovery and development were awarded an honorary title, such as 'Product A-Champion Team', and received a special bonus from the company. Paying the taxes that came with this increase in revenue was his/her responsibility.

To avoid the enormous energy required to battle disputes, Japanese firms are incorporating various measures. One measure is to provide a monetary reward not only to the individual inventor, but to all the employees who cooperated in developing the product as a group. I believe this is an excellent method. The amount rewarded may depend upon the size of the firm, the market size, and the potential diversity of the product.

Once again I would like to look outside of Japan. In the U.S., biopharmaceutical research has continued to deepen and evolve to the point of requiring an immense amount of investment. To ensure that the investment value of a discovery or invention

竹葉 — 1杯の酒
Bamboo leave – a glass of Sake

is protected, there is talk that it may be necessary to return to the 'first-to-invent' principle. One cannot neglect to watch what may occur. On the other hand, the EU intends to establish a unified patent for all member countries. I wonder what will happen with Brexit in motion. This also cannot be neglected.

第8話

薬価——誰のため

　2017年6月9日日経新聞朝刊に、政府の骨太方針最終案から"薬価引き下げ"削除とある。自民・製薬の反発とも書いてある。自民の反発は解る。選挙があるし、日本には米国のような正式のロビイスト（lobbyists）がいないので。ここでの製薬とはどのカテゴリーの製薬なのか解らない。薬価の引き下げにも、利害関係により、都合の良いもの良くないものがあるのだろうが、薬価は誰のためにあるのかと言えば、患者のためである。

　2017年5月17日、中医協において日本製薬団体連合会、米国研究製薬工業協会（PhRMA）、欧州製薬団体連合会（EFPIA Japan）が意見陳述を行った。関心が向くのは、現在の新薬創出・適応外薬解消等促進加算制度の現状維持を訴えた点である。後者の維持は賛成であるが、筆者は新薬加算の新薬の位置付けに疑問をもっている。当初、ここにおける新薬とは、ブレークスルーあるいはイノベーションに絡む薬剤を指すと理解していた。が、新薬申請であればミーツー（me too）クラスでも適用されている。予算がゼローサム（Zero-Sum）の中で、折角の当局の良い製品には高い薬価をという政策の継続が難しくなりはしないかと心配である。現に一部実行されているが、再生医療製品やブレークスルーの抗がん剤など。

健康に人間ドックhd

Narrative 8

Drug Prices – Who are they for?

The Nihon Keizai Shimbun's morning edition of June 9, 2017 reported that within the final version of the government's policy of 2017 topic of the "The reduction of drug prices" was deleted. Resistance from the Liberal Democratic Party of Japan (LDP) and pharmaceutical manufacturers was written as the reason. The LDP's aversion is understandable. Although reference is made to the resistance of pharmaceutical manufacturers, it is unclear as to the category of pharmaceuticals being referred to. The reduction of drug prices may be convenient or inconvenient to interested parties, but it is for patients that drug prices exist.

On May 17, 2017 opinion statements were made to the Central Social Insurance Medical Council by the Federation of Pharmaceutical Manufacturers' Association of Japan (FPMAJ), Pharmaceutical Manufacturers of America (PhRMA), and the European Federation of Pharmaceutical Industries and Associations (EFPIA Japan). Attention was focused upon the current status for the development of new drugs and the system of including and promoting off-label uses of drugs. Although I am for maintaining the latter, I do have doubts on the positioning of new drugs-Premium Maintenance when the new drug pricing system is applied. Originally, my understanding was that what is referred to here as new drugs were breakthrough drugs or those which were related to innovation. However, me-too class drugs that submit applications as new drugs are also eligible for the new drug status. With the budget at its current 'Zero-Sum', I am concerned that it may be difficult for the authorities to continue with their policy to reward superior drugs with high prices if the me-too drugs continue to receive new drug status. This concern has become a reality for a number of regenerative medicines and breakthrough cancer drugs.

The Nikkei's May 31, 2017 morning edition ran a full page article for the column "Safety Net over the Sand" of an interview of Mr. Masayo Tada (President, Sumitomo Dainippon Pharma Co., Ltd. & Chairman of the Federation of Pharmaceutical Manufacturers' Associations of Japan (FPMAJ)). During the opinion statement session to the Central Social Insurance Medical Council, all but the FPMAJ were of the opinion that the current drug pricing system, including transparency, needs to be reconsidered.

日経新聞2017年5月31日(水曜日)の朝刊一面(砂上の安心網)に多田正世氏(大日本住友製薬社長・日薬連会長)のインタビュー記事が出ている。中医協における意見陳述では日薬連以外は、今の薬価体制は透明性も含めて見直す必要があるとの意見であった。しかし大日本住友製薬社長としての思いが先行し、解っちゃいるけど…と苦しい胸の内がうかがえる。日薬連会長として、もうすぐ日本にもやってくるZero-Sumの時代、医療費抑制の必要性に言及してほしかった。ただし、薬価を研究投資の報酬として位置付けるのは賛成である。第2章第7話で記したように、研究投資としての価値として、特許も先発明主義に戻すべきであるという議論が、米国にあるように。業界3団体の総論には賛成でも、個々の企業利益優先では、産業としての成長は望めない。インタビューにおいて、成長のためには、国には政策を考えてほしいと言っている。がしかし、いざとなると国に頼る産業は枯れてしまうだろう。業界の成長戦略は、政府でなく業界が創るべきものである。

　薬価とマーケットの課題は、世界で起きているのはご承知のとおりである。まず欧米よりもお隣の中国を見てみたい。中国は、WTO、WHO、パリ条約などに入り、中国元もUSドル、ユーロ、英ポンド、日本円と共に基幹通貨に仲間入りした。そして人口の20%(3億人)が、公務員として官制保険に入っている。2016年度で、医薬品のマーケットは＄116.7bn(11兆円強)になった。しかし、政府の厳しい薬価削減対策により欧米の大手製薬企業は軒並み販売が落ちている。米国において、皆保険を目指したオバマ・ケアの恩恵でマーケットは上向きとなることを期待していた業界は、トランプ政権下オバマ・ケアは廃案となりそうで、マーケットは下向きかとの懸念が出ている。

　世界の地域別薬価などは、夢であろうか。日本は、製薬産業を成長産業と位置付けするためにも、産業界がイニシアティブをとってほしいと祈りたい。

However, as the president of Sumitomo Dainippon Pharma, it was evident that, although Tada also perceived the necessity, he was in a difficult position. As Chairman of the FPMAJ, he was aware that the age of Zero-Sum would be upon Japan in the very near future. I was hoping that he would touch upon the necessity to reduce healthcare costs. However, I agree that drug pricing should be positioned as a reward toward research investments. As written in Narrative 7 of this series, it may be necessary to direct value toward research, development, and patents, and return to the 'first-to-invent' principle, which is also being debated in the United States. I am in favor of the general opinion of the industry's 3 associations, but if priority is on the profits of respective individual corporations, growth as an industry cannot be hoped for. Within the interview, Tada states that in order to attain industry growth, he would like the government to think of policies. However, for an industry which relies upon the government, there is the potential that the industry will wither. The growth strategy of the industrial sector should not depend upon the government, but should be developed by the industrial sector.

The issue of drug pricing and the market is, as many of you are aware, is a global matter. Before discussing the West, I would like to take a look at our next door neighbors, China. China has joined the WTO, WHO, and the Paris Convention (International Convention for the Protection of Industrial Property). The Chinese renminbi, as with the U.S. dollar, the Euro, the English pound, and the Japanese yen, has become a member of the hard currencies. Twenty percent of the Chinese population (0.3 billion) is covered by a government funded insurance plan because they are government employees. In fiscal 2016, their pharmaceutical market amounted to $116.7bn, (a little over 11 trillion yen). However, with the government's severe drug pricing reduction policy, major western pharmaceutical corporations' sales have dropped from company to company. In the United States, Obamacare, with its goal to provide universal healthcare, generated expectations that the industry would benefit, providing a lift to the market. However, under the Trump Administration, there is a strong possibility that Obamacare would be scrapped, raising concerns of a potential downturn in the market.

It would probably be a dream to imagine drug prices based according to the various regions of the world. In Japan, for the pharmaceutical industry to be positioned as a growth potential industry, I pray that the industry takes the initiative.

Chapter II   Changes in the Trend of Globalization ●——— 159

第9話

火中の栗を拾え！

ジュリアス・シーザー
Julius Caesar

　危機は英語ではdanger（危険）だが、日本語では"危険と機会"となる。危機はチャンスということで、"火中の栗を拾う"という諺に行き着く。

　今回、洋の西（West）と東（East）から火中の栗をあえて拾って成功したジュリアス・シーザー（Julius Caesar、古代ローマ）と織田信長（戦国時代、日本）を取り上げたい。性格もよく似たところがあり、部下に討たれた最期も共通している。ただ信長が本能寺で跡形もなく消えたのは、筆者は火薬による自爆・爆死だと確信している。自らが殺めた他人（ひと）の扱いを自分がされてはいたまれないと考えたに違いない。

　まず、BC49年1月12日ルビコン川（The Rubicon）を渡った——火中の栗を拾った——シーザーであるが、BC100年7月13日に生まれBC44年3月13日に暗殺されるまで、ローマ共和国の中央集権化を図り、大きな役割をした。ローマ共和国のガリア地区総督であったシーザーは、ローマの支配が及ばないアルプス以北のガリア地区（現フランスなど）に遠征・平定して（ガリア戦争）、ローマの領土は英国海峡からドイツのライン川まで拡大した。シーザーは無敵の将軍としての名声を確立。当時ローマ共和国の執政官（BC58〜BC55）であり、ポンペー大王（Pompey the Great）と言われたポンペイウス・マグナス（Pompeius Magnas、BC106〜BC48）の地位を脅かすまでになった。

　元老院は、シーザーにガリアにおける軍司令官から降格し、ローマ（イ

Narrative 9

Pick the Chestnut out of the Fire

In Japanese, the word for 'crisis', is formed from two characters: 'danger' and 'chance'. A crisis can be seen as a chance, resulting in the proverbial phrase, "Pick the Chestnut out of the Fire".

Kiyosu Castle
信長の居城、清洲城

This narrative will provide examples from the West and the East of individuals who succeeded in picking up the chestnut: Julius Caesar (ancient Rome) and Nobunaga Oda (Age of Warring States, Japan). Both men possessed similar personalities, but that is not all they had in common. Both were murdered by men under their command. However, there was no trace to be found of Nobunaga's remains at Hon Noh Ji Temple, which leads me to believe that when he realized that there was no escape, he utilized gunpowder to commit suicide. It is highly likely that Nobunaga did not want his remains to receive the cruel and degrading treatment that he had previously delivered to those he had killed.

Let us start with January 12, 49BC. It is said that Caesar crossed the Rubicon River (picking the chestnut from the fire) on this date. He was born on July 13, 100BC. Until his assassination on March 15, 44BC, he played a major role in centralizing the Roman Republic. As the Roman Republic governor of Gaul, he invaded and conquered territories in the northern area of the Alps (currently France) where Roman rule did not reach (the Conquest of Gaul), expanding Roman territory from Britain's shoreline to Germany's Rhine River. Caesar earned fame and recognition as an unrivaled commander. He became a threat to the position of the Consul of the Roman Republic (58BC~55BC) of the time, Gnaeus Pompeius Magnus (106BC-48BC), or Pompey the Great.

The Senate relieved Caesar of his military command in Gaul and ordered him to return to Rome (Italy), which he disobeyed. Leading his army, he crossed the Rubicon River, even though it was forbidden to do so. When crossing, it was said that he

Chapter II Changes in the Trend of Globalization ● 161

タリア）に戻れと命令したが、シーザーはこれを拒否。軍を伴って渡ることを禁じられていたルビコン川を、"さいは投げられた"の名セリフとともに軍を率いて（不法に）BC49年1月12日に渡った——危険を冒して火中の栗を拾ったのである。市民戦争が起きたが、シーザーが勝利しポムペーを殺害、無敵な力をもつ執政官となった。永遠の君主（Dictator in Perpetuity）と言われローマ共和国の中央集権化を図ったが、政治的利害もありBC44年3月15日ブルータスに率いられた反乱元老院に暗殺された。もちろんその間、シーザーは、エジプトでクレオパトラと灼熱の恋におち、ケーザリオン（Caesarion、BC47〜BC30）という息子までもうけている。

　さて、信長の桶狭間の戦いは、筆者が述べるまでのことは無い。これを"火中の栗を拾った——ルビコン川を渡った"としたのは、何故なのかについて述べたい。信長は非常に繊細な感情の持ち主でもあった。妹を思い、娘を思い、姪たちを思い、そして息子たちを思う人柄でもあった。もちろん、延暦寺を焼き討ち、将軍・公家をも恐れなかったのは、彼の究極の目標・目的がアレキサンダー大王の東征を、極東からヨーロッパに攻め上がり実現させることであった（西征）からかもしれない。戦国武将として死を恐れない信長は、不利と知りながら、豪雨の中、今川義元の本陣に正面攻撃をかけた。戦いに勝っても義元を討たねば意味はない。だからこそ本陣でなくてはならないのだ。信長のことだから日ごろ、この決断は練りに練っていたに違いない。

　さて、シーザーと信長の共通点に触れたい。共に高貴な女性が一目惚れする男の魅力をもっていたことである。クレオパトラ、そして関白近衛前久（さきひさ）の御妹君。先頭に立つ勇気も共通している。

素心遊士の会
Soshin Playmate

made the famous statement, "The die is cast". During the January 12th crossing, he was accompanied by only one legion; defying peril, he picked the chestnut from the fire. Although a civil war was ignited, Caesar was victorious when he assassinated Pompey to become the all-powerful Consul of the Roman Republic. Although Caesar endeavored to centralize the bureaucracy of the Republic and was proclaimed "Dictator in Perpetuity", underlying political conflicts resulted in his assassination on March 15, 44BC by a group of rebellious senators led by Brutus. Of course, prior to this, Caesar met Cleopatra during a campaign in Egypt. After a passionate affair, he fathered a son Ceasarion (47~30BC).

Although I hesitate to write about Nobunaga's battle at Okehazama, I will explain why I chose this particular example of "picking the chestnut from the fire". Nobunaga possessed extremely sensitive emotions. He cherished and thought of his younger sister, his daughter, his nieces, and his sons. Of course, from the notorious burning of Enryaku Ji Temple and his fearlessness toward generals and nobility alike, perhaps Nobunaga possessed an ultimate goal / objective of conquering Europe from the Far East. It could be seen as similar to that of Alexander the Great, who endeavored to conquer the world by advancing eastward. As a military commander during the Age of Warring States, Nobunaga was fearless of death. Fully perceiving the disadvantages, he made a full frontal attack upon the main camp of Yoshimoto Imagawa at Okehazama in the pouring rain (picking the chestnut from the fire). Winning the battle would be meaningless if he failed to kill Yoshimoto, making it absolutely vital to attack the main camp. It is easy to assume that Nobunaga meticulously and repeatedly reviewed plans for this attack after he had made the decision to do so. Thus, he was successful in his quest to kill Yoshimoto during the battle.

Let me touch upon the similarities between Caesar and Nobunaga. Both possessed an allure that women of nobility such as Cleopatra and the younger sister of Senior Regent Sakihisa Konoe found difficult to resist. Another similarity is that both men possessed the bravery of being in the front lines of their respective campaigns.

Chapter II   Changes in the Trend of Globalization ●———**163**

第10話

新英国10ポンド紙幣と
Jane Austen（逝去200年記念）

樋口一葉
Higuchi Ichiyo

　2013年、破格の待遇でカナダ中央銀行総裁から英国中銀総裁に就任したマーク・カーニー氏（Mark Carney注）は同年、作家ジェーン・オーステン女史（Jane Austen）の肖像を10ポンド紙幣に起用し、2017年から発行すると発表した。オーステン女史は今年（2017）没後200年を迎える。

　このカーニー総裁の決心を、当時の財務大臣オズボーン氏（Chancellor George Osborne）は、配慮・分別（sense and sensitivity）があると称賛している。

　それでは、200年も前のオーステン女史とは、一体どういうお方なのだろうか。その前に日本では女性が紙幣に登場したことはあるのかを検証したい。現在通用している紙幣・硬貨はすべて中央銀行が発券したものである。日本における中央銀行は明治15年（1882）設立の日本銀行（日銀）であり、英国のそれは1694年設立のイングランド銀行である。

　明治政府が最初に紙幣を発行したのは明治11年（1878）であり、日銀設立以前であるので政府紙幣である。驚くなかれ、それは女性肖像であった。神功皇后（仲哀天皇の皇后、3世紀）である。面白いことに、原版はイタリア人技術者が作ったので、神功皇后はヨーロッパ系の美人になっている。明治41年（1908）、日本系の顔に刷りなおしているが。神功皇后以降、日銀が正式に発券した紙幣の肖像は、藤原鎌足、菅原道真など男系である。

　英国では、前述のごとく、今年（2017）から一般人オーステンが取り

Narrative 10
The New British 10 Pound Note and Jane Austen(200th Commemoration of Her Death)

In 2013, an exceptional move was made by the former governor of the Bank of Canada and newly appointed Bank of England governor Mark Carney (Note: Please see Insight Track, Chapter 2, Narrative 8 by Toshihiko Kobayashi) when he announced that the portrait of novelist Jane Austen would be featured on 10 pound banknotes beginning in 2017, which marked the 200th anniversary of her death. Governor Carney's determination was praised by then Chancellor of the Exchequer, George Osborne, as a move that showed "sense and sensibility".

Ms. Jane Austen (200 years death, 2017)
ジェーン・オーステン女史

Just exactly who was Jane Austen of 200 years ago? Before delving into this question, let us examine whether a woman has appeared on a banknote in Japan. Currently banknotes and coins in circulation are all issued by the Bank of Japan. The Bank of Japan was established in 1882 (Meiji year 15). In the U.K., the Bank of England was established in 1694. The Meiji government issued the first banknote in 1878 (Meiji year 11), which preceded the establishment of the Bank of Japan. Thus, it was actually a government note. Surprisingly, it was adorned with the portrait of a woman. The portrait was that of Empress Jinkou (wife to Emperor Chuai, 3rd Century). Interestingly, the plate was made by an Italian technician, resulting in Empress Jinkou represented as a European beauty. In 1908, (Meiji year 41), reprints were made to enhance her Japanese features. However, after Empress Jinkou, only male historical figures, such as Fujiwara No Kamatani and Sugawara No Michizane, appeared on banknotes officially issued by the Bank of Japan.

During 2017 in the U.K., as aforementioned, a new banknote was introduced that featured an ordinary person, Jane Austen. In Japan, in 2004 (Heisei year 16), Ichiyo Higuchi, a renown female novelist, was represented on the 5,000 yen Japanese banknote. In retrospect, comparing The Bank of England's establishment in 1694 and the 1882 establishment of the Bank of Japan, the introduction of the Ichiyo Higuchi

上げられる。日本では樋口一葉が平成16年（2004）に5千円札に登場している。英中銀の1694年設立と日銀設立1882年を比べると、樋口一葉の登場は随分早い。英国ではある意味、階級意識があるからだろうか。

さて、ファイナンシャル・タイムズ2017年6月17～18日週末版（執筆者キャサリン・サザランド、Kathryn Sutherland）によると、オーステンは、彼女の死の100年前の英仏戦争などを題材にした女流小説家で、名声も高かったらしい。小説界への貢献の一つは、その作風——ある田舎の村を舞台に、戦時のヒロイン・ヒーローをセットし、心の奥底からオーステン自らの思い（inner lives）を吐露させるという書き方である。オーステン自身は、今ではロンドンからタクシーで10英ポンドで行けるチョートン（Chawton）という田舎町に住んでいた。しかし、絆の強い家族、従兄弟等を通して、世界の最先端の出来事を知ることができ、小説を書く上で大変役に立ったと思われる。例えば、1780年代パリ在住の従兄弟のエリザ・ハンコック（Eliza Hancock）は、バスティーユ（Bastille）のフランンス革命を体験し、ギロチン（guillotine）も目撃していたかもしれない。

さて、その暮らしぶり、彼女の小説家としての収入を見てみたいと思う。彼女が生涯稼いだ約650英ポンドは、当時としては穏当なものであったという。

こうして彼女が200年後に、若く美しい顔で新紙幣に蘇るというのは、筆者のいうミトコンドリア説かな。英中銀カーニー氏とオーステンのミトコンドリア（母親）が千年位前に一緒だったかもしれないのだ。

注）筆者著作『国際人になるためのInsight Track』第2章第8話参照

banknote was extremely early. Perhaps this is a reflection of Britain's class-conscious society.

In the Financial Times June 17-18, 2017 weekend edition, an article written by Kathryn Sutherland portrayed Austen as a popular and famous female novelist who based her novels in the period about 100 years prior to her death, when Britain was at war with France. One of her contributions to literature was her style of writing which centered on the heroine during the war in country village settings. Her heroines have inner lives, represented on the page as a kind of conversation with the self. Austen herself lived in Chawton, a country village located a distance of a 10 pound taxi ride from today's London. However, strong family ties, through her cousin and brothers, enabled Austen access to events that were occurring in corners of the world far away from England, which presumably were extremely helpful to her in writing novels. For example, her cousin Eliza Hancock, who was residing in Paris in the 1780s, experienced the storming of the Bastille during the French Revolution, including seeing the use of a guillotine.

Let us examine the lifestyle and income of this female novelist. Her lifetime earnings totaled about 650 English pounds, which at the time was reasonable. Two centuries later, her youthful, beautiful face adorns a banknote. Personally, it is my view of mitochondria, perhaps. Another way of looking at this would be to imagine the possibility of Bank of England's Mr. Carney sharing the same mitochondria (maternal) with Austen, dating back thousands of years ago.

第11話
教育の無償化

　このテーマで書こうと決めてから、すでに数カ月が過ぎた。なかなか書き出せず、逡巡していた。学会で海外に出かけることもあったので、友人と話をするとその複雑さに戸惑ったのである。日本の義務教育は6歳〜15歳であり、米国、オーストラリア、英国（ロンドン）などの義務教育は5歳〜16歳である。そして授業料は原則無料である。しかし、実際の政府負担の教育費はかなり高い。例えば日本において義務教育を私立校で受けると、年間の授業料は百万円単位であることからも理解できる。オーストラリアでは、200万円位かかるという。どの国も、国家（連邦）予算と州（県）予算で半々負担のところが多い。一日毎に科学・技術と文化の進化が進む今日の基本になったのは、教育である。では、その財源はとなると、異口同音に、それが問題なんだよね、That's a problem！となる。後で触れたいと思う。

　さて、日本における教育無償化は、現政権の憲法改正の中で考えるということなので、私学の義務教育を支援するのではなく、公立高校の授業料でも（数十万円と低額であるが）負担をするのかな思ったら、そうではなかった。大学の授業料無償化をしようとしているのだという。あきれてものが言えないとは、まさにこのことか。一方で政府は、人材養成を声高に唱えている。産業競争力会議は、成長戦略において人材育成も決めた。まさか、人材育成と大学教育の無償化を連動させようとしているとは思えないが。真の人材育成とは、求められる人材を時の状況・要望に合わせて育成することである。必ずしも大学教育の中で育成するものではない。日本でも、刀鍛冶等伝統を守っている家がある。英国では、誇りをもって家業を継ぐという伝統がある、そして高等教育を受ければ、

168――●第2章　Changes in the Trend of Globalization

Narrative 11

Free Education

After deciding to write about this theme, several months have gone by. It was difficult to get started, and I was undecided about what issues to discuss. While attending academic seminars held abroad, I spoke with friends about the subject and found that there were numerous complexities involved, which caused a sense of hesitancy to arise within me. Japanese mandatory education is required for individuals between the ages of 6 to 15 years old. In the United States, Australia, and the U.K. (London), it is required for people between the ages of 5 to 16. In principle, it is free education. However, in reality, government funding for education is quite substantial. For example, the tuition cost for a child to receive mandatory education at a public (government funded) school in the US in 2016 was about US$12,500 (1.4 million yen). In Australia in 2013, it is said to have cost about AU$15,500 (1.3 million yen) per student. It is easy to comprehend the enormous cost of 'free' education. The majority of countries share the cost of providing free public education between the national (federation of states) budget and state (prefecture) budgets equally. Education is the foundation that has supported the steady progress in science and technology that we see today. So, when it comes to the required financial resources, it becomes an issue on almost every front. Voices can be heard saying, "That's a problem!" I will address this later.

Let us examine free education in Japan. The current administration has stated that it intends to make revisions to the current law related to education. The revisions are not intended to support private school tuition, nor are they intended to provide free public high school education (even though the cost is currently a relative low amount of several hundred thousand yen per student). Rather, they are intended to provide free university education. This is precisely a situation that can be described as being too absurd for comment. Please allow me to explain.

The administration emphatically stated that there is a need to cultivate human resources. The Council for Industrial Competitiveness has concluded that cultivating human resources was to be included in the strategy for growth. However, it is hard to image that they are endeavoring to connect free education with the cultivation of hu-

Chapter II   Changes in the Trend of Globalization ●——— 169

それを生かして伝統を守るのである。日本においても、職の選択の自由がある。家元に後継者がいないときは、伝統技術や伝統芸術に興味のある外部者が守ることを奨励し、家元も家系に拘らない新しいインフラを構築したい。お役に立てたら良いなと思っている。歌舞伎の世界では、すでに愛之助の例がある。

　大学教育の無償化については、大学数の問題がある。募集定員数に満たない大学・学部はどんどん廃止すべきである。政府も助成金など出さない。資本主義的民主主義の日本では、大学の淘汰が急務だと思っている。求められる人材を養成する教育機関は高専、IT・芸術・料理・美容の各種専門学校などなど数えきれないほどある。誰もが大学に行く必要はない。そのかわり、学生個人個人が自らに責任をもって、選択をしていくのが基本である。もちろん、どうしても大学と称する機関で教育を受けたいという父兄や学生もいるだろう。自由に選択すれば良いのである。

　さて、財源に戻そう。日本政府は教育国債を考えていると聞くが、賛成である。米国では、減税（個人・法人）を行うことで企業が繁栄し、減税法人税より納税が増える、個人消費が増える等で、トータル税収増加と読んでいるらしい。トランプ氏らしい。現に株価は上がり、史上最高値2万5,000ドルを更新している。

　また財源を使うからには、大切なことは教育をどの様に位置付けするかである。筆者は、オフィス（東大）でCenter of Career Counseling and Consultingなるものを無料で開いている。30分もすれば、学生の性格などはわかる（解析できる）ので、相談に応じたアドバイスをする。そして言う、決めるのは君だよと。

man resources. To truly nurture or cultivate human resources, one must recognize the demands on individuals and the conditions of the times, and then cultivate human resources in accordance with these elements. In addition, university education does not necessarily foster the use of human resources. It can be done in other ways. For example, in Japan, there are those who honor, protect, and continue to be sword-smiths. In the U.K. there exists the tradition of proudly continuing the family trade, and pursuing higher education in order to protect or expand the family business. In Japan, individuals are free to choose their profession. In the event that there is no successor to the head a long standing house, it may be necessary to enlist an outside individual who possesses the passion and interest in undertaking the task of sustaining and protecting the traditional techniques and crafts of that house. This is a method of establishing an infrastructure that would minimize the head of house and lineage system that has become tied to traditional crafts and skills of Japan. I just hope that the suggestion is useful. In Kabuki circles (traditional Japanese theater known for stylization of its drama and the extensive make-up worn by artists), the actor Ainosuke is an example of one who is continuing the lineage of a household in this manner.

In regards to providing free university education, the sheer number of universities is a problem. There is a growing number of universities and departments that do not have a sufficient number of applicants, and thus are being closed. The government does not provide grants to these institutions, nor should it. Within Japan's capitalist democracy, I believe that there is an urgent need to curtail the number of universities. There are countless educational/training institutions which are cultivating sought-after human resources in fields such as IT, art, food preparation, and beauty. Not everyone needs to go to a college or university to be trained in these fields. Of course, there are parents and students who seek to pursue an education provided by an institution referred to as a university. However, fundamentally it is the responsibility of each individual student to make their own decision. It is the freedom of choice.

Let us return to the issue of financial resources for education. It is rumored that the Japanese government intends to issue education national bonds, which I approve of. In the United States, tax reductions for individuals and corporations allow corporations to prosper, which some say provides a tax revenue that is greater than the corporate tax reduction. When combined with a projected increase in consumer spending, predictions are that the total tax revenue will increase. This is the approach advocated by President Trump. It is evident through the rise in the US stock market, which reached a new historical high above 24,000 near the end of 2017, that investors believe this will happen.

Chapter II   Changes in the Trend of Globalization ●————**171**

2番じゃダメです。無償化は1番です。
Free Education be Number One !

If valuable government financial resources are to be spent, it is vital to confirm the positioning of education. Personally, in my office at the Univ. of Tokyo, I have opened the Center of Career Counseling and Consulting, which is free of charge. Within 30 minutes, a visiting student's personality becomes evident, which allows for an analysis of that student's goals and ambitions. This is vital in order to be able to provide advice regarding the issues the student came to discuss. I always end the session by saying, "It is you who makes the decision."

第12話

AI（人工知能）につき一考

　AIという用語は、1956年ダートマス大学のジョン・マッカシー（John McCarthy）がThe Dartmouth Summer Research Project on Artificial Intelligenceにおいて用いたのが始まりと聞く。

　一方で生産性向上のためにいかにAIを応用するかを検討している企業は多い。仕事の効率化・合理化が益々進むと同時に生産性が上がる。結果、余った従業員は何処に吸収されるのかが次の課題である。それには、ワーク・シェアリング（Work Sharing）を活用することである。少し収入が減っても、その分余暇が生まれ、家族や友人と過ごす時間が取れる。パートの仕事もできるかもしれない。ものは考えようである。

　ワーク・シェアリングと言えば、オランダが本場である。1980年代、オランダの所得税は50％以上で、アカデミアの人もよくボヤいていた、何もしない失業者（遊び人）の面倒をみるなどマッピラ御免だと。今は多分、失業保険なども改善され上手く運用されているに違いない。

　さて、今スペインで話題沸騰のサルヴァドール・ダリ（Salvador Dali）と彼の家政婦との間に生まれたと主張しているマリア・マルチネー（Maria Pilar Abel Martinez、TVの占い番組担当）の10年越しの裁判は、結局ダリの遺体を発掘してDNA鑑定をするという結論になった。そして実行に移された。シュールリアリスト（surrealist）の旗手であったダリには気の毒なような気がする。彼の墓地は、有名なダリ・ミュージアム・シアター（The Dali Museum－Theater in Figueres, 1974）の中心部にあり、大変な労力・費用を要したに違いない。AIを応用すればこんなことしないで済んだはずである。

　というのは、東京大学特任准教授松尾豊氏によれば、ロボットに目を

174————●第2章　Changes in the Trend of Globalization

Narrative 12

Thoughts on AI (Artificial Intelligence)

©ZUMA Press/amanaimages
Surrealisme,
Salvador Dali (1904-1989)
サルヴァドール・ダリ

Will AI (Artificial Intelligence) take over jobs and displace workers? Personally, I don't think so. My opinion stems from the fact that human beings will be using AI for a variety of purposes. I will address this further below. To begin, it seems that the term AI was first used by John McCarthy of the Massachusetts Institute of Technology (MIT) in 1956 at The Dartmouth Summer Research Project on Artificial Intelligence, where the field of AI was born. Since then, a significant number of corporations either use or are considering the utilization of AI to increase productivity. The streamlining and rationalization of labor will continue to progress, which will simultaneously lead to an increase in production. As a result, the next issue that will develop is where to absorb the surplus of employees. This is where Work Sharing can be put into practice. Work sharing is a practice in which employers reduce employees' hours and wages instead of laying them off. Although there may be a slight reduction in pay, there would be the reward of additional leisure time to spend with family and friends. In addition, employees always have the option of taking on another part-time job. Thus, there are many ways to approach the employment issues related to AI.

Speaking of Work Sharing, the Netherlands is the center of this method of employment. In the 1980s, the income tax rate in the Netherlands was over 50%, and members of academia were complaining in discontent, saying that they were fed up with paying for those who were unemployed and doing nothing. Currently, it is highly possible that improvements have been made through unemployment insurance and the wise use of government funds.

Now let us look at the debate surrounding Spain's famous artist Salvador Dali and the lawsuit by the woman who alleged that she was born from an affair between Dali and his housekeeper. The woman, Maria Pilar Abel Martinez (who is a Tarot

Chapter Ⅱ Changes in the Trend of Globalization ●———175

付けたのがAIだと申されており、目から鱗であった。すなわち棺の蓋を開けるのでなく、片隅に穴を開け内視鏡的に生体採取をして、DNA鑑定にまわせば良かったのではないのかと思ったのである。

　なお、本件のDNA鑑定結果が出るのはすぐと思うが、次に大問題が控えているので、発表は当分ないのではないだろうか。それは遺産相続という難題である。

　それでは、筆者はAIをどの様に考え、応用しようとしているかを述べたい。世界の経済は、益々グローバル化していく。TPP（米国無しでもやるべし）、一帯一路（One Belt、One Road）、二国間経済協定などなど。AIを応用することで日本株式会社の生産性を上げなくては国際競争でメダルは取れない。前にも述べたが、生産性向上で余った人材をどこが吸収するのか。これは、政府の上から目線でなく、経団連、経済同友会、日商などがAIのメッカであるアカデミアと協調すれば素晴らしい提言が出来るはずである。できれば、橋渡し位したいと思う。

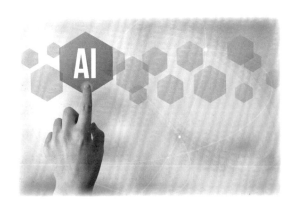

card reader and responsible for a TV fortune-telling program), waged a 10-year legal battle that finally resulted in a judge's decision to exhume Dali's body for a DNA test. The exhumation was conducted in July 2017. It was a moment that called for sympathy for the flagbearer of surrealism, Dali. His grave site is in the center of the famous Dali Theatre and Museum in Figueres, Catalonia, Spain, which opened September 28, 1974. It surely must have required a significant amount of labor and funds to build. If AI were utilized, there may have no need to exhume his body. According to University of Tokyo Specially Appointed Associate Professor Yutaka Matsuo, AI is a robot with eyes. With this revelation, a different process could have been utilized. In short, instead of opening the casket lid, a small hole could have been drilled into a corner of the casket. Then, a small instrument that resembles an endoscope could have been inserted to perform a biopsy for DNA testing, which I imagine would have been much better. In the end, the results of the DNA test, which were announced in September 2017, proved that Martinez was not the daughter of Dali. Fortunately, this made it unnecessary to discuss the extremely difficult issue of inheritance.

Now I would like to mention how I perceive AI and how it should be utilized. Unfortunately, I am a total amateur when it comes to IT. However, the world's economy is progressively becoming more globalized. Examples of this include the Trans-Pacific Partnership or TPP (which must proceed even without the U.S.), the One Belt, One Road Initiative (which combines the Silk Road Economic Belt and the 21st Century Maritime Silk Road), and the many bilateral economic agreements that have been put into place. Japan cannot succeed within international competition unless Japanese corporations utilize AI to increase their productivity. As I mentioned above, the increase of productivity due to the integration of AI creates an issue of how to absorb surplus workers. Resolving this issue depends upon the government not taking a superior attitude, but being willing to hold discussions with organizations such as the Japan Federation of Economic Organizations, Japan Association of Corporate Executives, and Japan Chamber of Commerce and Industry, along with the Center of AI, the academia. I believe this would result in a marvelous proposal. If at all possible, I would like to offer my assistance as a mediator.

第13話
AI（人工知能）につき一考（その2）

　第12話で書ききれなかったので、その続き（その2）を書きたい。"AIが人間を超える日"と言う文字が躍っている（日経新聞8月22日、2017）。人間あってのAIであるのに。が、しかし、記事を読むと実によくAI下の未来を大胆に予測し、課題を提供している。その内容は豊富である。一読を薦めたい。とにかく、あらゆるところでAIが語られ、そうゆう動的流れの中で、業態に応じたAIのプラットホームが決まっていくのだろう。

　Time is Money（お金で時間を買う）と言って、M＆Aを行ってきたが、AIを使って何を買うのだろうか。生産性向上を買うのである。企業も政府も、AIをいかに応用するかの研究・実践に資金・人材の投資を惜しまない。

　今回、企業の取り組みの一端を眺めてみたい。物流関連（ヤマト運輸、佐川急便など）と稲作農機具関連（井関農機、クボタ、ヤンマーなど）を取り上げてみたい。AIを縦に使う物流と横に使う農機具との対比である。すなわち、物流では、道路の先頭にAI搭載の運転手が乗っているトラックを配し、その後ろに無人のトラックが列をなして付いてくる仕組みである。何台繋げるかが他社との勝負である。

　一方、稲作農機具は、有人苗置きトラクターを配し、左右に、または一方に無人のトラクターを並列して苗を植えていく。こうして苗植えが半分・それ以上の早さで終了する。この時、AI搭載の有人トラクターがいかに早く動けるかが、競合メーカーとの勝負である。日本の田畑の広さは、小回りが利き、稲作にはもってこいである。米国や東南アジアでもこのシステムは十分応用可能である。また、物流システムは、まさ

178———●第2章　Changes in the Trend of Globalization

Narrative 13

Thoughts on AI (Artificial Intelligence), Part 2

As I was unable to completely address this topic within Narrative 12, I have decided to extend it into a second part. The Nikkei of August 22, 2017 published an article entitled "The Day AI Surpasses Human Beings." This is interesting to think about considering that it is through the presence of human beings that AI exists. However, upon reading the article, I found that it provided an extremely bold prediction of a future that includes AI, as well as a projection of the issues that will ensue. The content of this article is abundant, and I strongly recommend that it is read thoroughly. The fact of the matter is, AI is being talked about in many places, and it is within this dynamic surge that AI platforms will be established in order to respond to the demands of the industrial sector.

While chanting the slogan of 'Time is Money,' companies have been conducting Mergers & Acquisitions (M&A) with the desire of decreasing the time needed to provide their final product. It makes one wonder, what is to be acquired when AI is bought? The answer is an increase in productivity. Corporations, as well as governments, will not hold back on funding AI research, including the funds to develop AI, determine how to utilize it, and provide the human resources necessary to accomplish this.

To further our understanding, let us take a look at a corporation's potential use of AI. I would like to focus on distribution-related companies such as Yamato Transport and Sagawa Express, which utilize AI longitudinally, and agricultural machinery-related companies such as Iseki, Kubota, and Yanma, which utilize AI crossways. In short, the distribution sector may use AI in a method in which an AI-equipped lead truck driven by a human is followed by several unmanned trucks. The number of trucks that make up this convoy could provide the winning edge over the competition. In addition, this distribution system is ideal for America where the highways run throughout the nation.

The rice making agricultural sector could use unmanned tractors operating on the left and right sides of an AI-equipped manned rice planting tractor, progressing in unison through the fields. This could cut the time required to plant rice in half or

Chapter Ⅱ　Changes in the Trend of Globalization　●──────**179**

映画『ベン・ハー』(チャールトン・ヘストン、1959)
Charlton Heston in Ben-Hur (1959)

にハイウェイが縦横に走る米国向きである。

　筆者は、この苗植えトラクターをイメージした時、あの映画ベン・ハー(Ben-Hur)(1959)のシーン：ベン・ハーが宿敵メッサラ(Messara)と死を賭したチャリオット・レース(Chariot Race：12頭立)を思い浮かべていた。

　さて創薬の技術革新の一環として、医薬基盤・健康・栄養研究所の創薬デザイン研究センターは、アンメット・メディカル・ニーズ(UMN)領域の創薬を、AIを活用し、後押しする仕組みづくりを開始したという。時間の短縮を狙っているようだ。この仕組みづくりは、資金・人材投資が必要である。一時期、Time is Money：時間を金で買う、すなわち、製品だけをアクイゼッションはできないので、会社ごと買ってしまう、買わざるを得ないM＆Aが流行した。上記センターは、AI is Money：AI投資で、創薬の時間を買うと言ったところか。成功を祈って止まない。

　さらなるAIの真価発揮の応用を述べたい。ビッグ・データを読み込ませたAIに投資先を選択させている投資選択会社が、投資効率の成績を上げているという。これこそAIが技術の生産性を上げるだけでなく、サービス業の生産性を上げることのエビデンスでもある。

　第12話でも述べたが、AIは、単独では動けない。人間(その脳)が居てこそ本領発揮である。すなわち他人(ひと)との付き合いの距離感を上手く掴めることが大切である。空気が読めない(KY)とまずいのである。対人関係こそAIの基本である。

more. In this process, the speed at which the AI-equipped manned tractor operates will be the area in which competing manufacturers will focus. Because the size of Japan's farming space is limited, it requires the ability to make small tight turns, making this AI-driven method ideal for rice production. This system can also easily be applied in the U.S. and Southeast Asia.

When I envisioned the image of the rice planting tractors, it brought back memories of the film classic Ben Hur (1959) and the chariot race in which Ben Hur defeats his old enemy, Messara. The chariots raced side-by-side around a tight circle.

In the pharmaceutical industry, as part of the technological innovations in developing new drugs in the areas of unmet medical needs (UMN), drug development design/research laboratory centers, which encompass pharmaceutical basis, health, and nutrition, have begun utilizing AI. They have initiated the establishment of a structure to support the endeavor. The objective is to reduce development time and bring new drugs to market more quickly. To establish the structure, funds and investment for human resources are necessary. With the understanding that 'Time is Money', acquisitions cannot be conducted purely for the possession of a specific product, which ultimately leads to the purchase of the entire company. This has set the trend for the structure of M&As. In the case of the above-mentioned centers, 'AI is Money.' Thus, investing in AI is comparable to buying time in developing new drugs. I cannot help but pray for their success.

I would like to introduce a contrasting valuable AI application example. In the financial sector, an investment firm could upload big data to an AI system which selects where to make investments, increasing the successful results of this investment firm. This provides evidence of how AI not only could contribute to the increase of production in technology, but also the increase of production (delivery) in the service sector as well.

As I have noted in Narrative 12, AI does not operate independently. It is through the presence of human beings (the brain) that the real ability of AI becomes evident. In short, it is important to become skilled in understanding the sense of personal space when interacting with other people. A poor sense of perceiving the surrounding atmosphere will not do. Being able to analyze relations with other people and adapt accordingly are necessary fundamentals when implementing AI.

第14話

ダ・ヴィンチ（Da Vinci）と
ミケランジェロ（Michelangelo）

レオナルド・ダ・ヴィンチ
Leonardo da Vinci(1452-1519)

　三菱一号館美術館（千代田区丸の内）にてレオナルド×ミケランジェロ展が開かれている（2017年6月17日～9月24日）。筆者は8月に2度学びに行った。レオナルド×ミケランジェロで、すなわちルネッサンス期を代表するイタリアの両巨匠、静のダ・ヴィンチと動のミケランジェロの格闘技である。歳はダ・ヴィンチが23歳上と聞くが、お互いの類まれな価値を認め合う2人である。だから、闘うのだ。その上で、両雄並び立とうとするのである。

　それでは、展覧会場における、ダ・ヴィンチとミケランジェロのナレーションを引用しながら、話を進めたい。ダ・ヴィンチいわく"画家は、優れた師匠の手になる素描を模写することに習熟しなければならない"と、そしてミケランジェロ、（弟子のアントニオに）いわく"アントニオ、素描をしなさい、アントニオ、素描をしなさい。時間を無駄にしないで"と。いかに基礎が必要かを共に強調している。

　にもかかわらず、ダ・ヴィンチは言う"平らなものを立体的に見せるという技量…画家はこの点で彫刻家を凌駕している"。対してミケランジェロは言う"彫刻というのは削り取っていく種類のものを言っているので、付け加えていく種類の彫刻は絵画と同じようなものです"と、絵画を低く見ている。ふざけ合っているのか。仲が良いのだろう。

　ミケランジェロも痛烈だ、"あなたは騎馬隊の素描はなされたが、そ

Narrative 14
Da Vinci and Michelangelo

The Mitsubishi Ichigokan Museum (Chiyoda-ku, Marunouchi) held an exhibition entitled "Leonardo × Michelangelo" from June 17th thru Sept. 24th, 2017. Personally, I studied the exhibit twice in August. The exhibit highlighted the two great masters who represent the Renaissance period, and was presented as an encounter between the passive Da Vinci and the dynamic Michelangelo. It was noted that Da Vinci was 23 years older than Michelangelo, but they mutually recognized the other's unparalleled talent. Thus, a combat developed between them, in which the two great men endeavored to be on par with the other.

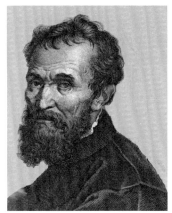
Michelangelo Buonarroti(1475-1564)
ミケランジェロ・ブオノリッチ

Now, going back to material from the exhibition hall, I would like to proceed by quoting from a narration on Da Vinci and Michelangelo. According to Da Vinci, "An artist must devote to sketching from the works of a skilled master." On a similar note, Michelangelo repeatedly told his apprentice Antonio, "Sketch Antonio, sketch. Do not waste time." The two masters mutually stressed the importance of becoming skilled in the fundamentals.

However, the two artists were not always in agreement. Da Vinci stated, "The skill to reflect on a flat surface and give it dimension . . . an artist, in this respect, surpasses a sculptor." To this, Michelangelo replied, "Sculpting is an art process of carving away, if additions could be made in sculpting, then it would be the same as painting", reflecting his low opinion of painting. Perhaps they were chiding each other, or perhaps they were merely teasing each other. They may have been friends.

Michelangelo was also severely critical when he stated, "You sketched an equestrian form for a bronze cast, unsuccessful at making the cast, you shamelessly had the statue placed as it was." According to Da Vinci, ". . . . it is through countless paintings that divinely beautiful representations have been preserved . . . . an artist's work has left

落語家・五代目柳家小さん
Kosan Yanagiya(1915-2002)

れをブロンズに鋳造しようとしたが、鋳造できず、恥知らずにもそのまま放置した"と。ダ・ヴィンチいわく"…どれほど多くの絵画が、神々しい美の似姿を保存してきたことか…。そのおかげで画家の作品は、その師匠である自然の作品よりも優れたものとして残ったのだ"と。

この辺で、2人の売り言葉に買い言葉はお開きにしたい。肝心なのは、ミケランジェロは純粋な彫刻家であったが、ダ・ヴィンチの絵画は彼の生涯の業績・タレントの一部にとどまることである。みなさまご存知のとおりである。

ミケランジェロの"彫刻は、無駄なものを削り取ること"という言葉に、感銘を受けた。筆者は実験化学者の端くれであった。一番無駄のない化学反応に行きつくために、どれだけ多くの試行錯誤を繰り返してきたか。毎回のこの一ページのためにも、数百ページの原文を読むことがよくある。削りに削って良いものになる。その神髄は、何といってもミケランジェロのダヴィデ（David）の像である。これこそ削りに削った結果、これ以上削ってはいけないボトムラインまで来た作品であると思う。

もう一つ、日本の古典芸能で無駄を削りに削った例を挙げたい。落語の五代目柳家小さん（小林盛夫、1915～2002）の話である。高座での食べる仕草は、天下一品。小さん師匠が自ら試行錯誤――削りに削って仕上げたものに、豆甘という食べ物がある。底の寒天、赤えんどう、そして最後にかける黒蜜の選択と量。小さん師匠はこれらの構成成分が複雑に絡んだ方程式を完成させるのに何年位かかったのだろうか。詳しくは息子である六代目小さん師匠に伺ったらよいのだろうが。この話はミケランジェロに通ずるものがある。

us with images that surpass that of the master, nature."

It is now about time to put an end to writing about the exchange of cynicism between the two. The importance is, although Michelangelo is known for his exceptional talents in the fields of sculpture, painting, architecture, and poetry, for Da Vinci, painting was a lifelong achievement, but only a segment of his talents. As many are well aware, he had extraordinary talents in inventing, sculpting, science, mathematics, and engineering, to name a few.

I was impressed by Michelangelo's words, "Sculpting is carving away useless matter". I am but a minor experimental scientist. Pursuing the most efficient chemical reaction has been an infinite repetition of trial and error. And as a writer, each time I endeavor to write a single page, I frequently read several hundred pages of reference material. What remains on the page is the product of carving and carving away. The essence of this is undoubtedly reflected in Michelangelo's sculpture of David. This sculpture is the ultimate result of relentless carving to the extent of reaching the bottom line.

One more example of carving and carving away I would like to introduce is from a form of classic Japanese entertainment called Rakugo (comic monologue). Ko-san Yanagiya the 5th (born Morio Kobayashi, 1915 to 2002) was the first rakugo comic storyteller to be named a living national treasure by the Japanese government. His use of mimicking gestures to convey eating food is unsurpassed. Master Ko-san, in perfecting these gestures, went through the process of trial and error – carving and carving away until finding perfection in making a Japanese traditional sweet, mamekan. At the bottom of the treat is a jelly, in the middle are sweet red beans, and finally on top is the choice amount of brown sugar-based syrup. Master Ko-san had combined these complex ingredients countless times during the process of perfecting his performance. Just how many years did it take him to do so? We would only learn of the details if an inquiry were made to his son, Ko-san the 6th. This episode possesses an essence which relates to Michelangelo in how they both carved and carved away until perfection was achieved.

第15話
弱い人と強い人

Cats-Mice-Collaborations
素心会のロゴ——みんな仲良くしようぜ
Logo of Soshin Association—Let's mingle together!

　弱い人、強い人と、言われても解らないよね…。これが本音であろう。弱い強いと言うと腕力を思い出すが、動物社会同様に、人の社会でも立ち位置の違いで、弱いと思われた人が現実には強い人だったということはよくある。何を軸にするかでも変わるので、考えてみたい。

　本章の第12話（参照）で取り上げたダリ（Dali）の婚外子として世間の同情を呼んだマリア・マルチネーは、弱い人のイメージがあった。が、DNA鑑定の結果は"否"であった。ダリとの親子関係は否定されたのである。彼女こそ、黒幕の張本人だったのだ！彼女は、DNA鑑定（科学的に正当）は、イカサマと騒ぐであろう。The Dali Museum Theaterが請求するであろう、ダリのお墓を開き棺を取り出した莫大な費用負担なんか、何とも思わないだろう。開き直った悪党！強い人を超えて怖い人になった。

　強い人がいる。1930年11月11日にポーランドの貧しいユダヤ家族と共にニューヨークに着いたミルドレッド・スピーワク（Mildred Spiewak, 1930～2017）である。1958年物理学者のジェーン・ドレッセルハウス（Gene Dresselhaus）と結婚してドレッセルハウス姓となった。彼女は、炭素の研究に生涯を捧げ、炭素の女王（Queen of Carbon）とまで呼ばれた。しかし、1996年のノーベル化学賞は、カーボン60（フ

Narrative 15

Weak People and Strong People

Weak people, strong people - what are you talking about? This is probably the honest, candid reaction of many of the readers of this narrative. Weak and strong are terms that can be associated with bodily strength. However, similar to the animal kingdom, in human society, the perceptions of weak and strong can be established through a difference in social standing. Those individuals who are thought to be weak were, in reality, often once a strong person. Because the perception can change depending upon what the situation is, I would like to ponder upon this.

Within Narrative 12 of this series, I discussed Dali and Maria Martinez. Martinez, who received sympathy from the general public for being his illegitimate daughter, reflected the image of being a weak person. However, the DNA test results were negative so parent-child relations with Dali were denied. She, herself, was the mastermind behind the fiasco. She will probably argue that the DNA tests (which are scientifically sound) were fraudulent. She could care less about the enormous sum that the Dali Theatre and Museum will probably bill her for the cost incurred to excavate Dali's grave and open his casket. She has proven to be a defiant villain. Beyond being a strong person, she is a fearful individual.

An example of a strong individual is Mildred Dresselhaus (née Spiewak; 1930 to 2017). She was born on November 11, 1930 in New York to poor Polish Jewish immigrant parents. In 1958 she married physicist Gene Dresselhaus, taking on the Dresselhaus name. She devoted her life to the research of carbon, and earned the title "Queen of Carbon". However, in 1996 the Nobel Prize for Chemistry was awarded to the discoverers of Carbon 60 (also known as fullerene), Harold W. Kroto, (whose father was a Polish Jew who had escaped to Britain), Richard E. Smalley, and Robert F. Curl. Under the leadership of Kroto, the three spent 11 days at Rice University conducting joint experiments and verifying the existence of the soccer ball shaped Carbon 60. They announced their findings in Nature magazine. Mildred, who was at MIT, was not invited to participate in the research. In the event she had been invited and there were four involved in the discovery, it would have been difficult to have been awarded the Nobel Prize due to the Nobel Foundation's established maximum of

Chapter Ⅱ　Changes in the Trend of Globalization ●————**187**

ラーレン　fullerenes）の発見者、ハロルド・クロトー（Harold W. Kroto、父親はユダヤ系ポーランド人、英国に逃れる）、リチャード・スモーリー（Richard E.Smalley）とロバート・カール（Robert F. Curl）に与えられた。クロトーのリーダーシップで、3人はライス大学（Rice University）で11日間の共同実験をして、サッカーボール型（Carbon 60）を確認し、公表（Nature 誌）したのである。マサチューセッツ工科大学にいたミルドレッドは呼ばれることはなかった。もし、呼ばれていて4人で発見したのなら、ノーベル賞はマックス3人なので3人を選ぶのは困難である。なので、クロトーともう一人の2人授賞——ポーランド系ユダヤ人2人——だったかもしれない。もちろん、過ぎたことに"若し"はない。そして彼女は"いいじゃないの"と言って本年（2017）86歳の天寿を全うした。真に強い人であった。合掌。

　日本のスポーツ界に、"気は優しくて力持ち"の本物の強い人がいる。柔道界の井上康生六段である。日本男子柔道監督である彼が奨めた"勝利の改革"というのがある。そのためにスポーツ科学を活用する。そして量より質を…。稽古一点張りの前任者に対し、改革者としての強さがよく出ている。

　最後に、そういう君（筆者）はどうなんだと聞かれれば…。私のオフィスに訪ねてくれる仕事関係の方々、友人そして学生などは、ニコニコしながら美味いコーヒーとお菓子を出してくれて、楽しいと言ってくれる。弱い人である。とにかく人（ひと）皆、程度の差はあっても、内に強い人・弱い人をもっていて時と機会によって、どちらかが表に出るものである。NHK 日曜日午後7時半の「ダーウィンが来た」という番組においては、小さな動物が子を守るために大きな動物に歯をむき出して向かっていく姿をよく映すことがある。普段はおとなしい動物でも、途端に変身できるのである。人間も同じ、私も強い人になれることがある。

three awardees for a specific accomplishment. This is perhaps why Kroto, Smalley, and Curl were awarded the prize. Of course, there are no ifs in events of the past. In an interview on the matter, she stated that she was "Not at all" bothered by not receiving the Nobel Prize. She passed away this year (2017) at the age of 86. She was truly a strong individual.

In Japanese sports circles, "Gentle in nature, and strong" is said to represent a really strong individual. This is embodied in the judo practitioner Kosei Inoue, 6th Dan. As head coach of the Japan men's judo national team, he introduced the concept of the "Reform of Victory". To put this concept into practice, he is utilizing sports science. In addition, his focus is upon the quality of training instead of the quantity. In comparison to his predecessor's policy of sheer training, the strength of the reformer is evident.

Lastly, I must do a little self-reflecting on what I would say if I were asked, "How about you?" I welcome friends and students related to my work to my office, where I am told that they enjoy the delicious coffee, sweets, and a happy atmosphere. I feel that generally I am a weak individual. However, although there may be a certain disparity, all people possess within them, a strong individual and weak individual, and depending upon a specific event or circumstance, one or the other will emerge. There is a NHK (Japan's National Broadcaster) program which airs every Sunday evening at 7:30 named "Darwin Came". The program, as evident by its name, focuses upon wildlife. In one of its episodes, it showed how small animals, in protecting their young, will bear their teeth and attack a far larger animal. Ordinarily benign animals can change in an instant if provoked. Human beings are the same; there are times when I become a strong person.

第16話
クール・ビズで良いのですか

　2017年9月15日金曜日、北朝鮮によるミサイル発射（午前6時57分）について、朝7時の記者会見に臨んだ菅官房長官はネクタイ無しのオープンシャツであった。何とも締まらない姿だった。国民には緊張感を要請しているのだから、ネクタイ位締めるべきである。インドから帰国した安倍首相は、ネクタイをちゃんと締めての記者会見だったが。菅氏は10月4日の会見でもまだ開襟シャツだったが、翌日の記者会見では黄金色（こがねいろ）の威厳のあるネクタイをしていた。その翌朝は（10月6日）、ブルーの品の良いタイ。衆院選挙や国際情勢の重大さに気が付いたのか、結構です。

　国会と政府（霞が関）は、違うと言えばそれまでであるが、英国・EU・USでも政府関係者は、地味だがしっかりとスーツにネクタイをしている。何か仕事のプロという感じがする。霞が関も、管理職はスーツにネクタイくらいは締めたら良いと思う。平和ボケの日本に、政府くらいは緊張感があって良いと思うが。一方、訪問者は正装が多いのでは。夏期に室温を2度上げることによるクールビズの経済効果は、箱モノを作って放置している無駄使いに比べれば、大した節約ではない。箱モノを作らなければ、良いのだから。官僚も年度を通して快適な仕事環境があれば、日本の生産性も上がるというものである。

　ちなみに、筆者が米国イ・リリー社に入社した時（1994）、リリースタイルはダークスーツに、地味タイ、そして白のワイシャツと言われたものである。今は本社も変わったと思うが、研究所や工場では、事故が起きないよう、服装は厳しい。

　また、クール（cool）と言えば、オードリー・ヘップバーンとグレゴ

190————●第2章　Changes in the Trend of Globalization

Narrative 16

Is it okay to go with Cool-Biz?

When North Korea launched a missile on Friday, September 15th, 2017 at 06:57 AM,Chief Cabinet Secretary Yoshihide Suga conducted a press conference at 7:00 AM without a tie and an unbuttoned shirt-collar. A lot can be said about how he looked. Although Kasumigaseki (government) is said to be unlike the Diet (Japan's bicameral legislature), he was conveying to the general public that they should accept this news with a sense of apprehension. This message should have been delivered with great formality; he should have at least worn a tie. Prime Minister Abe, who held a press conference immediately on his return from a trip to India, wore a tie. In a recent press conference on October 4th, again Chief Cabinet Secretary Suga appeared in an open-necked shirt. Finally, behold, he wore a dignified yellow-gold necktie for the press conference of October 5th. For the morning of October 6th, he chose a sophisticated blue tie. It is good to see that he finally realized the gravity of the general election and international affairs.

To say that the Diet and government (Kasumigaseki) are different is one thing. Government officials of the United Kingdom, the EU, and the United States dress in subdued colors, and the men wear suits and ties. This code of attire gives off an air of professionalism. In Kasumigaseki as well, I think that the men who are at a management level should wear a suit and tie. Japan may be peace-addicted, but the government, at least, should sustain a sense of decorum. On the other hand, the majority of those who visit government offices are in formal attire. The economic effectiveness of Cool Biz (increasing the room temperature in the summer by 2 degrees) is nothing in comparison with the amount of money wasted in constructing buildings that are later abandoned. Cool Biz's economic effectiveness is seen when the building of unnecessary structures is avoided. However, if government officials were able to work in a comfortable environment throughout the year, their productivity would increase.

When I joined America's Eli Lilly in 1994, the Lilly dress code required a dark suit, a somber tie, and a white business shirt. Although I believe that the head office has subsequently changed its policy for office workers, strict rules are enforced regarding clothing in their laboratories and manufacturing plants to avoid accidents.

Chapter Ⅱ　Changes in the Trend of Globalization ●───191

映画『ローマの休日』より
1953 - Roman Holiday - Moviestills

リー・ペック主演の「ローマの休日」で、ローマを満喫中のオードリーにグレゴリーが、ローマは如何ですかと聞くと、クール（cool）と答えていたのを覚えている。

　ここで思い出すのは、本年度（2017）ノーベル文学賞に輝いたカズオ・イシグロ氏である。5歳まで長崎で暮らしたイシグロ氏の英語は、難しい言葉を使わず解り易い言葉で話してくれる。突然、発想が大転換するので一瞬戸惑うが、説明の話が続くとあーそうかと納得がいく。

　話を戻そう。菅官房長官のコメントは、当然であるが言葉を慎重に選び、簡潔に政府の見解を伝えている。10月10日に選挙公示となる衆院選挙前の党首・代表の討論では（10月8日）、話が解りにくい方もいた。特に小池氏の話は解らない。憶測を呼ぶための手段ならなおさらだ。日本語の解る外国人記者も戸惑うのではと思う。今日10月9日、公示の前日であるが、政権交代を目指すなら、小池氏は衆院選に立候補すべきである。都知事として1年が過ぎたが、何もしていない。舌を使っただけである。都知事は、もっと時間のある人に代わるべきである(注)。今日の時点では、枝野新党が伸びそうな感じがする。とにかく安倍首相の過信が招いた思いつき解散（Snap Election）がこの混乱を招いたので、少しはお灸をすえる必要がある。明日の国民の反応が楽しみである。

　10月10日、小池氏は立候補出来なかった。第一幕は彼女の敗北である。

(注)この稿は編集子に、後で書き換えていないことを保証してもらっている。

Furthermore, when I hear the term 'cool', the film classic "Roman Holiday" starring Audrey Hepburn and Gregory Peck comes to mind. I recall the scene in which Gregory asks Audrey, who is thoroughly enjoying Rome, what her thoughts are of the city, to which she replies, "cool".

It is also interesting to note how this year's (2017) winner of the Nobel Prize in Literature, Kazuo Ishiguro, communicates. He resided in Nagasaki until he was 5 years old. When speaking in his now native English language, he does not use difficult words. Instead, he chooses words that are easily understood. However, it seems that his thoughts often make a sudden change in direction, which causes the listener to become perplexed. Upon further listening to his explanations, a sense of recognition develops.

Now let us return to the original theme. Chief Cabinet Secretary Suga's message was appropriate and was delivered concisely with words which reflected the gravity of the government's views. Prior to the October 10th Lower House election announcement, a debate between party leaders and representatives was held on October 8th. During this debate, some comments were difficult to understand. In particular, Ms. Yuriko Koike's comments were unclear. If her comments were a tactic to raise speculations, it probably failed because comprehension of her comments evaded the listener. Foreign correspondents who could understand Japanese must have been perplexed. If her goal was to change the current administration, Ms. Koike had the opportunity on October 9th (the day before the official election announcement) to become a candidate for the Lower House elections. A year had passed since she became the governor of Tokyo, but she had done nothing but use her tongue. The position of governor of Tokyo is a post that should be passed on to someone with more time to devote to their duties. Prior to the election announcement, it felt like Yukio Edano's new party (the Constitutional Democratic Party of Japan) would exceed expectations. It was Prime Minister Abe's overconfidence which led to his decision to hold a Snap Election, which caused major confusion in the political landscape. On October 10th, Ms. Koike did not announce her candidacy. Thus, the first act in this political play ended with her defeat. [Note]

[Note]I have secured a guarantee with the editors that there have been no additions, or alterations made to this manuscript.

Chapter II   Changes in the Trend of Globalization ●————193

第17話

習政権の中国は一党支配の
立憲共和制である

　習政権の中国を共産党国家と呼んだり、書いたりするのを目にすることがよくある。しかし、習政権の中国は共産主義王朝 (Communist Dynasty) かなと思い紐解いていくと、どうもそうでもなさそうな気がしてきた。

　清王朝の崩壊から毛沢東にいたるまでを、振り返ってみたい。孫文らによる辛亥革命 (1911〜) により、宣統帝が退位し従来の王朝制度が廃止される。1912年1月1日共和制国家である中華民国が発足した。孫文が初代臨時大総統となった。日本の明治維新に習って中華民国も、明治天皇が君主という日本とは内容は違うが、制度上は立憲君主制になったかにみえた。

　その孫文の後を就いた毛沢東が最高指導者 (President) であり、周恩来が首相という立憲共和制である。そこで狂いが生じたのは、毛沢東が現実主義の実力者劉少奇・鄧小平を追放し、毛沢東の江青夫人を中心とする四人組に文化大革命を実行させたことである。毛は病を患い現実が解らなくなっており、中国は紅衛兵による破壊と混乱の極みの状況になっているのを知る由もなかった。毛の死去 (1976年9月9日) により華国鋒が後継者 (党主席) になり、四人組の逮捕を実行した (同年10月6日)。そして文化大革命の終結を宣言。華国鋒は、良識派の周恩来首相の進言により、鄧小平の復活を認めたのである (劉少奇は下放中に死去)。鄧小平は華国鋒を激賞したと言われている。

　しかし、鄧小平もさる者、華国鋒を追い落とし胡耀邦を党首席に趙紫陽を首相に据えた。自らは最高ポストにはつかず、文化大革命後の中国を統括したのは、何度かの失脚の経験と下放から学んだ知恵からであろ

194————●第2章　Changes in the Trend of Globalization

Narrative 17

China's Xi Administration is a Constitutional Republic Ruled by One Party

Often when I hear and read about China under the Xi Administration, it is referred to as a Communist Party nation. However, upon further examination, perceiving Xi Administration's China as a Communist Dynasty does not necessarily seem to be accurate.

Let us review the period from the collapse of the Qing Dynasty to Mao Zedong. The Chinese (Xinhai) Revolution of 1911, led by Sun Yat-sen, brought an end to the imperial rule of Emperor Xuantong and the Qing dynasty. On January 1, 1912, the Republic of China was inaugurated. Sun Yat-sen became the nation's first provisional President. Although the Republic of China basically followed the example of Japan's Meiji Restoration in which Emperor Meiji was the head of state, it looked as though the nation was institutionally going to adopt a constitutional monarchy.

The Great Wall (万里の長城)

Upon succeeding Sun Yat-sen, Mao Zedong became the nation's executive leader (the President), with Zhou Enlai as Prime Minister. This was institutionally becoming a monarchy republic. Then disarray set into motion. Mao banished the powerful realists, Liu Shaoqi and Deng Xiaoping, which allowed his wife, Jiang Qing and the other members of the 'Gang of Four' (Zhang Chunqiao, Yao Wenyuan, and Wang Hongwen to initiate their Cultural Revolution through their control of the power in the Communist Party. Due to ill health, Mao was unable to comprehend reality. He was completely unaware of the deplorable state of destruction and chaos brought on by China's Red Army. Following the death of Mao (September 9, 1976), Hua Guofeng was chosen as his successor (Chairman of the Communist Party), and he had the 'Gang of Four' arrested (October 6, 1976). He went on to announce the end of the Cultural Revolution. Hua Guofeng, with advice from Prime Minister Zhou Enlai, reinstated Deng Xiaoping (Liu Shaoqi had passed away). It is said that Deng Xiaoping had highly praised Hua Guofeng.

Chapter Ⅱ　Changes in the Trend of Globalization ●―――― 195

"一帯一路"時をつげた
One Belt One Road ― declared!

う。しかし胡耀邦が走資に走りすぎると判断すると、1987年1月、胡耀邦を追放してのけた。そして胡耀邦の死を機に天安門事件（1989年4月）が発生し、鄧小平は容赦なく弾圧をする。結局のところ、鄧小平の基本は共産党を中心の立憲共和制だったのである。そして江沢民・李鵬／朱鎔基、胡錦濤・温家宝と続く。

　そして2012年、現在の習近平（President）・李克強（Prime Minister）政権が誕生する。この政権の立憲共和制はどうなっていくのだろうか。興味が尽きない。

　ここで何故、筆者が本稿を書こうとしたのか、説明をしたい。実は、現在トランプ政権から外れたが、トランプ氏の側近であるスティーヴ・バノン（Steve Bannon）が私人として北京を訪問し、習・李に次ぐ第6位であるが、汚職追放で習の信任熱くNo2と言われている王岐山（Wang Qishan）と会っているのである。北朝鮮に絡んでいるのは間違いないであろう。良い結果を生むと良いのだが。

　話を戻そう。習近平は、妻で国民的歌手である彭麗媛との間に、一人娘の習明沢がいる。ハーバード大学を卒業し、米国在住である。これが何を意味するかは、皆様お分かりのはずである。ところで習氏には男の子はいないので家族から後継を選ぶことはできない。しかし、筆者は、習氏は健康である限り三期、四期と続けるのではないかと思う。一対一路の完成には、数十年は必要である。

　一時は、毛沢東と鄧小平を賛美していたが、最近の核心の称号などから大分強権ぶりを発揮している。七上八下も無視。しかし2017年10月18日からの中国共産党大会あたりで、党規約を改正し正当化するのであろう。共に下放の苦難を経験した前述の王岐山を政治局常務委員に留任させる意向という。一方王氏自身は、健康に不安ありと言っているら

However, Deng Xiaoping proved to be quite an individual. After sidelining Hua Guofeng, he made Hu Yaobang the Party Chairman and Zhao Ziyang the Prime Minister. Even though he personally avoided taking on a high ranking position, he virtually controlled post Cultural Revolution China. This was probably due to knowledge he had obtained from his experience of repeatedly being purged and reinstated. When he concluded that Hu Yaobang was aggressively pursuing free market economic reforms, he had Hu Yaobang banished in January 1989. The death of Hu Yaobang triggered the Tiananmen Square protests (April, 1989) which were strongly oppressed by Deng Xiaoping. In retrospect, Deng Xiaoping, with the Communist Party at the core, was the architect of the monarch republic. He was followed in succession by Jiang Zemin(President) and Li Peng(Prime Minister) / Zhu Rongji(Prime Minister), Hu Jintao(President) and Wen Jiabao(Prime Minister).

A Painter
画家

In 2012, the current administration of President Xi Jinping and Prime Minister Li Keqiang was born. One cannot help wonder what the future holds for this monarchial republic. I, for one, am extremely interested.

Here I would like to explain what I was trying to express through writing this piece. Steve Bannon, who has left the current Trump administration, visited Beijing as a private individual in September 2017 and met with Wang Qishan. Because of his position as Xi's anticorruption tzar, Wang Qishan is 6th in the succession line, following Xi, Li, and several others. However, because of his strict and successful enforcement of Xi's policy to banish corruption, Wang has won firm confidence and is said to actually be No. 2 in line. There is no doubt that the meeting between Bannon and Wang involved the North Korean issue. Hopes are that positive results about this difficult issue will develop from this meeting.

Let us return to the topic of Xi and the monarchial republic. Xi Jinping and his wife, Peng Liyuan, a renowned singer, have one daughter, Xi Mingze . She graduated from Harvard University and currently resides in the United States. What does this reflect? I am confident that many of you already know the answer. Xi does not have a son; thus, choosing a successor from the family cannot be done. However, I believe that as long as Xi is in good health, he will serve a third and fourth term. He may feel this is necessary in order to complete the One Belt One Road initiative, which will perhaps take several decades. At one point, Mao Zedong and Deng Xiaoping were praised for what they accomplished for China. However, recently upon receiving the

米川弁護士夫人（ダンスの折）と妻
Dancing madam of lawyer Yonekawa and Junko

しい。いずれにしても、ぶれないが家庭では優しい習氏には悩みは尽きないであろう。習政権の立憲共和制が混乱なく進むことを願うのは、中国には中国合衆国 (United of China) はないであろうからである。中国は、米国のような新しい国ではなく、4000年の歴史をもつ多文化・多文明の国なので、透明性のある中央集権が必要なのである。

　今、世界で最もリラックスしている政治家は、誰あろう、ロシア大統領プーチン氏である。氏はかつての帝政ロシアのツァーが夢である。

'core' title (which designates him as a leader who is central to the leadership of the Communist Party in China), Xi has rigorously invoked the power of his position. He has totally disregarded the retirement age of 68 years. However, at the Communist Party General Meeting, held on October 18, 2017, revisions were made to the Party rules, perhaps in an effort to justify his actions. Having experienced the hardship of expulsion repeatedly, Xi seems intent to keep the aforementioned Wang Qishan on the Politburo Standing Committee. For his part, Qishan has mentioned Xi's concern about his ill health. The unwavering Xi is said to be a kind figure within his family, but there is probably no end to his worries. Hopefully the Xi administration will continue its monarchial republic rule smoothly, for in China, there is no United China. In contrast to the United States, which is a relatively new nation, China is a nation of multiple cultures and civilizations, spanning over 4000 years. It seems necessary to have a central administration that is transparent in order to have the country function.

Right now, the most relaxed politician in the world is probably Russia's President Putin. He dreams of becoming the Tsar of Imperial Russia.

第18話

ノーベル文学賞に本命 カズオ・イシグロ氏

　2017年のノーベル文学賞は、英国のカズオ・イシグロ氏が並み居る世界の文豪を抑え一足飛びに授賞した。ここ数年気になっていた作家である。2015年の来日時のインタービューをみても、とてつもない発想の持ち主であることがよく解る。

　出版関係の賭け率（オッズ）は、本が売れることが基本・目標なので、ノーベル賞委員会のリストとはだいぶ違うと言われる。ノーベル文学賞を待ち望んでいる世界の文豪と言われる候補者が列をなしていると言われるなかで、日本の候補者の位置は決して高くないと言われていた。

　ノーベル医学生理学賞・物理学賞・化学賞においては、その授賞歴が前提であるような賞がそれぞれ存在する。文学賞にはそれがあるのか。イシグロ氏は英国の最高文学賞と言われるブッカー賞を受賞している（1989、35歳）。他にも王立文学賞協会賞（1982）、ウイットブレッド賞（1986）と総なめにしているが。イシグロ氏の経歴から、英国のブッカー賞が最も重きのある賞のような感じがする。

　ここでブッカー賞について、少し触れたいと思う。インターネットによると、（the Booker prize）ブッカー賞：毎年英国で発刊された最も優れた小説に与えられる賞；英国の企業Booker McConnell社とPublishers' Association 主催でBook Trust の審査委員会が選ぶ　とある。また英連邦及びアイルランド国籍の著者によって英語で書かれた長編小説ともある。ブッカー賞の正式名称は、Booker McConnell Prizeというが、通称はブッカー賞、すなわちBooker Prize である。外国人にも門戸を開くため、国際ブッカー賞を2005年に立ち上げている。後述するが、米国人も授賞している。

Narrative 18

Favorite for the Nobel Prize in Literature, Kazuo Ishiguro

©共同通信／アマナイメージズ

The 2017 Nobel Prize in Literature was awarded to Britain's Kazuo Ishiguro, who left in his wake some of the world's foremost leading authors. In the past few years, I had been drawn to this author. While viewing the interview he gave when visiting Japan in 2015, I saw that his exceptional approaches and ideas were evident.

Mr. Kazuo Ishiguro blanlced by his wife and daughter, December 10, 2017
カズオ・イシグロ氏　妻と息女にかこまれて

The standard established by the pub-lishing sector on whether or not to publish a book is based fundamentally on whether the book will sell, which would be their main objective. However, this criterion very likely differs from that of the Nobel Committee when compiling a list of candidates. For the world's renowned authors who eagerly wait in line to be awarded the Nobel Prize in Literature, it has been said that the position of a Japanese candidate within this line is not high.

There are precursor awards that lead to Nobel Prizes in Medicine, Physics, and Chemistry. Does one exist for the Literature Prize? Mr. Ishiguro was awarded England's prestigious Booker Prize in 1989 when he was 35 years old. He has also been awarded the Winifred Holtby Memorial Prize (1982) and the Whitbread Prize (1986). When evaluating Mr. Ishiguro's career prior to his receiving the Nobel Prize, England's Booker Prize would presumably be the most coveted prize.

At this point, let us take a look at what the Booker Prize is. The official name of the Booker Prize is the "Man Booker Prize for Fiction", but it is popularly known as "the Booker Prize" or simply "the Booker". According to the internet, the Booker Prize is awarded each year to the author of the best original novel written in the English language and published in the UK. The Prize was originally known as the Booker McConnell Prize after the company that had sponsored it. An advisory committee appointed by the Booker Prize Foundation selects the judging panel. From its incep-

Chapter Ⅱ　Changes in the Trend of Globalization ●————**201**

この賞の権威は、どうもその選考過程にあるような気がする。ノーベル賞選考員会(全領域)と全く同じプロセスである。絶対に漏れない公正なシステムで行われている。

　さて、今年(2017)、ノーベル文学賞がアジアに来るならこの人かなと思っていた人がいる。オーストラリアのタスマニア州在住のリチャード・フラナガン氏(Richard Flanagan)である。アイルランド系オーストラリア人である。タスマニア大学文学部を卒業、オックスフォード大学にて文学修士取得。オーストラリアの文学賞を総なめにして、2002年に英連邦作家賞を受賞し、一躍世界の人となった。そして2014年英国の最高文学賞ブッカー賞を受賞した。今回イシグロ氏の授賞により、英語系作家の授賞は少し遠くのか、いつアジアに回ってくるのかも興味深い。

　もう一人、筆者の一作目『国際人になるためのInsight Track』第1章第9話「An Independent Thinker」(2014)で取り上げたフィリップ・ロス氏(Philip Roth)である。氏は、2001年に第1回フランツ・カフカ賞(Franz Kafka)を授賞。2011年には、国際ブッカー賞を授賞している。いずれノーベル文学賞に輝く作家の一人であろう。

　イシグロ氏の父親の石黒鎮雄氏は(理学博士、東大理学部)夫人と共に英国に帰化している。イシグロ氏は、1983年英国人のローナ・アン・マグドゥーガルと結婚し、1992年に長女ナオミ(Naomi)に恵まれている。時に両親を尋ねると3人で日本語で話すという。長崎弁？　微笑ましい。

素心館素心会(水海道一高 友人)
Soshin Club (Mitsukaido High School)

tion, only Commonwealth, Irish, and South African (and later Zimbabwean) citizens were eligible to receive the prize. However, in September 2013 it was announced that future Booker Prize awards could be given to authors from anywhere in the world. Later, I will go into detail about an American who has been awarded this prize. To allow authors of any nationality to gain recognition, the International Man Booker Prize was established in 2005 for books that were translated into English.

The prestige that surrounds this particular literary prize seems to stem from its selection process. It is exactly the same process undertaken by the Nobel Committee for Literature, which is conducted in an absolutely fair system.

This year (2017), if the Nobel Prize for Literature had not been given to an Asian author, there were many who probably thought of a specific author as the most likely winner. That author would be Richard Flanagan, who resides in Tasmania, Australia. He is an Australian of Irish decent. After graduating from the University of Tasmania with a BA, he went on to study at Oxford University where he received the degree of Master of Letters in History. After winning numerous literary prizes in Australia, in 2002 he was awarded the Commonwealth Writers' Prize, becoming world renown overnight. Then in 2014, he won the literary world's coveted Booker Prize. With Mr. Ishiguro being awarded the Nobel Prize for Literature, this may indicate that English language authors may be from a distance and still receive the awards. It may also reflect a possibility for additional candidates from Asia. It is interesting to speculate about this.

Another individual, Philip Roth, who I wrote about in Insight Track – To Become an Internationally-Minded Person, Chapter 1, Narrative 9: "An Independent Thinker" (2014). In 2001, he was awarded the first Franz Kafka Prize. In 2011, he was awarded the International Man Booker Prize.

Mr. Ishiguro was born in Nagasaki, Japan on November 8, 1954. His father, Shizuo Ishiguro, was a physical oceanographer (Doctor of Science, University of Tokyo, Department of Science) who moved to the U.K. with his wife, Shizuko, and children in 1960. In 1983 Kazuo married British Lorna MacDougall, and in 1992 they were blessed with the birth of their daughter, Naomi. When visiting his parents, it was said that the three conversed in Japanese. Was it in the Nagasaki dialect? Just envisioning this get-together makes me smile.

Miss High School
(ミス ハイスクール、2016年撮影)

第19話

後継者は要らない

　後任は要らないではない。これは、ベンチャーを立ち上げた人の壮絶な戦いの話である。立ち上げたベンチャーは、自らが守っていく——自らが完成させるという覚悟の話である。今年 (2017) も、10月21日 (第3土曜日) に、東大ホームカミングデイ (Home Coming Day) が開かれた。同日東大薬友会も総会と講演会を開催した。講演会のプログラムの一つがキャリヤーガイダンスである。日本の医薬品・食品・衛生関係の標準を創生する国立医薬品食品衛生研究所薬品部長である合田幸広博士をコーディネーターとして、また学部3年の佐藤玄謙君をアシスタントとして、卒後15年の産・官・個人 (2人のベンチャー運営者) の4人を招き、活発な議論 (戦い) を展開した。ここで取り上げたいのは、前述のベンチャー経営の2社である、徳渕慎一郎氏と土田薫 (関水薫) 氏 (Ms) である。2人とも、死ぬかと思うほど睡眠時間を減らして仕事に集中したという。共通点は、(1) 卒後大手企業に勤め、商品開発の面白さを知ると同時に、大きさ故の非効率・非合理性に気づき、それを外部から改善したいと(2) 共にコンサルテイング会社に転職している。(3) 土田 (Ms) 氏は、ご主人の関谷氏の香港転勤で共に香港に行き、多くを学ぶ。帰国後、場所と時間を確保するためコンサルタントとして独立。"自分らしいキャリアは自分で築く！" と手を振り上げている。凄いですね。(4) 徳渕氏は、2013年に (株) ハビタスケアを設立し、日常生活と科学研究をつなぐヘルスケアサービスを目指して、JR駅を中心の実証実験 (歩け、歩け) を行っている。やはり科学者の目線ありありですね。

　さてここで、海外に眼を移そう。筆者は、米国アサシス社 (クリーブランド、オハイオ州) の専任上級アドバイザーをしている。この会社の

204───●第2章　Changes in the Trend of Globalization

Narrative 19

There is No Need for a Successor

This narrative is not about not needing a successor to fill a position. This is about an individual who fiercely fought to establish a venture business. It is also about how the individual resolutely determined to protect and complete the venture business on his own.

On October 21 (the 3rd Saturday), 2017 the University of Tokyo held its Home Coming Day. On this same day, the Alumni Association, Pharmaceutical Sciences, of the University held its general Assembly and lecture meeting. As part of the lecture program, a career guidance segment was included. The coordinator of the segment was Professor Yukihiro Gohda, Director General of the National Pharmaceutical, Food, and Hygiene Research Institute, which is the organization that is responsible for establishing Japan's standards for pharmaceuticals, food, and hygiene. He was assisted by Haruki Sato, who was in his 3rd year at the Department, and several invited individuals who had graduated 15 years ago and represented industry, government, and the private sector (two of whom were venture business operators). These four individuals conducted an extremely stimulating (battle) debate. What I would like to bring up here, are the aforementioned venture business operators: Mr. Shinichiro Tokubuchi and Ms. Kaoru Tsuchida (Kaoru Sekimizu). Both of these individuals had concentrated so hard on their work that they had deprived themselves of much-needed sleep, to the point that they thought they might die. What they have in common is the following: (1) Upon graduating, they both went to work for a major corporation and found product development fascinating. However, at the same time they discovered that because of the corporation's large size, product development was both inefficient and unpractical, so they wanted to improve it from the outside. (2) Both joined consulting firms. (3) Ms. Tsuchida accompanied her husband, Mr. Sekimizu, when he was transferred to Hong Kong, where she learned a great deal. Upon returning to Japan, to keep developing her career, she established her own consultation practice. "For a career that I feel comfortable with, I had to build my own!" She is quite a remarkable individual. (4) In 2013, Mr. Tokubuchi established K.K. Habisucare, which is focused upon providing healthcare services by joining everyday life and scientific research. He

Chapter II   Changes in the Trend of Globalization ●———205

CEO・会長（Chairman）のギル・ヴァン・ボッケレン博士（Dr. Gil Van Bokkelen）は、正直、品格、聞く耳をもっている。思いやりもあり、決断も早い。筆者との信頼関係は深い。しかし、人間時に間違いは当たり前、お互い気づいたらすぐにゴメンナサイである。

　ボッケレン氏はスタンフォード大学医学部で遺伝学のPh.Dを取得し、カリフォルニア大学バークレー校で経済学と分子生物学の学位を取得した。多様な学歴の典型的な米国人である。ボッケレン氏は、アサシス社がベンチャーキャピタルによるスタートアップ（1995）からナスダック上場企業へと成長するまでを統括してきた。その主たる製品である幹細胞 マルチステム（MultiStem）の世界展開に全力を尽くしている。日本における臨床も開始された。日本が大好きで、PMDA理事長の近藤達也博士とは気さくな友人である。アサシス社での職務に加え、同氏は複数の施設による共同事業である全米再生医療センター（NCRM）の理事会会長を務めている。2010年から2012年は、ワシントンD.C.を拠点とする非営利団体の再生医療連合（ARM）の会長を務めた。ARMは、主要な政策立案者に再生医療の将来性について知識を深めてもらう活動を行っている。ボッケレン氏はまた、バイオテクノロジー産業協会（BIO）（現バイオテクノロジーイノベーション協会）の役員を務めており、これまでにその他の様々な組織でも役員会のメンバーを務めてきた。EYアントレプレナー・オブ・ザ・イヤーやBlue Cross主催のビジネスアワードSBNビジョナリー賞など、数々の受賞歴がある。

　彼もこの強靭な身体と精神力を要するCEO・会長職を自らの目標達成まで頑張り続けよう。その達成とはアサシス社を、小さいバイオベンチャーからメジャー製薬会社にまで育ったジェネンテックやアムジェンのようにすることであろう。時間を要するのは百も承知、後継者を探すなど考えられない。氏はオハイオ州ハドソンで妻と3人の子供と一緒に暮らしている。成功を祈って止まない。

is conducting actual experiments (walk and walk) centered on Japan Railway (JR) stations. His desire to join everyday life with scientific research is a reflection of a scientist's way of thinking.

Here I would like to look to overseas. I am currently a full-time senior advisor at an American company, Athersys (Cleveland, Ohio). The company's CEO and Chairman, Dr. Gil Van Bokkelen, is honest, dignified, and caring. He listens to people and is quick at making decisions. He and I have a relationship based on trust. However, it is human nature to make mistakes, and when one occurs, if either one realizes the mistake; they offer an immediate "I'm sorry".

Dr. Van Bokkelen received a B.A. in Economics and a B.A. in Molecular Biology from the University of California at Berkeley. He received a Ph.D. in Genetics from the Stanford University School of Medicine. He is a typical American with a diverse academic background. Dr. Van Bokkelen has been in control of Athersys since co-founding it in 1995 as a venture capital start-up. He has helped develop it into a corporation listed on NASDAQ (stock symbol: ATHX). The firm's main product MultiStem® is in the process of a bold and dynamic worldwide launch. Clinical trials have started in Japan. He really likes Japan, and he has become an open-hearted friend with Japan's Pharmaceuticals and Medical Devices Agency (PMDA) Chairman Dr. Tatsuya Kondo. In addition to his responsibilities of overseeing Athersys, Dr. Van Bokkelen is also the Chairman of the Board of Governors of the National Center for Regenerative Medicine (NCRM), a joint enterprise which is structured from a multitude of organizations. From 2010 to 2012, while residing in Washington, D.C., he served as Chairman of the non-profit organization, Alliance for Regenerative Medicine (ARM). ARM's activities were focused upon increasing the awareness of major policy makers of the future potential of regenerative medicine. Dr. Van Bokkelen is also an executive member of the Biotechnology Innovation Organization (BIO), as well as having served on the boards of numerous other organizations. He has been awarded with the Ernst & Young Entrepreneur of the Year, Blue Cross Sponsored Business Award, SBN Visionary in Business Award, as well as others.

He mirrors the strong body and mind that is proof that, in his position as CEO and Chairman, he is striving toward a goal that he has set for himself. Perhaps his goal is to see that Athersys grows from a small bio-venture into a major pharmaceutical corporation, possibly similar to the likes of Genetech and Amgen. Because he knows that this will take time, looking for a successor does not cross his mind. This can be summed up by saying "Post Gil is Gil!" He lives with his wife and three children in Hudson, Ohio. I always pray for his success.

第20話
新世界に七色の虹を

新世界と言えば、ドヴォルザーク(Antonin Dvorak)が、ナショナル音楽院院長として、ニューヨークに滞在中の1893年に作曲した交響曲第9番ホ単調作品95である。この曲を聴くと、ざわついている気持ち(脳)も静かになる。ドヴォルザークによると、この響きはチェコの民族と文化そのものであるという。まさに音のヒーリングである。

若き日のバーンスタイン
Bernstein on a young day

この荘厳さと共に、21世紀の新世界にふさわしいのは、レナード・バーンスタイン(Leonard Bernstein、1918～1990)の世界である。その名の示すとおり、彼はユダヤ系米国人2世であり(ウクライナ系移民)、作曲家、指揮者そしてピアニストでもあった。若くしてアメリカ生まれの指揮者(25歳)として名声を得、ヨーロッパの著名なオーケストラを指揮している。そして実にハンサムでもてたであろう！

彼のレパートリーの一つである宗教的香りの交響曲もさることながら、興味があるのは、彼のミュージカルである。シェークスピアのロミオとジュリエットを題材にしたウエスト・サイド物語(West Side Story)。ニューヨーク・マンハッタで白人グループとプエルトリコ系グループが対立し、主演女優マリアの兄としてプエルトリコ系グループのリーダーを演じたジョージ・チャキリス(George Chakiris)のリズム感あふれるダンス。チャキリス自身、1962年アカデミー助演男優賞を受賞した。

208——●第2章 Changes in the Trend of Globalization

Narrative 20

The New World, Over a Seven Colors Rainbow

In the title of this narrative, the words "The New World" are inspired from The Symphony No. 9 in E minor, Op. 95, popularly known as "New World Symphony," which was composed by Antonin Dvorak in 1893 while he was the director of the National Conservatory of Music of America and residing in New York. Listening to this piece brings about a sense of certain calm to the agitated mind. According to Dvorak, this melody embodies the Czech people and their culture. This is undoubtedly an excellent example of 'sound healing'.

DARUMA: a budism priest— Symbol of Patience
ダルマ太子―忍耐のシンボル

In addition to the solemnity of his work, an appropriate example of the New World of the 21st Century is the work of Leonard Bernstein (1918-1990). As can be deduced by his surname, he was a 2nd generation Jewish American(Ukrainian emigrants), a composer, conductor, and pianist. After attaining recognition as an American-born conductor at the early age of 25, he went on to conduct prominent orchestras of Europe. With his exceptional talents and good looks, he must have been popular!

Although within his repertoire there are symphonies that carry religious undertones, what are interesting are his musicals. He wrote the music for West Side Story, which takes the story of Shakespeare's Romeo and Juliet to a contemporary level. The stage is set in New York, with the ethnic conflict between a white gang and Puerto Rican gang. In the film version, the leader of the Puerto Rican group and brother to Maria was played by George Chakiris, who performed the rhythmical dances. For his performance, Chakiris was awarded the Academy Award for Best Supporting Actor in 1962. During his lifetime, Bernstein received many awards, including eight Grammy Awards and a Grammy Lifetime Achievement Award.

Slightly off the narrative, Chakiris, who was born to

Seven colored cup, Japan
七色のカップ、日本製

Chapter Ⅱ Changes in the Trend of Globalization ● ——— 209

バーンスタインもアカデミー賞を受賞している。

　話がそれるが、チャキリスは日本のTVドラマで壇ふみと共演し、ラフカデオ・ハーン（Lafcadio Hearn, 日本名：小泉八雲、ギリシャ生まれ）を演じているのを思い出した。2009年（再放送）のNHK総合TV「日本の面影──小泉八雲とセツの物語」である。

　話を戻そう。バーンスタインは、1日たばこ100本とウイスキー1本というから、これはかなりの大トラである。　最期は肺がんというのも宿命か。多くの弟子を送り出し、日本の小澤征爾氏、大植英次氏、そして佐渡裕氏もそうである。詳しくは、佐渡氏のトーク「こだわり人物伝"衝撃の出会い"」(2010)NHK教育TVをご覧になることをお薦めしたい。

　さてもう一つのキーワード"7色の虹"にそろそろ触れなくてはならない。恵みの雨の野原にかかる7色の虹、まるで天から新世界が降りてきそうな感じがする。目をつぶるとその光景がカラーで浮かぶ。生きている喜びを感じる瞬間でもある。虹という漢字は、虫と工からなる。中国では古来、虹は龍を意味したらしく、7色の昇り・下り龍である。龍は、紐（ひも）すなわち虫の一種と考えられてきたので、虹なのである。また虹と言う漢字の工は、匠が柱を創るという意味があり、天と地を結ぶ柱すなわち龍虹である。漢字は、ラテン語に始まる表音文字にはない創造の楽しみがある。

　では何故、虹は7色なのだろうか。雨上がりの澄んだ空では、光が7色に分光する。波長の短い方から（下から）紫─藍─青─緑─黄─橙─赤の順である。光の分光（プリズム）がもたらすマジックである。

　さて表題に戻ってまとめると、荘厳にして若さ溢れる新世界に向けて人（ひと）それぞれが七色のどれかを自由に選び、そして一緒に勇気をもって、新世界の安らぎ（安心）・安全を目指して飛び出すことかと思う。

　本シリーズも、第1章20話・第2章20話が終了し、ホッとしているところである。しばらくの間エネルギーを補給し、再び皆様に誌上でお会いするのを楽しみに筆を擱きたく存じます。編集の皆様、ありがとうございました。心から感謝申し上げます。

Greek immigrant parents on September 16, 1934, co-starred in a television drama with Fumi Dan, in which he played Lafcadio Hearn, known as Yakumo Koizumi in Japanese. The 2009 Japan's NHK television drama was titled, "The Memoir of Japan—The Story of Yakumo Koizumi and Setsu".

Let us return to the main theme. Bernstein was known to smoke 100 cigarettes and drink a bottle of whiskey a day. A heavy smoker and big drinker! As a result, he was destined to pass away from lung cancer. He mentored and oversaw the development of many, including Japan's Seiji Ozawa, Eiji Ohue, and Yutaka Sado. Details can be observed from the NHK Educational TV broadcast (2010) of a talk by Mr. Sado entitled "An Electrifying Encounter", which I suggest be seen.

It is time that the other key phrase in the title of this narrative, "A Rainbow of Seven Colors," is explained. After a life-giving rain a seven-colored rainbow often arches over the fields. It is almost as though a New World has rained from the heavens. If I close my eyes, I can envision the scene in color. It is a moment that is concentrated with the joy of being alive. The Japanese character for rainbow is a combination of the characters for insect and engineer or job. In ancient China, it was said that the rainbow was a seven-colored dragon flying up and down the sky. The dragon, as its form resembles a string, has been thought of as an insect, and that is the Chinese character for rainbow. The other character in Japanese, which represents engineer or job, incorporates the meaning of a master carpenter carving out a beam. Thus, a dragon rainbow resembles a beam that binds the heavens and earth. Kanji (Japanese characters) provides the pleasure of imagination that cannot be attained by Latin or other phonetic languages.

Why does a rainbow have seven colors? In a clean, clear sky after rain, water droplets become prisms that separate light into seven colors based on wavelength. The wavelengths of light, in order from short to long, are seen as purple, indigo, blue, green, yellow, orange, and red. It is the magic brought on by light prisms.

Returning to the topic of this narrative, for those young and impressive individuals, I would like to think that they would freely select one of the respective seven colors as a favorite and with courage, endeavor to go out into the New World's security and safety.

This series, which includes Chapter 1, Narratives 1 to 20 and Chapter 2, Narratives 1 to 20, is now concluded, which I am thankful for and relieved to be able to say. I will be taking some time to replenish energy, and look forward to an encounter with you readers through the publication. I thank everyone who was involved in the editing process. Allow me to convey my heartfelt gratitude to each of you.

感謝とあとがき

『素心』上梓にあたり、次の方々に心から感謝申し上げます。

・編集関連
吉見知浩氏、能登谷勇氏、松村藤樹氏：(株)日本医療企画
岩垂宏氏、後藤麻衣子氏：国際医薬品情報
吉川将史氏：公益財団法人薬学振興会
・写真
布施敏夫氏：(有)善美写真
・イラスト
三宅留美氏（Ms）：童画展
・英語監修
T. J. ガンブルトン氏（T.J. Gumbleton、前 米国ファイザー社
メディカルライター）
シェリー藤沼氏（Ms）、後藤忠良氏：C.C.コンサルタンツ

今回、『国際人になるためのInsight Track』(2014年)に続き『素心』を
上梓出来たのは、上記以外の多くの先輩、同僚そして学生からエネルギー
をいただいたおかげと感謝しております。特に畏友 国枝武久氏(熊本大
学名誉教授)並びに市川和孝氏(元厚労省大臣官房審議官)には、日ごろ
励ましをいただき、感謝いたしております。

また、常に気にかけご指導とご支援をいただいた米国アサシス社
CEO・会長 ギル・ヴァン・ボッケレン（Gil Van Bokkelen）博士、元東
大総長 小宮山宏 先生、PMDA理事長 近藤達也 先生、北海道大学病院
長・脳神経外科教授 寶金清博 先生、ロンドン大学（UCL）名誉教授 ロ
ビン・ガネリン 先生、東京大学名誉教授 柴﨑正勝 先生 (現 公益財団法
人微生物化学研究所 理事長)・松木則夫 先生 (現 東大副学長)、国立が

A Message of Gratitude and Acknowledgements

In publishing (Soshin) I would like to express my heartfelt gratitude to the following individuals.

·Editorial
Tomohiro YOSHIMI, Isamu NOTOYA, Fujiki MATSUMURA: K.K.
Japan Medical Planning
Hiroshi IWADARE, Maiko GOTO: International Pharmaceutical Information
Masashi YOSHIKAWA: Tokyo Foundation for Pharmaceutical Sciences

·Photographs
Toshio FUSE: Yoshimi Photo Studio
·Illustrations
Rumi MIYAKE (Ms):Dohga Ten
·English Supervision
T. J. GUMBLETON, former medical writer of Pfizer (U.S.)
Sherrie FUJINUMA, Tadayoshi GOTO: C.C. Consultants

In publishing (Soshin), which follows (Insight Track – To Become an Internationally-Minded Person (2014), in addition to those mentioned above, I would like to express my deep gratitude to; my seniors, colleagues and students from whom I acquired the energy to see this endeavor through. In particular, I would like to take this opportunity to extend my deep gratitude to dear friends Takehisa KUNIEDA (Professor Emeritus Kumamoto University), and Kazutaka ICHIKAWA (former Councilor to Minister of MHLW), for their frequent words of encouragement.

A special note to express my gratitude to individuals such as; Athersys Inc (USA) CEO and Chairman, Dr. Gil Van BOKKELEN, former Chancellor Professor Emeritus Hiroshi KOMIYAMA, The University of Tokyo, Hokkaido University Hospital President and Professor, Department of Neurosurgery Dr. Kiyohiro HOUKIN, Pro-

ん研究センター病院副院長 藤原康弘先生、東京大学老年病科 小川純人先生、米国大使館 花輪弘之 上級商務専門官、そしてお世話になっております主治医の東大病院循環器内科 大関敦子 先生並びに大森病院 石川みずえ 先生に感謝いたします。

米国アサシス社、ジョン・ハリントン博士(CSO)、ビージー・レイマン弁護士(COO)、ローラ・キャンベル公認会計士(SVP)、マナル・モルシ博士(SVP)に感謝します。また、かつてお世話になったPhRMA(W-DC)のデビット・ウィードン博士に感謝したい。

いつもお世話になっております我孫子市在住の東大の先輩、林盈六先生に感謝いたします。先生は物療内科医、整形外科医と漢方専門医で、前日本相撲協会診療所長でした。

三菱関係でお世話になりました三菱化学元社長 三浦昭氏・前社長 小林喜光氏（経済同友会代表幹事）、サウジ石化元社長 佐々木和男氏、元三菱銀行 田中昭彦氏に感謝いたします。また日頃お世話になっております我孫子市の隣人青木勝哉様にお礼を申し上げます。

さて、私は一つの会社に長くいたことは無く、会社や組織を5回ほど経験してきました。現在の東大薬友会会長は6回目になります。各組織にいた5年〜10年の間は、体を張って全力で組織に貢献いたしました。ただ、10年近くになると垢（マンネリ）が溜まります。一度心身を洗い直して、新しく招いてくれた組織で頑張るという繰り返しでした。しかし、人それぞれ自分に合った生き方をするのが良いと思います。

筆者(12月10日、2017)

妻・順子（3月15日、1965年 筆者との結婚日）

fessor Emeritus Dr. Masakatsu SHIBAZAKI (currently Director of the Institute of Microbial Chemistry), Dr. Norio MATSUKI(currently Vice Chancellor of the University of Tokyo), and Professor Emeritus Robin GANELIN (London University-UCL), National Cancer Research Center Dr. Yasuhiro FUJIWARA/ Vice President, The Uniberctiy of Tokyo Hospital / Aging medicine Sumito OGAWA, and American Emberssy Senior Commercial Specialist Hiroyuki HANAWA, who constantly provided guidance and warm support. Grateful also to PhRMA, David WEADON M.D., Ph.D.

Also grateful to my senior in The University of Tokyo, Dr. Eiroku HAYASHI living in Abiko-City and supporting me as always. Being a Chemotherapeutic physician, Osteopaedician and Chinese medicine expert, he was Director of Clinical Institute of Japan Grand Sumo Association.

And also grateful to Mitsubishi-related, former President of Mitsubishi Chemicals (MC), Mr. Akira MIURA, currently Chairman (MC), Dr. Yoshimitsu KOBAYASHI (currently Represidentive of Economic Executives Society), former President of Saud Petrochemicals, Mr. Kazuo SASAKI, and a former Mitsubishi Bank Mr. Akihiko TANAKA.

Last but not least, I am grateful to my physician, University of Tokyo Hospital Cardiovascular Internal Medicine Department, Dr. Atsuko OZEKI and Dr. Mizue ISHIKAWA, Ohmori Hospital. Also grateful to a good neighbor in Abiko-City, Mr. Katsuya AOKI. I must admit that I do not stay in one place for long, which has resulted in experiencing 5 different corporations and organizations. Currently I am the Chairman of the Alumni Association, Pharmaceutical Sciences, The University of Tokyo for the 6th time.

For five (5) through ten (10) years tenure, I put all my mental and physical power and energy to contributing for the success of organizations each. However, approaching to ten (10) years, there would be happened "MANNERISM". Then, wash out and move to the other kindly-inviting organizations and do best for the success of corre-

Canberra Grandma Kay, and our children Yoko-Kazuhiko-Natsuko at kobayashi Garden
キャンベラおばーちゃんと子供達
―陽子（次女）――彦（長男）―夏子（長女）小林家にて（1973）

今思えば、他人（ひと）との出会に偶然は無くすべての出会いが必然であると信じてきたということです。学生時代に始まった不思議な体験（必然）があり、このことを戯れにミトコンドリア・メッセージと呼んでおります。窮地に陥ると、かならず誰かが手を差し伸べてくれる幸せに感謝しております[注]。

　また、お世話になった薬友会秘書の和田留理子・柴田侑子・坂本朋子・堀江智早の皆さまに感謝いたします。

　最後に私事になりますが、召されて旅立った次女 陽子と妻 順子に深い感謝を。長男一彦（小児科）一家（妻 美千子、子供たち（孫）芙実子、美菜子、茉衣子）と長女夏子の大嶋一家（夫 尚／半導体、子供たち（孫）美希、宏一）の益々の発展を祈り、筆を擱きたく存じます。

[注]『国際人になるためのInsight Track』第2章第2話「天とは何か」を参照いただければ幸いです。

sponding organizations.

The above has been my carreer, and I believe that every individual has the right to choose their own carreer.

Looking back, it is no coincidence that we experience encounters with total strangers, I have believed that all encounters we experience within our lifetime are inevitable. Unexplainable experiences (inevitable) started during my student years, this can be expressed playfully as what I refer to as, the mitochondria message. When I am faced with a predicament, inevitably someone holds out their hand to help me, for this I am extremely grateful. (NOTE)

I am very grateful to the secretaries of the Alumni Association of Pharmaceutical Sciences; Ruriko WADA, Yuko SHIBATA, Tomoko SAKAMOTO and Chihaya HORIE.

Lastly, on a personal note, I want to express my deep gratitude to my late second daughter Yoko and wife Junko, who have made the trip to heaven before me. My eldest son Kazuhiko (pediatrician) and his family,(wife Michiko, and children (grandchildren to me), Fumiko, Minako, Maiko) and my eldest daughter Natsuko, the OSHIMA family (husband Takashi, semiconductor business), their children (my grandchildren) Miki, Kohichi, to which I pray that they all prosper and enjoy the good things in life.

(NOTE) Please refer to 「Insight Track – To Become an Internationally-Minded Person, Chapter 2 Narrative 2 : What is Heaven 」.

素 心
──ぶれない やさしい──　　【和文・英文】

2018年3月26日　第1版第1刷発行

著　　　者　小林 利彦
発　行　者　林　諄
発　行　所　株式会社日本医療企画
　　　　　　〒101-0033　東京都千代田区神田岩本町4-14
　　　　　　神田平成ビル
　　　　　　TEL 03-3256-2861（代表）
　　　　　　FAX 03-3256-2865
　　　　　　http://www.jmp.co.jp
印　刷　所　大日本印刷株式会社

ISBN978-4-86439-665-3 C0036
©Toshihiko Kobayashi 2018, Printed in Japan

定価は表紙に表示しています。
本書の全部または一部の複写・複製・転訳等を禁じます。これらの許諾については
小社までご照会ください。